Finding
her
Forever

ALSO BY CATHRYN BROWN

Finding her Forever

CATHRYN BROWN

For permission requests, write to the publisher, addressed "Attention: Permissions Coordinator," at the address below.

Sienna Bay Press

PO Box 158582

Nashville, Tennessee 37215

www.cathrynbrown.com

Cover designed by Najla Qamber Designs

(www.najlaqamberdesigns.com)

Publisher's Note: This is a work of fiction. Names, characters, places, and incidents are a product of the author's imagination. Locales and public names are sometimes used for atmospheric purposes. Any resemblance to actual people, living or dead, or to businesses, companies, events, or institutions is completely coincidental.

Finding her Forever/Cathryn Brown. - 1st ed.

ISBN: 978-1-945527-92-0

❀ Created with Vellum

DEAR READER

The idea for *Finding her Forever* came to me when my husband and I were driving to a small-town restaurant we like to visit occasionally. A Victorian-era house beside the road was charming but neglected. It needed someone to bring it back to life. By the time we had our food, I had this story.

For those of you who have read the Alaska romances, I included a character in *Finding her Forever* that you'll recognize —Mark from *Finally Matched*.

There's another wedding in Two Hearts in this book and a lot of fun. You'll want to keep an eye on Mrs. Brantley because she has good things coming her way.

I hope you enjoy Paige and CJ's sweet romance!

CHAPTER ONE

*P*aige's finger hovered over the keyboard. With one touch, she could complete the sale and own a house. She swirled her finger over the enter key, which all but flashed "Danger here!" in neon. She knew it really said, "Unknown here."

When she started to pull her hand away, the dream of home ownership flickered and began to die. How long would it take her to own anything here in New York City?

With a deep breath, Paige hit the button. And bought a house. A historic house in Two Hearts, Tennessee. The most spontaneous thing she had ever done in her oh-so-predictable life.

Fanning her face, she stared at the computer screen that said she'd finalized the online document.

What have I done?

Paige jumped to her feet and paced across the small room and back. She had never set foot in Tennessee. She'd never even been to the South. Not unless flying over it counted. As the child of an Army officer—a child who had moved eleven times, attended eight schools, and lived in multiple countries and states—that was saying a lot.

Passing the computer with its screen that had now gone dark, she wondered if she could contact the seller. Maybe if she asked, she could still get her money back.

Her phone pinged with a message from her boss.

Come in early.

That usually meant a long day. *Longer* day. She had left an all-consuming accounting position and moved to one that promised fewer hours and a stress-free environment. Her forty-hour weeks there had quickly become fifty or sixty. She had zero social life.

A car blasting a stereo approached her, growing louder before dying. Minutes later, a door slammed so hard it shook the building. Her neighbor in the other side of the duplex was home, and while she didn't have time to go to parties, he usually brought his party to her.

His stereo cranked up, and the vibration thumped through their shared wall and her body.

Surely, there would be peace and quiet in a small town. Two Hearts sounded quiet.

Paige grabbed her laptop and went outside. Someone had thoughtfully put a picnic table in the backyard in years past. That made a good escape from her neighbor's music choices. And his adorable dog was often there and needing attention.

Opening the laptop, she began the email to her boss—her soon-to-be-former boss.

Moving day finally arrived after two final weeks with a boss who wanted to get every hour of work out of her that he could. After work every day, she'd packed long into the night. Paige carried boxes to her small car, the one she'd bought instead of the bigger, more expensive one she preferred. Every bit saved got her closer to her dream of owning her own house and business.

She dropped the box in the trunk and pushed it to the side to make room for the many more still to come. As she turned to get another load, the dog from next door raced toward her with her tail wagging. Paige kneeled and held out her arms as the low-to-the-ground corgi rushed into them.

"Are you ready for breakfast?" She ruffled the fur by the dog's ears. "I saved some meat scraps from last night."

The dog woofed in response.

Laughing, Paige headed for her home's front door with the corgi at her side. "I'm going to miss you." Saying the words out loud, she realized that this dog had been the one bright light in her life recently. She set the scraps on a plate in front of her side of the duplex, and the small dog dove into them with gusto. "You're hungry this morning."

She stared with disgust at the opposite side of the building that she and the other tenant, the dog's owner, shared—the annoying part of her home sweet home for the past 363 days. He hadn't blasted his music the last couple of nights, breaking a months-long trend.

The pup, whose name she had only heard as "Dog," waited on the front step as Paige went inside for each box, then followed her to the car where she snugged that box in beside the one before. Paige soon stood at the trunk with the last box in her arms. Every square inch of space had already been filled.

"Now what?"

The back seat held clothes on hangers draped across her camera, tripod, and other photography equipment. She'd need to find time in her busy schedule as a bed and breakfast owner for her hobby.

"What do you think?" Paige turned toward the dog. "Should I abandon what's in here?" She held up the box for a second opinion.

The dog cocked her head to the side and peered up at her as if to say, "Is that really the best plan?"

Pulling back the taped-down flaps, Paige found kitchen tools, ones in still-new condition. Who had a spare moment to learn to cook? She scattered everything on top of the boxes and closed the trunk, relieved when the stuffed-to-the-top compartment clicked shut without protest. Her entire life—at least the parts of it she wanted to take with her—now filled her car. She did a quick walkthrough of the house she'd rented furnished, went out the door, and locked it for the last time.

Kneeling again, Paige petted the dog.

"Leaving?" A female voice she recognized spoke. Her across-the-street neighbor, Ethel, had been one of the few bright spots about living here.

Paige stood and turned toward the elderly woman. "Yes. I bought a house." Excitement bubbled up inside her whenever she pictured the adorable Victorian she now owned. She walked closer to the woman who had weathered the neighborhood's ups and downs—currently a down—over the past five or six decades. Paige had tried to talk her into moving, but this was Ethel's home, and she was staying.

"That happened faster than you expected."

That was because she'd cheated on her plan. Slightly. "Small towns have lower-priced houses."

"I thought you wanted to live nearby, maybe Brooklyn."

Paige frowned. "That's true. But I wanted my own place more."

"I'm glad it's working out for you. Where is it?"

"Two Hearts, Tennessee."

Ethel's eyes widened. "You're moving from New York City to a small town in Tennessee? That's surprising."

She'd been surprised too. Once she'd seen the picture of the house online, though, she'd fallen in love with it and known it was hers. The process of buying it through a real estate agent from the town had moved quickly.

The corgi leaned against Paige's leg.

"She's going to miss you."

Paige reached down to pet the dog. "I've been feeding her when her owner forgets." Paige kept her anger down at the reminder of the number of days the dog's bowl in the backyard went empty until she filled it. The dog didn't even get a place to eat inside.

"I'll do my best to take over feeding her. Now that he's gone." Ethel pointed toward the other half of the duplex.

Paige jerked upward. "He left?" That explained the recent wonderful, blissful silence.

"I watched him pack up on Friday. Loaded a truck with furniture—and everything else he owned, from the looks of it." Sad eyes gazed down at the dog. "Except for her." Ethel leaned forward, extending her hand. "Come here, girl. I'll be here for you."

The dog pressed tighter into Paige's leg. "You'll be okay." Paige crouched in front of the corgi. "Ethel won't let you go hungry."

"I'll do my best. My income only stretches so far, but I'll try."

Paige wrapped her arms around the dog and received a gentle lick across her cheek. With a deep breath, she stood and surveyed the neighborhood she'd called home for two years before going over to give Ethel a hug. Stepping back, she said, "You and this dog have been the only good things on this street. That and the cheap rent helping me save for my dream home. Once I'm settled, I'll send you my address and tell you about the town."

"I'd love that."

5

Paige walked toward her car, doing her best to ignore the dog, who sat watching her.

Inside, she adjusted her rear view and side mirrors. The dog kept her eyes on the car. Paige started the car, gave a final glance back, and swallowed hard as she pulled away from the curb and moved down the street. Ethel would feed the dog. *When she could.* And what if something happened to the elderly woman?

Paige hit the brakes. She couldn't leave her. Stepping out, she went around to the passenger side, opened the door, and said, "Are you coming with me?"

The dog ran over and stopped beside the car, looking up at Paige as if to ask if it was okay to jump inside.

"Let's go. We're going to have a girls' trip to Tennessee. Our new home."

The dog jumped to the floor, her short legs working overtime, then up to the seat, where she sat, waiting for their adventure.

Paige waved to Ethel who watched their progress.

The older woman smiled widely. "I'm glad she has a good home."

Starting the car again, Paige wondered for a second if she'd made the right decision. When she glanced to her side, the dog woofed and seemed to smile. Yes, she'd made the only decision she could.

CJ swung his pickup truck around the bend in the road. The clear sky overhead sent sunshine down that somehow made the overgrown city park he passed, and the street's abandoned houses, more cheerful. Just five minutes outside Two Hearts, this area felt rural. Barely visible through the thick brush and trees, glimmers of sunlight sparkled off the lake. The scene was close to poetry, and he wasn't really a poetic kind of guy.

"Pretty today," Greg Brantley, the town's often-serious sheriff, said.

The unfortunately painted-pink Victorian house came into view as they continued down the road.

"Are you sure you want to buy that dump? I mean 'historic house.'" Sarcasm oozed through Greg's words.

CJ laughed. "Don't let Cassie hear you talk that way about an old house."

Greg winced. "That's the truth. My fiancé loves the place she bought. But it was livable from day one, and I will happily live there once we're married. I don't remember seeing anything I'd call 'livable' here on the lake."

Livable. The building up ahead was anything but. The beauty —or the potential for beauty, once it was cleaned up—made up for it, though. And the details inside were amazing. Some of them were lost under layers of paint and grime, but he knew they were waiting to be rediscovered. Once upon a time, this must have been a beautiful street to live on, but time itself hadn't been kind.

"Do you remember coming out to the lakefront park when you were a kid?" CJ asked.

"Barely. Even then, Two Hearts didn't have money to keep up the picnic area. And no one cared enough to take it on."

"That's too bad."

"Yes, it is. But I think that's what happens when a town slowly fades away."

The large home became more visible as they drew closer, and so did his real estate agent Randi's *For Sale* sign out front. He'd all but decided to buy the house a couple of weeks ago. If Greg agreed with his assessment, then he would call her today and get the deal going.

Pulling to a stop in front of the house, he reached for his door latch. Greg's hand on his arm stopped him. CJ froze when he looked at where his friend had pointed.

A *SOLD* sign proudly perched atop Randi's sign. The sign he'd seen every time he'd driven out to see the house and ponder over it. First once a week and then every day. Last week, he'd been here twice every day. Moving slowly had served him well in the past. "Act in haste, repent in leisure," had been one of his grandmother's favorite sayings. Grandma had failed him this time.

"Who was willing to take on that thing?" Greg pointed at the big house. "It needs a massive amount of work."

CJ stared at the house in front of him. His house. But it didn't look like it would be his house after all.

He could picture the building brought back to life. Windows not replaced but restored so they kept their historic charm. Paint scraped, and the old wood siding and gingerbread details saved, if they could be.

But none of that mattered now. Not the house, not the brick walkway that would have been weed-free on his watch, and not the stunning view of the lake he'd have had once he'd removed the overgrown brush between it and the house.

"I'm sorry," Greg said. "I don't know anyone in town who wanted it."

CJ nodded and stared straight ahead. For the first time in his adult life, he'd found a place to turn into a home. But it looked like the charmer on the lake was going to be somebody else's.

He put his truck in motion and continued down the road. He just hoped whoever the buyer was knew how to fix up houses.

Greg's thoughts must have mirrored his own. "I wonder if the guy who bought it knows what he's getting into."

"I know you didn't see the inside—"

"The outside is bad. I can't imagine the amount of work on the inside, too."

"When I toured it with Randi, I realized that it would take all of my savings and a lot of sweat equity before it moved beyond basic living. That broken window upstairs lets in rain."

Greg gave a rueful chuckle. "And when it rains in Tennessee, it can be a sideways downpour. It may have flooded that side of the house."

"I would have had to pull it apart to check the full damage. The bird's nest in the kitchen was worthy of note, too."

"Are you saying there's a nest *inside* the house?"

"Yep." CJ laughed in spite of his disappointment. "Maybe I'm better off not having to repair everything." Besides, hadn't he, just a month ago, been ready to get out on the road again and go to a new place?

"I'm sure another house in town will be even nicer."

CJ didn't reply. This house had been the only one. With that gone, it was time to leave. He'd always wanted to see Oregon. A little voice in his heart whispered, *It's already fall. Maybe you could wait until after Christmas.* That thought brought a surprising smile to his face.

"Greg, has your mother said what she'll do about the holidays now that's she's in charge?"

"My mother the mayor? I have to tell you that I did not see that coming."

CJ came to a full stop at a stop sign. After a few seconds, he drove on. He was always extra careful to obey traffic laws when Greg was in the vehicle.

"I know she wants to have a fall festival to bring people to Two Hearts. I overheard her talking to Cherry and Levi about a corn maze at their farm."

Mayor Brantley would do whatever it took to revive this town. Now that she had been officially elected, she was doing even more good than usual around town. Christmas would be worth the drive from Nashville.

"Don't panic, but she did mention something about renovating a building or two on Main Street to try to attract more new businesses. Whatever she has planned, I'm sure she'll want your help with that and her fall-season fun."

And there was the problem. Well, one of them. He liked the people and this town.

But he'd already stayed here far longer than anywhere else. He knew he'd want to leave soon. He always did.

CHAPTER TWO

*P*aige woke up early. Who was she kidding? She'd barely slept. She loaded up the car. Yesterday's drive —her first with a dog—had gone surprisingly well. On their journey, testing dog names to see if the corgi would answer to any had become a game. She was still unnamed.

Today, they'd be in Two Hearts by mid-afternoon if her timeline was right, and it usually was. She could picture her house quickly turning into a home for herself and the guests she would serve in the bed and breakfast.

After a short section of interstate through Nashville, the city's hectic traffic faded away as subdivisions gave way to houses scattered on larger properties and, finally, farms with grazing cows and horses. Paige sighed. *This.* This was why she was moving to a small town. Well, that and the facts that she'd despised her former job and loved the low cost of the house she'd bought.

The sign to Two Hearts, freshly painted and hanging on chains, announced she'd arrived.

She was home.

Her real estate agent, Randi, had offered to take her to her new house, but Paige wanted to see it alone the first time. After much back and forth, Randi had decided to give her directions and leave the key under a flower pot. Paige wouldn't have agreed to the key being accessible where she'd lived a week ago, but in an idyllic place like Two Hearts, she didn't need to be so cautious. At least she hoped that was the case.

"We're almost here, girl."

Her excitement carried to the dog, who sat up and wagged her tail back and forth.

"Are you ready for our new life?"

"Woof."

Paige would take that as a yes. She drove down the highway, which became Main Street, and zigzagged through side roads to reach the lakefront. She, Paige Conroy, owned a house on a lake. The real estate agent had given her the contact information for the utilities, so they were all turned on and in her name now.

Some of the houses she passed were cared for, but many looked abandoned or on the verge of it. Yards were overgrown, and paint on the buildings and fences was faded and peeling.

Straightening, Paige put her shoulders back. She'd known this was a town coming back to life. The article she'd read about Carly Daniels' wedding had said as much. She would help rejuvenate it.

Coming around a curve, she saw flashes of light bouncing off water through the trees. She must be near the lake her house was on. Slowing the vehicle down, she passed a sign for a park that had been all but swallowed by vines. The first house she drove by had grass and brush so tall you'd never be able to get to the front door. She knew her house's yard had been mowed, but in the photos, it had still looked like it needed more work. She'd always dreamed of having her own garden, so that hadn't scared her away.

A roofline she recognized came into view. How could anyone resist a house with gingerbread trim? Being pale pink only added to its charm. Heart racing, she moved closer and closer to her dream home. With no driveway, her only option was to park beside the road. She climbed out and helped her dog to the ground. They walked over to the gate and stopped, and the dog sat beside her.

"We're here! Are you excited?"

"Woof! Woof!"

The three-story building rose from a weedy lawn and almost nonexistent landscaping, but brave flowers peered through the weeds in places. Her gaze moving up, Paige took in the wide front porch and sighed. Sitting on her front porch to take in a cool breeze and visit with the neighbors sounded so small-town Southern.

Paige opened the once-white gate, which creaked loudly and was attached to a rickety fence that boxed in the front yard but had multiple pickets missing. Fixing that so the dog could run freely would go to the top of her list. She started up the path toward her dream, but with each step, the porch—and the dream—took a turn for the worse. Some of the ceiling boards hung down.

A mixture of wood siding beneath peeling paint covered the front and eaves, with areas of what must be rot in places. The window on the second floor that she'd thought was only open was broken, based on the shards of glass still in the window frame.

Paige's horror deepened. Her dog whimpered beside her.

"We may have gotten ourselves into a mess, girl."

The dog barked.

Paige lifted the pot beside the front steps and fished out the key, as Randi had instructed. She picked up the dog and gingerly crossed the porch to the front door, her panic rising as she found a foot-sized hole in the decking. Once she'd unlocked the beautifully carved wooden door—one of the few bright spots so far—she pushed it open and surveyed the entry.

Original wood floors were, as they had appeared in the photos and video, in good enough condition to sand and refinish. They seemed safe for her pooch, so she set her down, but the dog stayed close to her legs. She must have sensed danger. Paige couldn't argue with her.

A wide staircase rose from the far left and turned right at a small landing. A fireplace to her left seemed to serve no purpose in the open area, but perhaps had provided necessary heat in times past.

Stepping inside, she spotted a room to the right she remembered from Randi's video, a parlor with paneled walls, a wide window seat, and a fireplace. She continued toward the back of the house. To the left, doors opened to a study with a desk—the only furniture she'd found so far—angled in the corner, and a bathroom that would take hours to clean. To the right, beside the parlor, she found what must be the dining room, and finally, the kitchen.

The bathroom had been dirty. The kitchen was worse. Was that a bird's nest on top of the refrigerator? Connecting the kitchen and dining room was a butler's pantry—a room with cabinets still filled with dishes and glassware and with a small sink—but it was all equally filthy.

How could rooms appear quaint and charming in pictures but disastrous in person?

Decades of grime covered every surface. While that hadn't bothered her too much in the other rooms, the substances coating everything made her question whether or not she'd want to enter the room again, let alone eat anything prepared here.

She cautiously crossed the kitchen, its floor covered with old-fashioned linoleum in a rust and probably cream pattern— the light color was barely discernible—to the big, old sink with a window over it. The green and brown—was that dirt or paint?

—cabinets rose almost to the high ceiling. Her research after seeing photos had told her they weren't original.

She might have to spend a week scrubbing this room alone. A twist of the faucet handle brought water—rusty, icky water. She must have to let it run for a while to clear out the stuff that had been sitting there.

Backing out of the room quickly, she almost tripped over a confused corgi.

"Woof! Woof!"

Paige took a deep breath. "This isn't going well, girl. Let's hope the upstairs is an improvement." She'd done hard things in her life. This would be just one more.

The wooden stair rail was smooth to the touch, worn that way from generations of hands, and much cleaner than the rest of the house. Randi and potential buyers must have used it. The stairs stopped in an open area with a long hallway and many doors that led to bedrooms.

She reached for the first doorknob. A water-stained ceiling topped a decent-sized bedroom. The next bedroom was similar. She knew from the information from Randi that there were two bathrooms upstairs, a luxury in a house this age and needed for her bed and breakfast. They both appeared functional, but only a scrubbing would reveal the tile's condition under the gray and brown coating.

The third bedroom gave her hope. The ceiling had a decorative plaster medallion around a glass light fixture and no visible damage. A good cleaning would make it livable. Even though she should rent out the pretty room in the future, she immediately chose it for herself.

Paige swung open the next door with high hopes. Her breath caught in her throat.

The broken window she'd noticed downstairs belonged to this bedroom. Rain—and critters—had been coming through the opening for a while, if the amount of damage was any indication. The plaster under the window had fallen off and to the floor. Birds' nests on window sills might be charming on the outside of a house, but not in here. This had probably been the access point for the bird that had taken up residence on the fridge.

When she stepped into the room, the floor creaked. Was this even stable? One thing she knew for sure after her tour: buying this house had been the biggest mistake of her life.

A single tear trickled down her cheek.

Realizing the dog had followed her, she picked her up and carried her out. Nothing in here should be stepped in or sniffed. She set the corgi down, and they went downstairs, Paige's vision blurring by the last few steps. Wanting to be somewhere, anywhere else, she opened the front door and realized she had nowhere to go.

"What have I done?" Paige sank to the dusty, bug-speckled floor.

The corgi climbed into her lap and snuggled close.

"We have gone from a not-great situation but a roof over our heads to one where I'm not sure the roof won't cave in while we sleep." Paige wiped tears with the back of her hand.

The dog crawled off her and into what Paige had learned was called a "corgi sploot," flat on her belly with her legs stretched out.

Paige laughed as she rubbed the dog's ears. "Thank you for being cute." Drying her eyes with her sleeve, she stood. "If I don't get to work, I won't have a place to sleep." She thought of the smallest rooms they'd seen. "Or a bathroom."

If she started now, she could get a bedroom and bathroom livable before dinnertime. After a quick phone search, she found one grocery store in town, and that she had a half hour before they closed. Hurrying out the door with the dog, she made it in time. While the dog waited in the car with the windows rolled down, Paige rushed down the aisles, grabbing cleaning supplies, sandwich fixings, dog food, and bottles of drinkable water.

After the supermarket near her old rental, the selection felt limited, but fellow customers gave her a smile and a nod when they passed her, and the cashier took the time to ask her how her day was going. She'd debated her answer, choosing "things are looking up." Because they would if her determination and elbow grease were involved.

At home, Paige poured food into the dog's bowl. With her crunching away, Paige set up the pieces of her own dinner— bread, sliced meat, brown mustard, and cheese—and assembled her sandwich in a small area of cleanliness she'd carved out on the kitchen counter.

The old-fashioned kitchen light flickered once, then again. She stared up at the ceiling fixture she didn't have a ladder to reach. "Please don't burn out!" It brightened and held, but it was a reminder of her tenuous situation. No ladder. *Alone.*

"Dog?"

The corgi kept her focus on her bowl of food.

"Tomorrow will be interesting. We need a hardware store and a truck to haul everything in." At this, the dog looked up and woofed.

Paige carried her own meal to the window seat in the front parlor, one of the few places to sit down. A table would have been a lovely luxury at this point in the project, but maybe she would come across one that would fit the meager budget she'd set for extras. Supplies like wood and paint must come first.

Sitting with her back against the side of the window seat and her feet up, she ate her sandwich as a bird flew by her garden. *Her* garden. Or what would be a garden soon. By the time she'd taken the last bite, the sunshine had been replaced by long shadows.

She grabbed the corgi's leash and clipped it on. "Let's go for a quick walk before dark." Her new dog pranced down the front steps.

They wandered together down the lane, and Paige observed with increasing dismay that every house on this road seemed abandoned. After a while, the night sounds grew louder, and darkness settled around them. Paige glanced over her shoulder to find her house the only area of light. The dog barked at a skittering sound in the brush to their left.

Paige spun around and sped toward home with the dog keeping pace with her. They both broke into a jog as they reached the open front gate. When Paige closed and locked the door behind her, checking to make sure it was secure, she leaned against it, panting.

"Stupid. Stupid. Stupid! You bought a house in the middle of nowhere. A house that needs work you don't know how to do!" She slid down to the floor and sat with her arms wrapped around her bent legs.

The dog licked her hand and woofed.

"We will be okay, won't we? Is that what you're telling me?"

She woofed again and showed that smile of hers.

Paige ruffled the dog's ears and then stood. "Thank you for your encouragement." She turned and peered out the window beside the door—or tried to, since all she found was her own reflection. True darkness engulfed the house, unbroken by even a slight glow from another house or a streetlight.

Ignore it, Paige. You have a dog.

A noise had her swinging to her right. The dog sat at the entrance to the room, licking her lips. She must have finished her dinner. Hand on her racing heart, Paige said, "Get a grip! You're safe here. The doors are locked." She went to the front door to test it. Again. Pulling her phone from her back pocket to check the signal, she added, "And your phone has surprisingly good service."

She debated calling her dad. The time difference between

here and Japan, the location of his latest military posting, made calling difficult. Between that and his marriage two years ago, she often wasn't sure what to do. Lorraine seemed like a lovely person, but she had no relationship with her. Paige decided on sending him a text. His quick reply with his nickname for her in the message—*Ladybug*—helped her quiet down.

~

Paige opened her eyes the next morning when something dropped on her shoulder. Reaching up, she found a wet tennis ball owned by a certain corgi. The ball's owner panted beside her ear.

"Time to go out?"

She barked once.

As they went downstairs, Paige noticed for the first time that she needed to repair some plaster beside the stairs. The house had far more problems than she'd realized, but she'd never open for guests if she didn't make it beautiful. Without income from people paying to stay in her bed and breakfast, she'd lose this dilapidated house she called home.

The corgi went to the door and looked back at Paige, her posture tense with urgency. Paige clipped on the leash. She'd normally be concerned about wearing the oversized T-shirt she slept in outside, but not here. There was no one else in sight. She probably wouldn't see another soul on this street all week. And being isolated didn't add stress, did it?

While they were out there, Paige tested classic dog names: "Fido! Lucky! Honey!" The dog happily wandered the yard with no response to anything but a bug that buzzed past her head.

Back inside, Paige tried to ignore the messes she passed on her way to the kitchen. First things first. Toast with peanut butter followed by cleaning . . . something. She had options. Many, many options.

Soon, armed with a bucket of soapy water, she stood in the center of the kitchen, knowing she'd be there for hours. The dog slept on the floor in the corner of the room, occasionally looking up then going back to sleep. Since she was sleeping so nicely and wouldn't run away, Paige decided to open windows and doors to air the house out. Instead of just being stuffy, it now smelled like a combination of everything she'd wiped up.

Finally, Paige stepped back from the area she'd just finished and rolled her shoulders. The kitchen sparkled in the light pouring through the now-clean window. Perhaps "sparkled" was extreme, but it was clean, and that was saying a lot given where she'd started.

The dog jumped to her feet and started barking. "It's okay, girl." Paige pulled a treat out of her pocket, but the dog didn't care. She raced to the nearest window facing the front of the house, thankfully passing the open door, and stood on her hind legs, trying to see through the glass. When she let out a low growl, the hair on the back of Paige's neck stood up.

CJ neared the pink house on his way to another one two doors down. Randi had suggested it might be similar enough that he'd love it too.

He doubted it.

He slowed when he reached the place he'd begun to see as his and found a small tan car parked out front. Had the new guy arrived? The door stood wide open. A dog barked furiously from inside. Then again, maybe someone had broken into the house. It was only right to make sure.

Being a good citizen could get him a dog bite, but he couldn't ignore this. And he wasn't stopping simply because he was curious about the person who had bought his house. CJ pulled in behind the car. He hopped to the ground from his truck and went toward the house, but the dog's barking increased. Taking a step backward, he wondered if he cared enough to continue. The worst that could happen was that he'd meet the new owner. He hoped.

CJ strode down the front path, the incessant barking growing louder with each step and warning him that he could end up with a lot worse than a meet and greet.

He swallowed hard as he reached the front porch and the dog's volume increased. When no dog shot outside to attack him, he tested his weight on the porch, ignoring the place where his foot had pushed through a few weeks ago, and moved toward the door.

Inside the house, a woman with a barking dog beside her, stepped out of what he knew was the kitchen.

"Girl, calm down." The woman reached for the dog. If anything, the dog's volume increased as it focused on him.

"She's afraid of me."

The woman jumped back.

CJ held up his hands. "Don't worry," he said loudly. "I heard the dog, saw the open door, and wanted to make sure everything was okay."

She warily stared at him. "I'm the new owner," she shouted over the barking. She came closer and into the light from the doorway, allowing him to see her more clearly. The view included the dirt smeared over her right cheek, halfway up both arms, and probably into her hair, if the long, brown, tangled mess was any indication. She must have already dived into the work.

He shouted back, "It's a lot of work!"

She moved closer, and he was grateful to be able to speak more normally, even with the barking continuing. "Let's just say that this house looks better in pictures."

"Doesn't the dog ever stop that racket?"

She sighed and shook her head. "Sometimes it seems like it goes on forever."

"You don't know how to make your own dog quiet down?"

She chuckled. "She's been my dog for, what's it been, girl?" She looked down at the dog. "Four days?"

The corgi stopped her noise-making for a moment as though evaluating the question. When the woman added, "Yes, four days," the dog seemed to know that a conclusion had been reached and she could go back to her earlier work. *Barking.*

He shouted above the din. "Are you going to pack up and sell the place?" He tried to keep the hopeful note out of his voice. It wouldn't be right to encourage her to do that if she really wanted to stay. But he hoped she didn't.

She looked around. "I admit that I do want to cut and run."

His heart beat faster. Maybe the pink monstrosity would be his after all.

"But I was raised to never—under any circumstances—be a quitter." The words sounded tough, but her expression said she wished she'd been raised otherwise and could run away.

"Sometimes giving up is just choosing a different path."

She looked at him for a moment. "That's very wise."

It was, wasn't it? The first thing he'd do once he owned the house—

"I've decided that I'm staying, though. I am going to fix up this place. Somehow."

His heart hit the floor. Before he had time to even consider doing something stupid like offering to help, he said, "Then it was nice meeting you."

"What?" she said loudly over the dog, whose barking had somehow increased in volume.

If she didn't want to sell, he should leave before he somehow ended up working for free when he needed to make his rent. That had happened more times than he could count. If he'd bought the house, it would have been sweat equity as he created his dream, but he wasn't about to renovate an entire house as a favor.

"I said, I'm glad to have met you. I'm leaving now." He pointed toward the street.

The corgi suddenly quieted and sat.

"But we haven't actually met," she shouted, then visibly realized silence now reigned.

"CJ McIntosh."

"Paige Conroy." She held out her hand, stared at it, then pulled it back. "Oh my gosh!" Paige flipped her hand over. "I'm dirty, aren't I?" She put that hand on her formerly clean cheek.

Completely. "Some. Yes."

"I'd better go wash up." She took a step back. "It was nice meeting you. CJ, right?"

He nodded.

She spun on her heels and started down the hall to the back of the house. "I need to get back to work. Yes, work. Um, now." With a glance over her shoulder, she said, "Please close the door when you leave." As she vanished into the kitchen, she added, "Thank you!"

The dog stayed behind. She cocked her head to the side and stared at him.

"Is she always like that?"

The dog grinned.

CHAPTER THREE

*P*aige sank to the kitchen floor. A handsome man had not only just seen her at her worst, he'd *met* her at her worst. Covered in who-knew-what from her feet to her hair. She reached up and found a tangled mess. A strangled scream brought the dog running.

She trudged upstairs for a shower with the dog beside her. Usually a lover of long soaks in a tub, she didn't want to sit in water that contained whatever now coated her body. Nothing about their meeting could be undone, but she'd feel better clean. Her guard dog curled up outside the door.

Keeping her back to the mirror, Paige stripped off and stepped under the hot spray. Having a hot water heater that worked in this old house was nothing short of miraculous, and she needed every miracle she could get.

Dressed, with her hair waving around her shoulders, she paused on her way out of the room for a swipe of lip gloss. The corgi sat watching her, cocking her head to the side when Paige also reached for the blush. "This has nothing to do with CJ," she told the dog. But that was a lie. At an inch shy of six feet tall, she often towered over men. CJ had towered over her, and she'd liked both that and his red, almost auburn hair and beard. He had a mountain-man vibe that she found appealing.

But he would steer clear of the grimy woman he'd met earlier.

Hammering brought her to the door. She went outside, and thankfully, the dog didn't bark this time.

"CJ?" she called from the porch.

He didn't look up from his work, which appeared to be mending the fence. "I didn't want your dog to escape."

She really needed to do the easy work herself to save money. "I can take care of it."

"No need. I'll be done soon." He glanced over at her. Dropping his hammer, he stared at her. "Paige?"

Heat washed over her. "I was cleaning earlier."

They both knew what she was explaining.

He nodded slowly and smiled. "You look . . . different."

She laughed. "That's an understatement." She crossed the yard to see what he had done.

The dog at her side, not wanting to be ignored, woofed.

"How are you?" CJ reached down and rubbed her ears. "Thank you for not barking this time." He went back to hammering.

Maybe he wouldn't charge too much. It *would* be nice to be able to have the dog able to play in the yard. She knew she should do one of the thousand things inside the house that were needed, but the sunny, late-summer day was too pleasant to spend inside. She decided to pull weeds. Crouching, she got to work.

"You know which is poison ivy, right?" he asked as he picked up another board.

Paige dropped the plants in her hands. "No! There's poison ivy?"

He hammered in that board and then came over. "Have you gardened much?"

"Some." She pursed her lips. "Okay, that's stretching it. I watered a neighbor's flowers for a week when she went on vacation." She'd been twelve at the time. And the military moved her and her dad so often that she couldn't have planted and cared for a garden if she'd wanted one, which she had. She wished her dad could be here now to see her new garden, but he was still active duty and stationed overseas.

Grinning, CJ pointed to weeds that were, thankfully, not where she had been working. She liked what the smile did to his already handsome face.

Focusing on the poison ivy, she admitted, "I would have grabbed that."

"And probably ended up itching. Garden gloves would help."

She sighed. "Another thing for my must-buy list."

"Albert can help you with most of it." At her puzzled expression, he offered, "The owner of the hardware store."

"Oh, good. I need to go there."

She stood when she heard car doors closing nearby.

Mrs. Brantley, Cassie, and Bella approached the gate. Her dog barked a warning a moment too late.

CJ winced. "Oh, no!"

"What?" The woman who'd bought his house out from under him leaned closer and whispered, "Are they mean?"

"Absolutely not." He hesitated for a second. "They're . . . involved in the lives of single people."

"Do you mean matchmakers?" At his nod, she said, "But why me? I just arrived."

"Two Hearts is a wedding-crazy town. *Everything* weddings! The woman with the red hair is Cassie. She's a wedding planner. The petite brunette is Bella, the owner of Wedding Bella, the bridal dress store on Main Street."

"That sounds harmless. Customers already have their significant other."

If only they'd stopped there. "I've heard tales of these three matchmaking a couple of other single men."

"Did the match work?"

Typical female response. The result was irrelevant. Meddling in the lives of others for good was still meddling. "One couple is happy. The male victim from the other attempt is considering a job offer in Spain to escape."

"I see what you mean. But I'm sure we can fend them off." She didn't sound as confident as her words suggested.

He hoped she was right. Their catching him here with Paige wasn't good. Not good at all.

The gate creaked as Mrs. Brantley opened it. She reached them first. To Paige, she said, "Hello dear, I'm Emmaline Brantley." The woman, who was about his mother's age, carried a covered plate of something delicious. Everything she baked was delicious.

"Mayor Brantley," Cassie added.

The dog's barking had not lessened. Mrs. Brantley passed the plate to Cassie, then kneeled and reached toward the pup. "We're all friends here. You don't need to yap at us anymore." The dog stopped, and a ringing CJ hadn't realized was in his ears slowly eased off. After a single last "woof," the dog stepped forward to be petted by the mayor.

"The mayor? I hadn't realized that a small town would send out someone so important to meet somebody new." Paige's voice rose. "Or have I done something wrong?"

"Of course not, my dear. And I actually forget I'm the mayor sometimes."

Paige's gaze narrowed. She probably thought she was dealing with a doddering older lady, but Emmaline Brantley was far from that.

27

"I've had the job for less than a week, so it's still hard to get used to."

"And I'm Cassie. The new mayor's future daughter-in-law. This is my close friend Bella. We wanted to welcome you to town. But it looks like CJ got here before us." Cassie's smirk did not bode well for the rest of the conversation.

Before they could conclude that he'd come to meet the pretty new owner, he said, "I actually didn't know anyone had moved in. I was looking at a house up the street. When I found out she had a dog, I didn't want it to escape." He pointed at the last section of the fence that was still missing boards.

Mrs. Brantley patted his arm. "That's good to know."

"I'm Paige Conroy." She put out her hand.

"It's a pleasure to meet you." Mrs. Brantley shook Paige's hand. "And who else do we have here?"

Paige—sighed. "I've just been calling her 'girl' or 'dog.'"

When four sets of startled eyes looked her direction, Paige added, "I'd been feeding her when my previous neighbor didn't. He moved and abandoned her days before I left, so the two of us hopped in the car and came to Tennessee."

"Well, she's going to need a name soon," Mrs. Brantley added in her always reasonable tone of voice.

"I know. I've tried many, but she doesn't respond to them. I'll keep working on it."

Mrs. Brantley stood. "If you need help with your renovation project, the first person you've met here is the best carpenter in town."

CJ cringed. The conversation he wanted to avoid descended upon him.

"I'm sure there are other capable carpenters in Two Hearts." Paige glanced over at him and took a half step away.

He realized he'd crossed his arms and pursed his lips as he waited for their worst. With his size, he could appear intimidating without meaning to be. Forcing a smile, he added,

"I'm sure there are too." Even though he hadn't met anyone, and everyone had welcomed his skills, surely in a town this size there was someone else who could do carpentry.

Mrs. Brantley frowned. "You would think so. Unfortunately that isn't the case." She gestured toward him and smiled.

Here it came.

"CJ, you know as well as I do that there's only a handful of people in Two Hearts who can hammer a nail straight into a board." She paused. "That may be a slight exaggeration. Nevertheless, you are an expert." Turning to Paige, she added, "This man can do everything from replacing a window to copying crown molding so it matches what's there. He's been a godsend to me since he drove into town early this year."

The other two women offered similar words of agreement.

Paige put her hand on his arm. "You can help me fix up this" —she looked around the room—"horrible mess I just bought?"

CJ gulped. How did he answer that? He didn't want to fix up the house he had actually wanted to own. He definitely didn't want to get caught up in a project this large. If things in Two Hearts weren't working out, he needed to be able to leave. He could not take on a job that was going to last months and occupy every waking hour.

"I think I'll be heading out of town soon." He smiled. At least he hoped it was a smile.

Mrs. Brantley completely ignored his comment and continued to sing his praises by describing, in detail, the work he'd done for her.

He held up his hands in a *stop* motion. "As I just mentioned, I'm planning to get back out on the road again and move on."

Paige's eyes filled with tears. *Not the tears.* His sisters had done that growing up, and he'd given in every single time. One sister had been able to turn it on automatically—she had wisely chosen to go into theater—but this woman seemed genuinely distressed. He looked up to find Mrs. Brantley glaring at him.

When he turned toward Cassie and Bella, he found similar expressions on their faces.

He was sunk. Maybe he could start the job and find someone to hand it over to. Even as he considered that, he knew that it was unlikely another carpenter would drive to this small town in the middle of nowhere.

Maybe she didn't have enough money to pay him. Yes, that was good. He had to eat, so he couldn't work for free.

Mrs. Brantley had probably planned this visit in part to suggest that Paige call him right away. But he'd been *here*. He'd feel set up if he hadn't done it to himself.

The matchmaking plot thickened. "Maybe the two of you could sit down and discuss your budget, Paige. You can talk while you eat brownies."

His favorite dessert. *Of course.*

She handed the plate to Paige, who lifted the cover to peer under it.

"They smell wonderful."

"They're still warm."

He knew she was pushing hard when she not only brought brownies, but *warm* brownies. They probably had chocolate chips in them too. Mrs. Brantley knew those brownies were his Achilles' heel.

She added, with a glance in his direction, "With chocolate chips."

He stifled the groan.

Paige smiled so widely that it pushed her cheeks up, and her eyes glinted with joy. She'd been pretty before, but she was stunning now. She reached down to pat the dog a couple times, then stood. How had he missed how tall she was before? With him at six-feet-four, she looked just about right for someone his height.

He realized he'd been staring when he caught a glance between Cassie and Bella. Cassie, probably wanting to extend the meeting, said, "Could we have a tour of your home?"

"It's . . . not what it will be when it's ready."

Mrs. Brantley asked, "Ready?"

"To be a bed and breakfast. That's my goal."

"How lovely! We need more businesses." Mrs. Brantley focused on the building in front of her. "I played with a friend who lived here when I was a child. I remember sitting with our dolls in the front yard. But I barely remember the layout. Does it have many bedrooms and baths?"

"Six bedrooms and three bathrooms."

She gave a nod. "I'd love a tour. And don't worry about the current condition. We all know you're working on it."

Paige perked up. "Okay. Let's go." She led the way, with everyone following.

CJ paid little attention because he'd already toured the house multiple times, but the mayor clearly felt otherwise. The kitchen got a *tsk-tsk* sound, as did the bathrooms. The butler's pantry earned a smile and the comment, "Great storage." When they reached Paige's bedroom, Mrs. Brantley stared at the stack of blankets on the floor. "No bed?"

Paige went red but held the mayor's gaze. "I'm saving money for renovations. And I have money set aside for beds for guests when it's time."

Mrs. Brantley tsk-tsked again, and they continued, but Paige did not open the door to the room with the broken window. CJ knew why: They would be too shocked. Back downstairs, Mrs. Brantley pointed to the kitchen and said, "Paige, I'm sure we can find a small table, a bed, and other basics."

Paige seemed about to protest, but Cassie added. "I think there's a small table in my attic."

"See? We'll help." Mrs. Brantley patted Paige's arm. "That's what a small town is for. We care about everyone." She glanced meaningfully from Paige to CJ.

Cassie said, "Absolutely."

Bella added, "We do everything we can for our neighbors."

~

CJ's phone rang. "I have to take this." Paige heard the words, "Yes, Mom," as he walked away.

Cassie smiled at her. "We're glad you've come to live in our community, Paige. I'm very happy here."

Bella laughed. "Because she found love."

Cassie nudged her. "You did too!"

They looked so happy when they spoke about this town. And love. Finding love was unlikely, but Paige did like the town. "I hope I get to stay."

All eyes focused on her, and Bella said, "What?"

"I have to open the bed and breakfast quickly." The rest of the words remained unsaid: *Before I run out of money.*

"You might leave?" Mrs. Brantley frowned.

"I already like it here, so I *want* to stay."

Cassie looked around the room. "I may be able to have brides stay here the night before the wedding. Whenever it's done."

Paige knew her mouth was hanging open, but she couldn't help it. Could finding business be that easy? "That would be wonderful!"

"It's . . ." Cassie wandered into the parlor.

Bella jumped in. "In need of help."

"Desperately." Cassie turned toward Paige. "I'm sorry! I shouldn't have said it that way. I love old houses."

Paige waved away the comment. "I know it's needy now, but I can see it as it will be."

Minutes later, Paige and CJ stood in the entryway and watched the women leave, with Paige clutching the plate of brownies. Cassie and Bella had not had an opportunity to say much. It hadn't been necessary—Mrs. Brantley had said it all.

Paige felt as befuddled as he looked. "Well . . ."

He glanced around the room with a practiced eye. "Before we do anything else, tell me exactly what you want to do with the house."

"Would you like a brownie first?" She held out the plate.

"After that."

CHAPTER FOUR

*A*s they ate while sitting on the dusty floor, Paige began to describe her vision for the house. Her dreams fired up, and a smile came from deep inside her. For the first time in a while, she felt something she'd have to call *joy*. "I want to bring the house back to life." When he started to speak, she held up a hand to stop him. "I know that doesn't tell you anything."

He shook his head and shrugged. Then he grabbed another brownie off the plate and took a bite.

"I want to save everything we possibly can from the original house. I want to feel like I stepped back in time—with the addition of modern appliances and plumbing."

"I like that idea. So, this old wallpaper?" He gestured toward the wall facing the stairs.

"It's in rough shape. I think we'll have to remove it and paint."

"Are you planning to take out the trim molding, the tile around the fireplace, or anything like that?"

"Absolutely not. It would have to be really ugly for me to want to remove it." She thought about it for a second. "You know, there is some very ugly tile upstairs in my bedroom around the fireplace. It doesn't look original, though, so I think I can trash that and put in something that's more appropriate."

CJ nodded thoughtfully. "I can see where you're going with this."

When he eyed the last brownie, she couldn't help smiling. "Split it with me?"

"Sure."

She broke it in two and extended the plate to him. "Can you help me with the house?"

"I would like to say yes to every project. There's one question that matters: How much money do you have for this?"

She hated that it would come back to money, but she knew it had to, eventually. Paige named the figure.

CJ stared at her for a few seconds before shaking his head. "That is barely enough for materials."

Paige gasped.

"Maybe it could buy the materials. If you were frugal." His tone didn't convince her.

"I can definitely be careful about what I do." That was how she'd been living for years when she wasn't traveling for business. Then she understood his full meaning. "There isn't enough for material *and* labor." She might be in more trouble than she'd realized.

"Could you do a few rooms and wait until you have more money for the rest?" CJ asked.

The numbers wouldn't add up. If she couldn't fill all three guest rooms at a time, at least occasionally, she wouldn't earn the income she'd need to stay in Two Hearts. It was all a long shot, anyway.

Her stomach sank at this immediate drain on her funds that did little to help her reach her goals.

They both stood.

"I'll help you secure the house from the weather. No charge for my labor. It's the neighborly thing to do."

"Thank you!" Paige started to reach out to hug him but caught herself in time. CJ didn't seem like the hugging kind.

Paige went to the hardware store right after CJ left. The small amount of work he had done in the yard had made her want to try working on the house. Maybe she could also make a big difference with tiny changes.

She entered the building, which looked like it had been there forever. Inside, time seemed to have stopped in about the 1950s, from the wooden floors worn where generations of feet had walked, to the wood shelves stacked with hardware goods, to the antique brass cash register.

A kindly man her grandfather's age greeted her from behind a wooden counter. "You're the woman who bought the old Samuelson house." He added, "The pink house on the lake?"

She smiled. "Yes. I'm Paige Conroy."

"People just call me Albert. That house needs a fair bit of work. You must need a lot of supplies."

Her heart sank. She did have a long list, but she had to start small since she was doing it herself and on a budget. "I'm starting with fixing up the butler's pantry." When his brow furrowed, she added, "It's a small room."

"That makes sense, I guess. Stripper and paint?"

"Just what I need to strip the wood, hinges, and drawer pulls. If the wood is pretty, I may not paint it."

"I like that plan." Albert quickly grabbed everything and brought it to the front. "Remember that if you have any questions, you can call me here. I should say that I don't have all the answers." He leaned closer. "But I have most of them."

Knowing Albert was on her team gave her confidence a boost.

Back at home, she found herself staring at the butler's pantry and wondering if she should have bought more paint stripper. Everything but the floor in here needed attention. It seemed every decade had brought a new layer, if the various shades peeking through peeling and worn paint were any indication.

The old colors would have been an interesting look at the history of home décor—if she wasn't the one who was trying to save this particular house.

Paige stacked two boxes to use as a makeshift step stool. Next time, she'd add a stool and ladder to her list. Maybe Albert could deliver the ladder. There was no way she'd fit something that size in her tiny car.

The container of paint stripper gave her the directions she needed, so, starting with the upper cabinets on the left side of the room, she applied the chemical with a brush, hoping to see a miracle before her very eyes.

And she wasn't disappointed. Paint bubbled up. When she scraped off the treated area, she realized that she had only removed a layer or two of the paint. She turned and looked around the room. This task alone was going to take a very long time.

Her dog whimpered from beyond the barrier she'd set up at the door, made from an old wooden pallet she'd found beside the house.

"Don't worry, girl. We're going to transform this house into something we both like living in." She silently added words that she couldn't even say out loud. *And we'll earn income from it.*

Two hours later, Paige had made headway on the project. She'd stripped the top row of cupboards on the left side of the room down to the bare wood. Even that slight progress gave her a thrill of hope. Her vision *would* come to life. She would soon have people wanting to come here to stay in her bed and breakfast.

Now she just needed to remove the hardware and doors from the cabinets she had already finished.

"That should be easy, right?" Though the boxes had felt sturdy during the first part of the task, when she climbed back onto her "step stool," it shifted back and forth. She held onto the cabinet door's handle, and the wobbling stopped.

As if sensing her foolishness, the corgi barked wildly as Paige unscrewed the first cabinet's hinges and dropped them onto the counter below. She climbed down and moved the boxes in front of the next cabinet, put her foot on the cardboard, and reached up. This time, when she pulled on the cabinet door, it wouldn't budge. After unscrewing and removing the hinges, she grabbed the cabinet door—now seemingly free—and tugged it.

Nothing happened.

"You are going to come off, because this is going to work." Paige shook her finger at the offending door. She grabbed the door with both hands and yanked it back with all of her weight.

This time, it started to give. "Woo-hoo!" She tugged harder and felt it loosen. Putting one foot against the cabinets to gain more leverage, she grabbed the piece of wood and gave it everything she had.

It immediately came off. But her foot slipped, and she flew backward. Holding her breath, she waited to hit cabinets on the other side. *Clunk!* She skidded off them, jerked to the left, and hit the floor with a dull thud.

Blinking, she stared up at the cabinet door she clutched in both hands. Unfortunately, the pain in her right arm overrode any joy at her success.

Paige rose gingerly to her feet. "Ouch!" The gash on her arm was bigger than the one she'd gotten when she'd taken a cooking class a couple of years ago, and that was saying something.

Pressure! Wasn't that the advice? She ran to the kitchen and grabbed a clean towel, pressing it against the wound and wincing in pain. This injury might not be one she could handle herself.

Was Two Hearts large enough to have a doctor's office? A search on her phone showed a veterinarian, but no human doctor. Great. She'd be in the waiting room between a goat and a dog.

Maybe a nearby town had one, but she wouldn't know where to check. A quick call to Randi gave her the information she needed: A new nurse practitioner's office had opened near the hardware store.

A half hour later, she sat on the exam table. *Daniel* was embroidered on the nurse's white coat. The man turned her arm from side to side. "How did you manage this?"

"Home repairs."

He nodded. "I understand. My wife and I just bought a house and have been making updates." He gestured toward the front desk, so he must mean the pregnant woman she'd met when she'd signed in. "Kitchen?"

"I haven't been brave enough to tackle that. Butler's pantry."

His eyes widened. "You must have a large house. Wait! You're the woman who bought the house on the lake, aren't you?"

This small town thing was weird.

"That's me. I may have fallen off a box I used as a step stool."

Daniel stopped, his hand in mid-air with a liquid-soaked piece of gauze. "Box?"

She winced when he touched her cut with the gauze. "Not my best choice."

He silently continued his work. After cleaning her wound, he said, "I'm not going to do stitches, but I need you to rest your arm for a couple of days."

Two days of not being able to work? The clock kept ticking toward when she had to open.

Seeming to know she was about to argue, Daniel added, "Or I can do stitches and charge you more, and you may hurt more."

When he put it like that . . . "I'll behave."

After bandaging her, he said, "You're patched up. Not that I don't want to see you again soon, but I'd like to suggest asking Albert at the hardware store about stepladders."

She jumped to her feet. "I'm on my way to do that."

"Maybe you need help. What about CJ?"

Perhaps CJ *was* the only carpenter in town. She didn't want to say he'd turned down her project, though. "I'm going to try working on it alone." Honest truth. Saving money was above getting help.

"Understandable." He stepped back. "You're done for now." As she walked toward the door, he added. "Baby it."

She nodded and frowned. It just wouldn't be easy.

Paige sat on the floor of the parlor, eating her sandwich—one she'd slowly made using only her left hand—and looked up and out the side window to tall trees that flanked the house. She could hear the dog upstairs barking furiously. She'd probably scramble down the stairs in a couple of minutes.

A knock on the door brought Paige to her feet. After peering through the window beside the door, she pulled it open. "CJ? What are you doing here?" She put her hand over her mouth. "That sounded rude. I apologize."

"I was told I needed to stop by. I received a call that you had hurt yourself trying to fix up the place."

Word had already gotten around town? "It was only a small cut. And I was able to get by without stitches."

His eyebrows shot upward. "You caused enough damage that stitches were considered? What happened?"

Paige focused on the floor. "I needed to remove a cabinet door in the butler's pantry. It wouldn't release, so I pulled harder, and it did. It was a short fall." She struggled against shuddering when she thought of what it had felt like to free fall through the air and bounce off cabinets. She looked up at him.

CJ stared at her, slack-jawed. "I found room in my schedule, and I've checked my finances. I am going to be able to do some work for you." He took a step forward into the house, but she didn't move out of the middle of the doorway.

"I'll need to pay you for your time."

"You can't."

He was right. But she wouldn't take charity. "Can I sign an agreement that says I will pay you over time?"

He seemed about to argue, then changed his mind. "I can do that if you won't just let me help."

That made her sound ungrateful. "It isn't that. It's that this is supposed to be for a business that pays its own way."

"Micah can draw something up for you."

"Micah?"

"Micah Walker. He's Bella's husband and the town's lawyer."

"The only one?"

He gave a single nod.

"I'll give you his contact information. But we can get started now."

Should she do this? She moved her arm and the pain from her wound made her wince.

"Paige?"

Of course, she wanted help. Needed it, really. CJ was qualified, but she always felt odd around him. There was something about CJ that made her want to be near him, but at the same time made her want to run far away. He intrigued her.

Since she could find no good reason to turn him down, and a million reasons to accept, she stepped to the side and gestured for him to enter. She kept the front door wide open, though. She told herself it was because she wanted to let in some of the wonderful fresh air, but she knew it was really because he seemed to fill a space and take control of it, and she wasn't ready to let go of any control of her house. She'd have to figure out a way to be clear about that.

The dog flew down the stairs as fast as her short corgi legs could carry her. Or maybe she just thought their guest was somebody who would play with her. Was she the defender or playmate?

When the dog stopped at CJ's feet, he reached down to scratch her ears. The pup all but sighed at his attention. So much for being a watchdog.

They all walked into the butler's pantry. He carefully checked the areas she'd been working on. "Paige, you've done great work in here. I'm impressed."

When she heard approval in his voice, joy bubbled up out of her. "Thank you!" She reached out, pulled him tight in a hug, and then stepped back with her arms fluttering in the air. "Oh my goodness, I am so sorry. Pretend I never did that." Mortification rushed through her. She had just hugged the carpenter, a virtual stranger.

He stared at her a moment before replying. "That's okay. I didn't mind at all." Then he smiled widely. "Feel free to hug the carpenter any time you believe he's done good work."

The ice between them melted. Smiling, Paige said, "I doubt that will ever happen again. But thank you."

"Then walk me through here and show me again what you want. We need to make the most of your budget. Tell me what your plans are for the house."

Her plans. She hadn't shared those with anyone. Not in detail. Paige leaned against the staircase's newel post. "So in here, I just want to bring back the wood of the staircase and the railing, remove the paint from the fireplace mantel—I don't believe it would have been painted when the house was built—take down that wallpaper we talked about, and put a good coat of wax on the floors." She brushed her hands together. "Done."

He looked around as she spoke and nodded. "We should

make a list. Then it will be easier for me to assign a price to each thing."

Money. She'd become so carried away with ideas that she'd forgotten there was a cost to them. That was odd for someone who had spent her life with numbers.

"Let's get started, then." She had naively factored in enough money for cosmetics like paint, but this house needed major work. Paige swallowed hard. She'd have to see what CJ would say when they were done with the tour.

They went past the small bath downstairs, CJ only stepping in for a moment before he backed out swiftly. "The floor boards are soft, they're probably rotten. This is a gut job." He shuddered. "I don't think there's anything in there we can save." As they walked away, she thought she heard him mutter, "And I hope I can hire someone else to help with the demolition."

He sounded so disgusted that Paige couldn't help chuckling to herself. When they stood outside the kitchen, he said, "Other than the bathroom, the work seems simple. We'll need to deal with the windows one by one to try to refinish them. That can be done over time, though. As long as we get some glass in that one upstairs by the end of today."

Her whole world felt brighter. She still didn't know what to do about the money, but at least she wasn't alone anymore.

In the kitchen, CJ walked around the perimeter of the room. "We could save the cabinets. They were probably installed in the 1940s or 1950s, so they aren't Victorian, but they are good quality. And the built-in cabinet, which may be original."

"I love that one. They're all solid wood." And keeping anything would be cheaper.

"The floor?"

"No matter what I try, it won't come clean."

"Okay, so a new floor. And countertops? Tile can be . . ."

"Gross. I can't get the grout between the tiles completely clean, either."

He frowned. "Are you a medical professional? Your love of cleanliness reminds me of my sister, the nurse."

"Accountant. I couldn't even patch up my own arm, remember?" She lifted it and winced.

"Don't worry. I'll get to work on this. You know, there's still plenty of room to add a Hoosier cabinet or another old piece of furniture like that."

Paige sighed as she pictured it. "Period furniture would be wonderful."

"Maybe you can find some at auction or for sale somewhere else."

She perked up. Here he was again, offering good suggestions. And auctions sometimes sold things for a low cost, didn't they? They certainly did on TV and in movies.

CJ opened the door to a back staircase, which she hadn't told him about.

"You *have* been here before."

He reddened and tugged on the collar of his shirt as though it had grown too tight around his neck. "I've walked through it."

Clearly, that wasn't the whole story. She wouldn't push him for it, though.

"These stairs could get by with just being cleaned." CJ's phone rang, and he absentmindedly reached for it while he checked a window in the kitchen. "McIntosh here."

"CJ? Is that you?"

The voice sounded familiar, but he couldn't quite place it. Looking at the screen, he saw the name of a man he'd worked with in Colorado.

"Mark! How are you doing?" CJ pointed to the phone. Paige waved him toward the back door, and he stepped out to speak to his old friend.

"I'm great. Back in Alaska where I'm from, and I got married not too long ago."

"That seems to be happening more and more."

Mark laughed. "It does. All my brothers have found their special someones and gotten married. It's been quite a year for our family. My mom is finally getting the grandchildren she's wanted for forever."

"It's great touching base with you again. I should have done it a long time ago—"

"I could have reached out too. I've met so many people along the way, but some of them, like you, became friends. I shouldn't let them go." After a slight pause, Mark continued, "Well, friend, I have a possible job for you."

CJ stood straighter. Mark had worked on some high-end houses. It had been a pleasure teaming up with him, not only because he chose fun construction projects—from a carpenter's viewpoint—but also because Mark was a great guy to have as a boss. "What do you have in mind?"

"I have a job that I've been trying to get somebody to take." CJ could picture Mark rubbing his hand over his face in frustration. "I don't think by some miracle you're in Alaska right now, are you? I know you've been traveling the country."

"That's one of the few states I haven't been to yet. I've wanted to go for years; I just haven't gotten on the road to do it." Excitement about traveling to somewhere exotic bubbled up in CJ. "What kind of job is it?"

"It's a remote home. Off the grid, so no utilities are running to it. It's going to be solar and wind, and luxurious."

"How remote is remote?"

Mark sighed. "This is the point when I lose everyone I tell about the job. The jobsite is a small plane flight away—probably an hour from a road. I would drop you off, and you would be there for about six weeks or until you finished your part of the job, and then we'd pick you up. Food would be brought in—

you'd have anything you wanted as far as that went—and you'd live well."

But he wouldn't be anywhere near Two Hearts, Tennessee. "I'm going to tell you now that it's probably a no—"

Mark groaned. "Are you sure you can't consider it?"

Could he? "How much is the job going to pay?"

Mark named a figure.

CJ's mouth dropped open. "Wow!" He could not only buy a house here in Two Hearts, but he'd be able to fix it up immediately and not have any debt. "Did I hear you correctly?" He repeated the figure back to his friend.

"You did. The man has a seemingly bottomless budget, high-end tastes, and a desire to have the good life in middle-of-nowhere Alaska. He's ready to pay for it."

"You just need someone to do the job."

"I do. Are you that man?" Mark's voice rose, clearly in the hope of good news.

Was he? "I . . . don't think I am, Mark."

"You don't sound like you mean it."

"Maybe I don't. Let's call it a no, though."

"I'm going to call you back in a week to see if you have the same answer."

"Hang on. Don't you think you'll have somebody for the job before then?"

"I've been trying to fill this thing for two months. I'll call you back in a week." Mark ended the call.

CHAPTER FIVE

$\mathcal{T}$he corgi bounded up the stairs behind CJ and Paige as they continued the what-to-tackle-first tour. The three of them walked down the upstairs hallway. Everything was as CJ remembered it from his own walkthrough with Randi last month and the more recent tour with the matchmakers. Other than a couple of rooms, the house was in decent shape. Old but okay.

Then he got to the ones that weren't. The bedroom with the broken window needed more work than anything else. Quite a lot more.

He entered the room and carefully stepped over to it. He'd brought the plastic and tape he'd need to temporarily repair this. This window had to be a priority.

"Unless you're wearing shoes with sturdy soles, don't come over here." He heard a "woof." "And don't let the dog in here until it's cleaned up."

He went downstairs, back to the room under that one, to evaluate any ceiling damage from the elements entering the broken window. The dog sat beside him and also stared upward as though trying to discern what the human found so interesting. Paige stood on his other side, just close enough for him to pick up a coconut scent that he thought could be shampoo or lotion.

"This doesn't look too bad. I'll need to open things up to be sure, but I'm optimistic. I see slight staining under the window, but I think we can easily fix that."

"Great. I can use good news about this house. Can I help with anything?"

The dog chose that moment to go to the back door, where she stood and whimpered. "I think she needs to go out." A way to keep Paige occupied and take her coconut scent away from him appeared. "Maybe you could clear an area in the backyard for her."

Paige stared at the back of the house. "Um, are there snakes in the grass?"

Only half paying attention to her words, he opened a cupboard and examined the paint-coated hinges. "There could be."

A yelp startled him. He turned to see her panic-stricken face. The dog whined louder.

"Maybe she'd like a walk."

She relaxed. "Good idea." With the dog leashed, Paige and the corgi went down the front walk as he followed them to get supplies from his truck. After covering the window, he grabbed a scrap board and put it over the porch hole to make that safer.

An hour later, Paige came around the street corner with the dog taking the lead. "Dog! Slow down. Corgi, stop! Please! Spot! Rose. Sky. Peaches. Dixie!" She spewed random words as she was pulled along with the exuberant dog.

The canine clearly already knew where she lived, because she turned into the yard and up the walk toward him. Just as he wondered if he was about to be bowled over by her, she stopped and sat, staring up at him. "Good walk?"

Paige dropped a large manila envelope to the ground as she panted and leaned against the fence for support. The glare she gave him and the dog said it all.

He chuckled. "Can I ask what the assorted words meant? Is it a dog code I'm unaware of?"

She sucked in air. "I thought that if she had a name she responded to, then she'd do what I wanted."

He almost asked how that was working for her. Her expression all but dared him to say something like that. He moved on. "Spot, I understand. It's a classic dog name, even if I may point out that this particular dog has no spots."

Paige kept breathing like she'd been in a marathon.

"And Rose?"

She replied, this time between gasps. "I passed a beautiful rose bush. And there's a pretty blue sky today. Not a cloud in it." She made a sweeping gesture above her.

"All true. And—"

"Before you ask, I thought Peaches and Dixie were perfect for the South."

"All solid logic." He crouched, and the dog ran over to him. "They just weren't you, were they, girl?"

"What's in the envelope?"

"I called Micah on the way, and he quickly drew up a contract."

He sat back on his heels. "That was fast. We can sign it after lunch."

"Lunch?"

After a final scratch behind the dog's ears, he stood. "If you get lunch for us from Dinah's Place, I can keep working. And I'll watch her. Whatever her name is." He grinned.

The dog wandered over to the mass of weeds and flowers and sat in the middle of them.

"I can do that. There's so much work to do in the yard and the house, along with everything I need to learn about running

49

a bed and breakfast. Sometime soon, I need to weed the garden. Maybe there are more pretty things in that mess. Right now, I only see a daisy or two."

"Woof!" The dog's ears stood up in alert.

"Daisy?"

"Woof! Woof!"

CJ stood. "She seems to like that."

"Daisy!" Paige patted her leg.

The dog hurried over and looked up.

"Daisy, you have a name!"

The dog grinned.

"As to dog sitting while I'm gone, CJ, are you sure about that?"

Was he? The dog moved closer. "No problem." What would he do with a dog while he worked? She couldn't be allowed to get into the middle of his tools. The dog stood lower than the weeds that had been growing all summer, and that gave him an idea. "I'll start on the yard. You can help us when you return with a cold drink."

She lifted an eyebrow. "I'm going to get you a beverage in addition to lunch?"

"Yep. Daisy and I will start clearing the overgrowth that's hiding the house and will make it difficult to paint. If we have time, we'll work on the yard itself."

"We?"

"Daisy and I."

She laughed. "If your payment is just lunch and a drink, you're on."

She ran down the sidewalk before he could reply and drove away.

∼

When she returned, she found the promised progress outside. The house was even more pink now that she could see areas the overgrown brush had hidden.

Coming down the front porch steps, CJ said, "At least there's one thing I know without asking: You're going to paint the house's exterior."

She pictured the pretty pink house as it had been when she'd driven up the first day. "I will, but I'll stay true to its history."

"What do you mean?"

"I want to respect the former owner's choice, so I'll repaint it the same color."

He grabbed the hand rail and stopped in mid-stride. "*Pink?*" His expression would have been comical if he hadn't been so serious.

"Pink's a nice color."

"For flowers, and frosting, and . . ." He seemed lost for words.

"And houses." Standing here, she also noticed that the front door needed to be sanded and restained or painted. Was there nothing that didn't need attention? "Look at the color. It's almost white." Her words were an exaggeration, but it was a soft pink. Maybe he'd be lured over to her side.

He walked down the steps and toward the street. Just as she started to wonder if she'd offended him to the point that he was leaving, he turned and faced the house, his elbow resting on his other hand in a thoughtful pose. He cocked his head to one side and then the other as though examining all possibilities. "No. It's pink." He returned to the porch, tapping one of the columns as he passed. "And if I were ever to forget that, the darker pink trim would remind me."

She laughed. "I'll consider the color when it's time to paint. When can we get started on the renovation?"

He grinned. "We may want to figure out the cost and decide which projects to tackle now."

"Right. Money." That made her remember the papers Micah had drawn up. "Let's sign the contract now."

He hesitated again like he wanted to argue with her about it. Then he walked toward the door. "Sure. Let's get that done."

CHAPTER SIX

*P*aige pulled out a chair at her new kitchen table, which Cassie's fiancé, Greg, had dropped off yesterday. New-to-*her* table. It showed its wear with scratches and scuffs, but the round, light wood surface was solid, and she liked it. A couple with a pickup had brought in a small couch, which was now in her parlor. Would she have chosen green and gold? Probably not, but it was comfortable. More people arrived through the day: one with a lamp, another with a side table she could set it on, and a teenager even dropped off a vintage kitchen clock with mushrooms on it, which somehow fit her eclectic decor.

Mrs. Brantley had tsk-tsked most over her lack of a bed, so she hadn't been surprised when a double bed had also arrived yesterday. The two older men who'd brought it had carried it upstairs for her. Sleeping had been much better last night.

Happily seated, she studied the video playing on her computer. Omelets appeared easy to make. But how many times had she said that before about cooking? The good news was that she still had five and a half weeks to get her cooking skills in shape.

Taking a break from that, she did another search on bed and breakfasts. She felt like she was on track for a successful B&B, but maybe she'd missed something. One site had a great list.

Quality breakfast. Check. Well, it would be a check before she opened. She hoped.

Comfortable beds and quality linens. Check. She had researched those, and they would be arriving before her grand opening. She wouldn't get the same for herself, though. Of course, the rooms needed to be remodeled and livable first. And the bathrooms had to be functional. But it would all happen before opening day.

A sign out front to welcome guests and tell them they were in the right place. Check. She would get that done on schedule.

She hadn't found any surprises yet. Everything was on track. She continued reading the website. This one was particularly thorough. It wasn't as if she was new to this concept, though. She had researched owning a bed and breakfast for what felt like forever.

As Paige scrolled downward, the word *website* jumped at her from the page. She knew she needed a website. Every business did, especially a travel business. But with her thoughts and her actions focused on getting this building in shape for guests, she hadn't begun working on it yet.

Photos would be important. The idea of stepping away from renovation even for a short time to get out her camera made her heart sing. But her house had to make a transformation first.

She refused to call it a money pit. That would give it power in her mind, and she didn't want it to hold that over her. It was simply an *almost* beautiful house.

Flipping through B&B websites, she found a distinct pattern. Not only did she need pictures of the rooms and outside, she also needed photos of her nemesis: Food.

Many of the establishments—especially the ones that seemed a little "higher end," as she wanted to bill herself—

showed off pictures of the food they served. Quite a few of them provided treats. Some even had an afternoon tea. That sounded like a lovely idea.

She was an intelligent, well-educated woman. She had worked with challenging clients at work time and time again and come out on top.

Paige closed her eyes and sighed. Then why couldn't she seem to make a meal anyone would want to eat?

She refused to be defeated. Even though her house had to be brought to life before she could have paying visitors, she still had to practice. Past attempts indicated that she'd have to practice *a lot*.

But if guests wanted treats in the afternoon, she was going to give them treats. With that in mind, she continued on with the search terms *easy sweet treat*. Options flew by as she scrolled down page after page. Unfortunately, *easy* seemed to be one of those words that was hard to pin down. If someone truly knew how to cook, these recipes probably would be straightforward.

Then a recipe caught her eye. It was as though a light shone above it. It used premade cookie dough that she could buy at the grocery store. The directions said to pat that into a pan and, when it was baked, cut it into small squares. The guests could have warm chocolate chip cookie bars. That felt a little more dressed up than just a cookie.

Maybe she could decorate them with whipped cream. No, that would be messy. Powdered sugar. It would be only a little messy and it would seem elegant. Or frosting. Frosting could work really well on a chocolate chip cookie dough bar. She scribbled a note on the pad next to her, adding the cookie dough to her grocery list.

After a half-hour's drive, she pushed a grocery cart around the store in a neighboring town. Stopping at the cold case, she was pleased to find multiple options for premade dough. Why hadn't this occurred to her before? They even had cinnamon rolls she could pop out of the container and put in the oven. Who would know they weren't homemade? They would bake in her oven, right?

She grabbed several kinds to test and left a short time later with a cart full of eggs, bacon, potatoes, and additional supplies she could use to try for the other portion of her breakfast. It was all well and good to have cinnamon rolls in the morning, but you couldn't just put one of those on a plate in front of somebody. There had to be more.

When she arrived at the house, she was pleased to see that no one else was around. She pulled to a stop beside the fence and hurried inside, where she quickly unloaded the groceries, and put them away before CJ came back from a run for more supplies.

She set to work. Glorious chocolate chip cookie bars would be ready in less than a half hour. With the dough patted into the pan, she stepped back and smiled. She could do this. Sure, she was good with numbers. But that didn't mean she couldn't do something creative like this, right?

Paige slid them into the oven. Then she put the light on inside it and leaned down to look through the window. They would be gorgeous. Checking her watch, she saw she had just enough time to get another square foot of weeding done before this deliciousness came out. Maybe she'd even be able to offer CJ a sweet treat when he returned.

Practically skipping out the front door, she went to the garden and got to work. A short time later, she stepped into the house and started running for the kitchen. Instead of chocolaty cookie deliciousness, she smelled smoke.

Paige whipped the oven door open, grabbed the pan with a potholder, and dropped it on top of the stove. Smoke billowed up from what should have been a golden cookie bar with dark-brown bits of chocolate. Instead, it was dark brown everywhere.

Almost, but not quite, black. An improvement over past baking attempts, but still inedible.

She threw open the kitchen windows, and those that would open in the front parlor, to blow the smell out. Returning, she stared at the fridge, which contained the other kinds of cookie dough. Should she try again? Or was she just wasting her time?

Paige straightened and eyed the pan of brown not-so-goodness.

Did she dare?

She cut a piece out of the center, thinking that might look nicer than a crispy edge. Setting it on a pretty plate, she also realized she could see the chocolate chips inside. The beauty of this was that the cookie was blackened slightly more on top but enough throughout that it appeared to be a delicious brownie.

She grabbed the package of powdered sugar and carefully sifted it through a strainer as she'd seen done on one video. The brownie now had a light dusting of powdered sugar and actually looked quite tasty.

Chuckling, Paige got out her camera and started snapping photos. She might be terrible at baking, but she could take a good shot. She soon had a selection to choose from, and, flipping through her options on the back of the camera, she knew she had the right one.

And it wouldn't be a bait and switch. She'd figure out how to make a real brownie before then. She could try a brownie mix. She ignored the voice in her head that said premade cookie dough hadn't worked. For the millionth time, she wished her dad had had basic cooking skills he could have shared with her. Or that she'd had time to learn as an adult, but work had always been too demanding.

~

CJ tossed a newly cut shrub over Paige's fence, adding it to the growing pile of debris he would haul off when he finished. Checking his watch, he found that he'd been at this for a long hour and a half. He stood up, stretched, and walked toward the porch with Daisy nipping at his heels. He paused for a moment and reached down to scratch her behind the ears. Satisfied, she raced off to chatter at a squirrel that had the nerve to be in a tree on her property.

He opened the door and looked around. "Paige?" No answer. He went toward the kitchen so he could get a drink of water from the sink.

As he passed through the kitchen entry, he noticed the windows were open, and an odd odor filled the air. A brownie on a plate, dusted with powdered sugar, caught his attention. "Wow." When he swung around to the left, CJ saw a pan of them on the stovetop. The single one was so pretty that she must have taken a photo of it. Maybe for social media.

Paige wouldn't miss a small sliver of brownie, would she? It seemed like she had everything she needed for the photo shoot. He leaned to his left to peer through the doorway. Finding no one, he took a knife out of a drawer and ran it down the brownie to remove what he hoped would be an undetectable strip.

When he picked it up and put it in his hand, melted chocolate smeared over his palm. "Warm chocolate chips." CJ closed his eyes and sighed. "Could anything be better than warm chocolate chips?"

The treat was an unusual darker brown on the outside and a lighter color on the inside. Must be a different recipe than he'd seen before. He popped a bite of brownie into his mouth, ready for the chocolate that would melt over his tongue and the warmth of the darker chocolate in the brownie itself, whether it was fudgy or cakey. He was open to either option.

The brownie hit his tongue.

CJ raced for the kitchen sink, spitting the bite out. "Oh! Yuck!" He stuck his face under the faucet and rinsed his mouth. The bitter taste wouldn't go away.

A box of crackers on the counter stood open, so he grabbed a few and shoved them into his mouth. Swallowing, he realized the nastiness hadn't gone away. He hurried over to the refrigerator and opened it to see if there was food or drink in there that he could use. It was filled with food, and he scanned it to find something—anything—stronger than the burned whatever-that-was.

Hot sauce called to him. Grabbing the bottle, he unscrewed the cap and dripped some of it onto his tongue. When he swished that around in his mouth, it lit on fire. He grabbed the glass of water and chugged it down.

Paige stepped into the kitchen. She stopped and looked from him to the brownies to his palm, which was still covered with melted chocolate.

"Did you eat that?" she said with horror and pointed at the pan.

Fanning at the noxious flames that must be shooting from his mouth, he said, "I thought it was brownies. I thought you wouldn't mind."

A mortified expression swept over her. She closed her eyes and opened them slowly. "I am so sorry, CJ. I stepped away from the oven when they were baking, and I shouldn't have."

When he saw tears welling in her eyes, he said, "It's okay, Paige. Don't worry." She still looked like her sorrow was increasing. "I'm sure the taste will leave my mouth soon." He put as much hope as he could in that last statement.

Paige swallowed hard. "I'm sorry," she repeated in a low voice he could barely hear.

"It's okay." The display on the plate caught his eye. "But why did you take a picture of it?"

She gasped and put a hand over her mouth. "Oh my

goodness. I forgot that I'd left that there." She hurried over and picked it up. In seconds, the pretty brownie had been dumped in the trash can. She held up the plate. "I'm surprised it didn't burn a hole in the china."

He chuckled. "That probably wasn't funny."

She looked heavenward. "I've learned that I have to laugh about the situation. I didn't mean to poison you, though."

He filled the glass again and took a few deep swallows. "Don't worry about it." He hoped that sounded happy.

Paige scrunched her eyes as she stared at him. "It was really bad, wasn't it?"

She seemed to want an honest answer. "It was the worst thing I have ever put in my mouth in my entire life. I have traveled and eaten at diners and all kinds of places big and small across this great land of ours. Bad."

Paige grinned. He was so startled that he took a step backward.

"I had a feeling it would be nasty. I do think it would have been tasty, though, if the chocolate chip cookie bars had come out right."

He slowly turned his head back toward the offending pan on the stove. "It wasn't even brownies?"

"Nope." A chuckle escaped her, surprising him again. "I tried so hard. I thought if I used premade dough that it would work out. I mean, what could go wrong?" She shrugged.

How did he answer that question?

Before he had a chance, she continued, "I have to keep going, though. A bed and breakfast needs to have baked goods. And breakfast." She grabbed the pan off the stove, carried it to the trash can, and dumped out the contents. "My next attempt will be better."

CJ held back against a shudder. He scraped his tongue across his top teeth, trying to rid himself of the last hints of hot sauce and charcoal. When it came time for another tasting, he would suddenly need to be elsewhere. Or full.

Turning toward him with a smile, she said, "Are you ready to start on the bedroom upstairs that we talked about?"

He would gladly take a break from yard work. "Let's do it. You're going to need a dust mask for this. Wall-to-wall carpet in a house that was abandoned? I don't even want to imagine what might be living in it. Or was once there."

"That sounds worse than burned chocolate chip cookie bars."

Maybe not. As they went upstairs, he wondered how many attempts she'd made at trying to bake something only to have it turn out like that. He felt sorry for her. But not enough to try anything until someone else had first.

Paige rubbed her hands together with glee. Today, she would have a delicious lunch. Breakfast had not gone well, but she'd researched how to recreate the carrot ginger soup she used to love in her favorite restaurant near her old office. It looked easy.

You cooked the carrots and ginger to death, put the mixture in a blender, and hit the button. They'd served it with a sandwich of avocado, cheese, and tomato, and she could certainly do that.

Something good would finally come out of her kitchen. And CJ wasn't here this morning, since he'd had to run to a neighboring town for additional supplies, so she wouldn't have the pressure of someone else's expectations.

"But I will not fail," she said forcefully.

She put the carrots and pieces of fresh ginger root on to boil exactly as the blog post directed. Some salt and pepper completed the easy project.

With that going—and a timer carefully set this time—she went into the front parlor to work for a few minutes.

Wallpaper hung in strips from some places and was still apparently glued to the wall in others, so she got to work ripping and pulling it off. She could at least make her job easier when she used the steamer to remove the rest. She was starting to catch on with all of this. By the time she was done, she might actually know what she was doing.

As she peeled the last strip from the wall, her timer went off, and she returned to the kitchen. Opening the pan, she saw a perfectly executed recipe. Nothing had burned. She drained the carrots exactly as the recipe directed and put them in the blender. Then she eyed the directions. They said to do this in several batches in the blender, but maybe they'd used a smaller blender. It seemed much easier to puree the whole amount.

She topped it with the lid on carefully, pressing it down to seal it tightly. Then she hit the Blend button.

The machine whirred. Smiling, she watched the mixture become the soup she loved. Then a *pop* sounded, and the lid and the still-blending carrot mixture flew into the air. She stabbed at the buttons to turn it off.

Silence reigned, and hot orange soup descended. Carrot puree covered the cupboards, the refrigerator, and the floor. When she looked upward and sighed, she saw that it also speckled the ceiling.

"So much for lunch."

Fortunately, CJ had been working downstairs yesterday afternoon, so his step ladder was where she could easily drag it into the kitchen. A few minutes later, she had wiped down half the cupboards and the fridge, and climbed the ladder with wet rags and a pail of clean water. As she reached up, she heard the front door open.

"Paige, are you home?"

Was there any way she could explain this mess without

admitting her failure? She eyeballed the orange splotches. No, probably not. With a sigh, she answered, "I'm in the kitchen, CJ."

He stepped through the doorway and stopped. "We didn't need to do any work on the kitchen ceiling, right?" Then his eyes opened wide, and he looked around the room, taking in the orange flecks that still speckled the floor and some of the cupboards . "What happened?"

"Let's just say I will not be having carrot soup for lunch. I was going to offer you some too."

When he took a step toward her, his arms windmilled, and his feet slipped out from under him. "Oomph." He landed flat on his back.

She carefully stepped down the ladder and onto the slippery floor. "Are you okay?"

CJ nodded from where he lay on the old linoleum. He tested his arms and legs and seemed to find everything working, because he sat up, then stood with only a wince. "Just don't tell anyone that I was felled by carrot soup."

She reached out her hand to help him up. "Since your secret is also my secret, it's safe with me." That level of humiliation didn't need to be shared.

His warm hand slipped into hers, and she struggled against a sigh. Using her for balance, he let go as soon as he was on his feet. "But I probably will have a few bruises tomorrow." He reached for the countertop to steady himself as he inched away from the messy part of the floor. "Paige, maybe cooking isn't for you. I mean, I know you're good at other things."

Not cook? "You don't understand, CJ. I want this to be a bed and *breakfast*. Food is in the title. And guests will expect edible food. That isn't too much to ask, is it?"

He went over to where the mop was and pulled it out, wetted it in the sink, and came back to run it over the floor. "While that may be true, evidence shows that this hasn't gone well for you. Maybe if someone showed you how to cook?"

She shook her head. "No! I don't want anyone to know I'm this bad at it. What if word gets around that the woman who owns the bed and breakfast is a terrible cook who destroys baked goods and shoots soup onto the ceiling?"

Holding the mop, he looked up at her, and she saw his lip twitch for a second before he caught it between his teeth. He swallowed hard, opened his mouth as though to speak, and closed it shut again. A moment later, he said, "Paige, did you listen to your own words?"

She thought over what she had said. A vivid image appeared. "It is kind of funny, isn't it?"

He grinned. "Other than my backside, there's no damage. Laughter wins."

She put her hands in the air in a shrug. "It's so much better than crying. But I'm still left without lunch, and I don't know how to serve a decent breakfast to guests. The clock is ticking, CJ." She tapped her finger on her watch.

"Why is the clock ticking?"

"I have to start earning income. I'd like to open by October."

CJ's eyes had grown bigger and bigger as she'd explained. "Do you realize the amount of work we have to do in this place? You're talking about getting three bedrooms and bathrooms ready, not to mention making the public spaces presentable."

She stood straighter. "I don't think I have a choice." Paige held her breath, waiting for his reply. She couldn't pull this off alone.

After a long minute or two, he nodded. "We can do this."

"It will help get money faster."

"I know. We've reviewed your budget, and there's just enough to get this done with me earning what I need to survive. Maybe it's best that we don't stretch out the project."

"I wish I could pay you more."

"Yeah, but this is the way it is. It may not be as fancy as it will be in a few years when you add more to it, but we can get you bathrooms that function and remove the danger." He muttered what sounded like, "I hope." He cocked his head to the side. "And it will be pretty. I added that for you. Not so much me."

She giggled. "Then let's do this. I'm all in." She gazed around her kitchen fondly.

"I do know how to cook a few things. I'm a bachelor, so I've had to learn to take care of myself. It's nothing fancy, but I can teach you how to make scrambled eggs and bacon and even pancakes. Would that help?"

Paige lunged at CJ, wrapping her arms around him and squeezing him tightly. "Thank you! I don't have to tell anyone new, and I get to figure out how to be a great cook."

His muffled voice against her cheek said, "Not great. But edible. Even decent." He brushed the hair off her face, and she felt the gentle whisper of his fingers on her skin. When she stepped back, they were just inches apart. He looked from her eyes to her lips. "Paige?"

This was a moment that would draw him across the line from contractor and maybe even friend to something that would be harder to back out of. She stepped away and turned toward her ladder. "I appreciate your help. I think this will go well."

After a moment's pause, he said, "You may be right." His voice held less optimism than hers did. Why did he sound that way? And should she be worried?

CHAPTER SEVEN

*C*J kneeled in front of the wooden bench he'd just built in Mrs. Brantley's backyard. He reached for the coarse grade of sandpaper to start his finishing touches. He still wasn't sure where the woman was going to put it. Only that she'd come to him yesterday and requested that he make it as soon as he could.

He jumped when a voice spoke from behind him.

"Sorry to startle you, CJ!" He turned to look up at Mrs. Brantley. "I just wondered if you would like to stay for dinner. I'm making a big chicken pot pie and some homemade biscuits."

CJ's mouth started to water. He'd never had a bad bite of food at this house. "Is Greg coming over?"

Mrs. Brantley fidgeted with her hands as she nervously rubbed them together. "I don't believe he'll be here tonight." She gave a laugh that seemed forced. Something about this felt off. "But he may stop by."

No matter what was going on, her chicken pot pie would beat the can of soup that he probably would have opened for dinner otherwise. "Then count me in."

After a single nod, she returned to the back door and

opened it. Delicious cooking scents wafted out. Mouth watering, he continued with the bench. After he finished sanding with the fine sandpaper, he stood and stepped back to admire his work. It was made of oak, wide enough for two people to sit down at one time, and it had a shelf underneath at an angle that you could rest footwear on. He was rather proud of the piece. But he still hadn't figured out why she'd needed it in a hurry or what she was going to do with it. Maybe it was a gift.

He reached upward and stretched with his hands over his head—first to the right and then to the left—and then toward the ground. Standing upright again, he arched his back to stretch out the kinks. He enjoyed the results of his work, but not always the positions he had to be in to get it done.

Cassie walked around the corner of the house.

"Has my future mother-in-law invited you to dinner?" She shifted from foot to foot. Cassie could stand up against bridezillas, so she wasn't usually the fidgety type. What was going on? And did he want to be involved with it?

"She did. And I'm looking forward to it." He heard what sounded like a question mark at the end of his own sentence.

Cassie laughed nervously. "I'm sure it will be wonderful." She went inside, and when she opened the door, he caught the scent of the food as it billowed out again. No matter what was going on, he had to stay. His stomach would never forgive him if he walked away from a meal that smelled that good.

CJ continued working, but the thought that something wasn't right kept tickling the back of his mind. Mrs. Brantley had acted like this bench was an emergency. And yet she didn't seem to be in any hurry to get it. But maybe he'd misunderstood. He got up and headed toward the house.

Mrs. Brantley answered his knock. "CJ? Is anything wrong?"

"I just wondered where you'd be placing the bench so I would know how to stain it."

And then, the impossible happened. The unflappable Mrs. Brantley started to shift on her feet in a nervous way.

"I think that bench will be a gift." She nodded vigorously. "Yes, definitely a gift."

She wasn't sure if it was a gift, yet she'd needed it built immediately?

"Stain it however you think is best. I trust your judgment."

"Okay. Then I will get back to work." He'd never had a client this insistent that a job needed to be done, but equally uncaring about how.

She smiled at him broadly. "How much time until it's finished?"

He glanced over his shoulder at the project, doing some quick calculations. "I'd say about an hour."

"That should be about right."

He would have normally asked *for what?*, but decided not to bother considering how this conversation had gone. Finally, a normal-sounding Mrs. Brantley asked, "Can I get you something refreshing to drink?"

He scrubbed his fist across his forehead. "It has gotten hot out here this afternoon. Lemonade?"

"On its way."

She closed the door, and then he heard whistling from what must be near the fridge. He wandered back over to his bench and eyeballed it. This was an odd situation that seemed to be getting odder by the second. But who was he to complain? Mrs. Brantley always paid him for his work, usually with extra added. A couple of minutes later, she opened the door and came out, carrying the glass of lemonade in one hand and a napkin with a cookie on it in the other.

"I brought you something small because I wanted to make sure you were hungry.

That's a new treat I'm trying. I know it's a lot of citrus in one place, but it's a lemon-flavored sugar cookie with orange frosting."

He took a bite, and it melted in his mouth. This woman knew how to bake. "Delicious," he said around a mouthful of crumbles.

She beamed. "I'm so glad. Cassie thinks some of her couples might like to have cookies served at their weddings. Maybe something special. What do you think? Are these right for a wedding?"

"I have no idea, ma'am."

"You're a young man who must be thinking about getting married at some point."

He gasped, the crumbs going down the wrong way. Coughing, he reached for the lemonade. When he could breathe again, he said, "Don't even consider that. I have no intention of getting married any time soon."

He wasn't sure if the expression on her face was disappointment or determination. The first one he could handle. The second one scared him more than he wanted to admit.

"I'm sure it's just that you haven't met the right woman yet."

An image of Paige came to mind. He banished it from his thoughts. He'd barely spent any time with her, and she certainly shouldn't be popping in at moments like this one.

She patted him on his shoulder. "Don't worry about it. I'm sure the woman of your dreams will appear when it's time."

She started to walk away, then turned back and said, "Dinner will be ready in about an hour."

CJ took a moment to drink his lemonade, wondering the entire time if there was a hidden message in what the older woman had just said. He knew his own mother would love it if he settled down and got married. If he got over what she called "his itchy feet." But there were always more things to see in the world, and he liked to stay on the move.

He finished up about five minutes short of the time he'd stated. Leaning back on his heels, he admired his work. The bench had come out very nicely, and the light stain on it should look good in almost any home. Including that of the mysterious gift recipient. As he wondered where he should put it, Greg pulled up in the driveway. When his friend stepped out of his police car, he did a double take at finding CJ in the backyard. "What did my mother talk you into doing this time?"

CJ chuckled. "She needed an emergency bench made. She called me last night and asked if I could come over this morning and do it."

Greg walked over and studied the project. "It's a nice bench. Did she tell you where she's planning to put it?"

"She *thought* it was going to be a gift. Although, between you and me, I think she made that up on the spot."

Greg stared at him. "That sounds odd to me."

"To you and me both. But your mom's a nice lady, so here I am."

Greg shrugged. "I'm sure there's a good reason for it."

"Besides, she invited me to stay for dinner."

His friend grinned. "When you're a bachelor, you have to take advantage of these things."

"That's the truth. How's Cassie's cooking coming along?"

Greg shrugged. "Good. Most of the time. There is an incident now and then, though . . ."

CJ sincerely hoped he found a woman that was a great cook. Would that be the only factor that would make him want to marry her? Absolutely not. But it would help sweeten the deal.

"Cassie's making dinner for me tonight. I'm only here to change from my uniform into what she calls 'less stuffy and more friendly and comfortable' clothing."

"That's a mouthful."

"I may have paraphrased it. Let's just say that when we're relaxing, she doesn't like it when I'm wearing my sheriff's uniform." Greg started for the hallway. "I'd better get going. Have a good dinner. It's Monday, so that usually means meatloaf."

"She said chicken pot pie."

"She does break the mold every once in a while." Greg went up the stairs to his apartment. Halfway up them, he added, "Why don't you put the bench for the unknown recipient in the garage? I think it's unlocked."

CJ reached for the now-dry piece of furniture and carted it over there, lifted the door to the garage, and stowed it off to the side where it wouldn't be damaged. Then he headed over to the back door and tapped on it again.

"The bench is done, Mrs. Brantley," he said when she opened the door for him and ushered him inside with her dog Cookie at her side.

"That's wonderful."

"Maybe I shouldn't have put it in the garage, as Greg suggested, without showing it to you first."

She waved away his comment. "I'm sure it's fine. Greg's here?"

"He's just here to change."

"That makes sense. He's not here as much as he used to be. But I did gain a daughter in the process, so I'm not complaining." She gleefully added, "And maybe grandbabies in the not-too-distant future."

Mrs. Brantley focused her attention on him. "Would you like to have children someday?"

His future seemed to be on her mind today. CJ replied, "I suppose at some point. I'm from a family of six kids, though. So I've already taken care of younger siblings. I've kind of done the parenting thing."

She pursed her lips together and shook her head. He had somehow failed her with that response. "Why don't you come inside and get cleaned up? Dinner will be soon." When he went toward the kitchen sink where he usually washed his hands when he had been working for her, she directed him instead out of the kitchen and down the hall. "You'll be more comfortable in the hall bath."

He was comfortable washing his hands in any sink. But she was the host. CJ walked to the bathroom, whistling a happy tune. He had completed a project, albeit a very small project, and he was about to enjoy a homemade dinner. All in all, this was a good day. When he returned with a clean face and hands, he heard women speaking in the kitchen. Cassie must have returned for dinner after all.

He stepped into the kitchen and froze.

Michelle from the diner was standing there, with a glass of what must be iced tea in her hand. She wasn't wearing her pink uniform shirt, but a pretty top that flattered her features. It was too bad that she didn't inspire any interest in him. She'd certainly expressed it toward him on multiple occasions.

"CJ, it's great to see you here," Mrs. Brantley said, as though she hadn't seen him for a week.

Michelle looked up from her tea with a wide-eyed expression.

CJ gulped. They'd been set up.

"I'm so glad that you could both come for dinner. I think you're going to enjoy it. At least I hope you do." Mrs. Brantley dropped a bite of what must be chicken down to Cookie, who caught it midair. The dog swallowed, then sat and stared up at her owner, clearly waiting for another treat.

CJ glanced at Michelle and shrugged. Maybe dinner wasn't the fix-up it seemed to be.

"It smells wonderful," Michelle said.

He could not argue with that.

"Have a seat." Mrs. Brantley paused. "I could have us move to the dining room to make it more formal."

CJ shook his head. The last thing he wanted was for this to feel more like a date. "I always enjoy sitting in your kitchen."

Michelle said, "Me too!" She appeared more comfortable than he did. But everyone in town knew that Michelle wanted to get married. At least, every single man knew. She was a great woman, but he didn't feel any chemistry. Paige came to mind, but they didn't work together any better than he and Michelle did.

When they were seated, Mrs. Brantley placed a casserole dish of chicken pot pie on the table. Then she added a basket filled with what smelled like homemade biscuits, followed by green beans with bacon, a Southern staple. They certainly wouldn't have any shortage of food for dinner tonight. There were only the three places set at the table, so it must be that Cassie couldn't come. He would have liked to have had Cassie and Greg at the table to help diffuse the matchmaker feel to the meal.

Mrs. Brantley still seemed nervous, not an emotion he was used to seeing in her. "Oh dear, I forgot to get you something to drink." She bustled over to the refrigerator, filled glasses, and returned with iced tea. But she didn't sit down. "Oh, and let me get you some butter for those rolls. There's nothing better than melting butter on yeast rolls fresh from the oven." She laughed anxiously.

Mrs. Brantley's phone rang from where it lay on the kitchen counter. She hurried over to it and picked it up. "Oh my! Really? You don't say!"

CJ couldn't help but overhear her half of the conversation as he reached for the pan and scooped some of the thick broth with the chunks of chicken and crust onto his plate. Then he passed the bowl to Michelle, and she did the same.

Mrs. Brantley continued to speak, many of the words followed by what sounded like very dramatic exclamation marks. By the time CJ and Michelle had their plates filled, Mrs.

Brantley was setting down her phone. She ran her fingers through her hair and pushed it back from her head, no mean feat since it was actually quite short to start with. Then she said the words that he'd thought might be coming but had hoped would not. "I'm sorry, but that was Cassie, and I need to run out for just a few minutes. If you two wouldn't mind, you just have a nice dinner there between the two of you, and I will be back, probably before you've finished eating." She giggled. Giggled!

Then she made a beeline for the back door, grabbing her purse along the way—which he hadn't even noticed was resting on the end of the kitchen counter, apparently ready for her escape. "Dessert is over there." She pointed toward the kitchen counter as she went out the door.

The screen door smacked shut behind her. He stared at it, hoping she would change her mind and return. When that didn't happen, he gulped. The bachelor alarm he had silenced came roaring to life.

Staring at his plate, he wondered if he could somehow box up his dinner and take it away gracefully in a way that wouldn't offend Michelle. His mother would come after him and smack him on the side of his head if he was rude to a woman. She'd do that to any of her boys. They had all been taught to respect women.

Before he had a chance to say anything, Michelle spoke up. "This isn't awkward, is it?"

He turned to her and saw glee dancing in her eyes. She really was pretty. It was too bad he wasn't attracted to her in the slightest.

"Now that you've broken the ice, maybe we can just have a nice dinner together as friends?"

"I'm all for that. I may eat well down at Dinah's—because Dinah is an amazing cook—but I have loved Mrs. Brantley's chicken pot pie since I was a kid. She'd invite my family over when we were growing up, and this was the dinner she made once she knew that I loved it so much."

A comfortable, friendly half hour later, they were both finished. Michelle started to stand with her plate, but he waved her back into her seat. "You serve people all day long. Let me do this for you."

She watched him take both plates to the sink. He could feel her eyes on his back.

"Are you sure you aren't available?"

He chuckled.

"Before you answer that, let me say that I'm kidding. I think we can both agree that we believe the other one is a nice human being, but we don't want to spend the rest of our lives together."

He focused on her so she would know he was sincere. "I wish it wasn't so, because you're pretty and easy to be around, Michelle. I know the right guy will come along for you."

"Yeah. Yeah. I keep hearing that."

"I kind of thought Mrs. Brantley would be back in time for us to have dessert." He paused for a second, but he couldn't hear a car coming or any movement outside.

"She would not want us to go without dessert."

"Agreed."

He grabbed the tin that Mrs. Brantley had gestured toward when she'd mentioned dessert and brought it to the table. Prying it open, he found several kinds of cookies, including the lemon-orange one he'd had earlier. He took one of those and so did Michelle, both immediately taking a bite.

"So, are you hanging around this town for a while, then, CJ?"

He swallowed. "I really don't know. I had thought about buying that house on the lake."

She laughed as she reached for a second cookie out of the tin. "Which house on the lake? There are so many empty places out there."

"The big gorgeous one that—"

"Paige bought."

He shrugged. "That's the one."

"There are other houses beside it and around the lake that are beautiful." She shrugged. "Or at least they could be if someone fixed them up."

"None of them have the same charm to me, the same potential. I walked in that house, and it just felt special to me." He felt his face burning as he realized he'd gotten a little too open with his emotions.

Michelle reached for another cookie. "I know what you mean. There's a little house in town that I've been admiring for a while. When Cassie moved here and bought hers, it made me think about the future and what I want to do."

Should he consider other houses?

Michelle continued before he could figure that out. "The least you can do, then, is help Paige fix it up." She grabbed a fourth cookie. "I don't have any restraint around anything Mrs. Brantley bakes. She should open a shop. She'd sell out every day."

CJ took a couple more.

Mrs. Brantley entered the house with her dog beside her. She looked at the two of them still seated at the table, laughing, and smiled widely. She clearly thought her work had been done.

CJ pushed back his chair and stood. "Thank you for dinner, Mrs. Brantley. I think that Michelle and I can agree that it was delicious and enlightening."

Michelle also stood. "Thank you. As always, it was wonderful. I think it's time for me to go now."

"I'll be on my way too," CJ added.

Michelle went out the door as he stepped closer to his host. "Thank you again." He leaned forward and kissed Mrs. Brantley on her cheek. "My mom has tried this trick with her boys before." He dropped his voice for the last words. "It didn't work then either."

The always in-charge and capable older woman sputtered a response. "I . . . I . . . I don't know what you mean."

He chuckled. "It's a matchmaking failure."

Her face dropped. "Oh. I had so hoped . . ."

CJ whistled as he stepped out the back door, reaching down to pat Cookie on the head as he went out. He barely heard her words when she said, "I'm sure we'll find the right person eventually," as he exited. What instinct did women have that drove them to try to make matches?"

His conversation with Michelle replayed in his head. He had wanted to buy that house. The money sat in his bank account, waiting. He did need to earn money, but not just to survive, as he'd been saying. He needed to keep his hard-earned savings tucked aside, because the idea of owning a house somewhere had grown on him the more he'd considered it. Now he just had to figure out if Two Hearts was the permanent place for him.

CHAPTER EIGHT

The wonderful thing about a small town was that Paige could walk almost anywhere if she chose to. The bad thing was that walking allowed her to focus completely and not be distracted by having to watch the road. As every step took her closer to Bella's, Paige became a little more nervous.

She'd only met the woman once, and now she'd been invited to dinner. Bella had called this morning and surprised her with the invitation. This sort of thing didn't usually happen in the city, and she wasn't sure whether it was a good or a bad thing.

As her footsteps slowed, she gave herself a stern talking-to. "Paige Conroy, you know you have wanted to move to a small town for years. You're here now, and people are being friendly and inviting you over. There's no reason to be anxious."

A car drove by, and the driver watched her as she passed. Now Paige would be known as that crazy lady who talked to herself while she walked. Wasn't that wonderful? Maybe they'd think she was talking on the phone. You could hide a lot of crazy behind that.

She reached the address that Bella had texted her. It was a cute older house in great shape—unlike many in this town, including her own. Seeing the ones that were in good shape gave her hope. She walked up to the door, boldly reached her hand up to knock . . . and froze. What did she say to someone she barely knew?

She rapped on the door. Unless she wanted to turn tail and run back to the city, she needed to embrace every bold cell of her body and step away from being an introvert.

The door opened to reveal Bella's husband, Micah. "Welcome to our home."

"I want to thank you and Bella for inviting me," she blurted.

Bella stepped out of the kitchen, drying her hands on a towel. "Paige! I'm so glad you could come." She had an infectious smile. "We're having my grandmother's lasagna recipe. I hope you like lasagna," she added more quietly.

"Love it." So far, the conversation was going well. Wasn't it? Being the only guest put pressure on her to find something to say.

"The food should be good. I talked over the menu with Cassie and Mrs. Brantley, and we all agreed this would be perfect."

Micah gazed longingly at the table that was set, but without any food. "Dinner's ready, isn't it, Bella?"

"It is. I'll have our salads on the table in a second, and I will bring the lasagna in when we're done with those." Micah directed Paige to a small table.

When they were seated around it, Bella looked from Paige to her husband and said, "Micah, did you introduce yourself to our guest?"

"We've met. He drew up a contract for CJ and me."

Micah stabbed a bite of his salad with his fork. Before putting it in his mouth, he said, "Is your project going well?"

Her house was a subject she was comfortable talking about. "We've just begun. Well, CJ has begun. I do what I can." Paige moved her salad around, too nervous to eat. "Isn't it unusual for a town to have only one attorney?"

"I'm not sure how much you know about Two Hearts. The town fell on hard times. It didn't need more than one attorney."

"And he's such a handsome one at that." Bella kissed her husband on the cheek. The two gazed into each other's eyes, breaking apart after a few seconds. "Don't mind us, Paige. We're still newlyweds."

Paige's nervousness dropped a notch. As long as she didn't drop food on the floor or anything else embarrassing, this might be fun. "How long have the two of you been married?"

Bella tilted her head to the side as though trying to come up with the right answer. "That should be a simple question, shouldn't it?"

"Usually," Paige said slowly.

Micah laughed. "The problem is that we got married because Bella was short on cash. My grandfather told me that if I married quickly, he would give me money and that, if I didn't, he wouldn't pay for my sister's college."

Paige gasped. "That sounds like something I would read in a romance novel." As soon as she said that, she realized that she had just admitted to reading a genre not everyone admired. Not all readers saw that as a positive thing.

Bella grinned. "I am so glad to have found a fellow romance fan. Maybe we can start a book club," she added quickly.

Instead of being awkward, this dinner was going very well. Paige might have a new friend.

When it was time for dessert, Bella fidgeted in her seat and seemed nervous. She picked up her water glass and set it back down without drinking anything. After a few minutes of that, there was a knock at the door.

With what seemed to be a forced smile, Bella stood. "We have another friend coming to have dessert with us. I hope you don't mind."

"Of course not. It's nice getting to know the people of the town."

She thought she heard Bella mutter, "I hope so," as she walked by.

"George! I'm so glad you could stop by tonight."

"When I'm told that you've made Mrs. Brantley's best cake recipe, you know I'm going to be here."

Micah chuckled, but even that didn't sound quite normal. Paige turned in her seat to see what she'd assumed would be another woman, and instead saw a single man about her age moving toward them.

This was clearly a setup and, judging from the expression in the other man's eyes, he knew it too.

He was handsome in a denim and plaid way, but even his tidy brown hair and warm smile weren't enough to make his sudden appearance feel any less awkward.

Micah gestured him inside as he had done with her a short time earlier, and the man stepped into the house. Bella hurried into the kitchen and returned with pieces of what looked like coconut cake, and placed those on the table before scurrying off for the other two. From the kitchen, she called, "Would anyone like coffee?"

Paige mostly wanted to get out of there as quickly as she could, but she'd be polite because that's just what you did in situations like this. "I'd like tea if you have it."

Bella chuckled. "I knew I liked you. Would you like a specific kind of tea? Or should I just choose one for you?"

Micah chuckled. "Believe me when I tell you that you have never seen this number of tea options in one place outside of a specialty store."

"Please choose one for me that goes well with the cake."

"I'm on it. And I know both of those men want coffee."

A few minutes later, Paige held onto a pretty mug filled with tea with a heavenly orange spice scent, and George sat across from her with a mug of coffee in his hands.

No one spoke. Micah glanced around the table, seeming to realize that he needed to do something to resolve the situation. "George, how's everything at your farm?"

Great. They wanted to fix her up with a farmer. Paige knew nothing about farming or the land. Not that she didn't like things to do with a farm. Pigs were cute. Cows and that whole pastoral thing were lovely, but she didn't have any idea what went into caring for them. Her yard still looked like it belonged to an abandoned house in a horror movie.

The man seemed to relax and told them about recent antics of goats at his farm.

By the time he finished his story, Paige had finished her dessert by shoveling it in as quickly as she could. Staying longer meant Bella and Micah would have more time to push them together, so she stood. "I want to thank you for this lovely dinner. It was so nice meeting you, Micah, and you." She nodded at George, edging toward the door as she spoke. "I'm sure I'll see all of you around town."

The startled faces of Micah and Bella watched her. Paige's supposed match sat eating cake. She really couldn't blame him. It was delicious. But it also proved how little interest he had in her.

"Thank you for a wonderful dinner." Paige gave a wave as she took a backward step.

Bella asked, "Are you sure you don't want to stay for conversation? Maybe a board game?"

"I'm sure there's some work I need to get done on the house." She took another step toward the door, hoping with every fiber of her being that there wasn't a piece of furniture or pair of shoes behind her that would trip her up. An awkward blind date was enough stress for one evening.

"Let me get you some leftovers. Some lasagna to have for lunch tomorrow?" Bella rose to her feet.

Paige took another step back. She could make a break for it, or she could stay and have some of this delicious food tomorrow.

Bella sensed her hesitation and decided to take command. "I'm going to get it for you. You just wait right there." Bella put one hand up in a stop motion, and that was probably a good idea, because Paige wanted to run away from here as fast as she could.

Paige continued toward the door, this time facing it. A cute pair of boots Bella must have worn earlier today stood by the door. One of these days, Paige was going to splurge on some new clothes for herself. Right now, the only things new were for the house. With one hand on the doorknob, Paige waited for Bella to return.

She emerged from the kitchen with a storage container in her hands big enough to hold food for a family of four. Paige noticed she was also carrying a bag in her other hand. "I thought you might enjoy some garlic bread and salad with it too."

Perfect. Toast for breakfast and this for the other meals would stretch her dollar. Every penny saved was a penny that could go into the house.

"Thank you very much." She turned the knob and pulled open the door, trying not to look like she was running out of the place as fast as she could, even if she was. She had made it about three steps out the door when she heard Bella's raised voice behind her.

"I forgot dessert. Wait a sec."

Paige wanted to tell her that didn't matter, but that dessert had been wonderful and would add to her bounty of leftovers. She stopped outside and swatted at a mosquito buzzing around her head. Bella returned with another large container and handed it to her.

"Thank you again for dinner! It was great!" Paige made a break for it and all but ran toward her house.

When she went up her own walk, Daisy barked furiously from inside. "It's only me!" The volume dropped a notch. Paige opened the door and kneeled to scratch the dog behind the ear. "I didn't get any leftovers for you—"

The dog woofed as if in protest.

"But I have leftovers for me, so that means that we can extend our food budget to a nice chew bone for you. How does that sound?"

Daisy snuggled close to her side. The house was important. But family was more important, and right now, Daisy was her family.

The next morning, CJ found her in one of the upstairs bedrooms stripping wallpaper. She'd finished the first room—finally!—and moved on, alternating between that and working on the fireplace.

CJ stepped into the room. "I had a strange evening. Have the matchmakers been after you too?"

"Yes! Bella and Micah asked me to dinner, and a farmer named George had been invited to join us for dessert." She was relieved to be able to talk to someone in the same predicament.

"They went easy on you for the first attempt. Mrs. Brantley left me alone with Michelle for my dinner." He crossed his arms and leaned against the wall. "It just isn't what I expected. Why not the two of us?" He motioned between them.

Was he interested in her? A smile began as she considered that.

"Of course, we don't have anything in common, but we're spending time together. I was sure we would be the match."

So much for romance. She didn't have time for that, anyway.

"I'm known as someone who moves around the country a lot, but you're stable and staying. You've been good for me." He rushed to add, "In their minds."

"Maybe they've made their attempt, and that's the end of it."

His laughter, as he walked out of the room, told her that was probably wishful thinking.

CHAPTER NINE

*P*aige opened the door and found George standing there.

Daisy barked a few times, but a butterfly flew by and distracted her watchdog.

George tipped back the brim of his ball cap to look her in the eyes. "Mrs. Brantley said I needed to come over to bush hog your yard."

Paige worked to process the sentence he had just said. "You're going to put pigs in my yard?"

He chuckled. "No. Bush hogging is cutting the tall brush. The stuff that's too much for a normal mower." He looked around the front yard. "There isn't any here, though."

"My backyard is still overgrown." Should she allow this stranger to work for her? She couldn't afford to pay him.

He seemed to understand her silence. "There's no charge for doing this. When Mrs. Brantley asks a favor, we help out."

It would be so nice to have a backyard that she could let Daisy play in. "Then I would love to have you do that." She turned toward the house and said, "Follow me."

"No, ma'am. I need to go around outside with the equipment."

She felt like smacking herself on the forehead. Of course, he had to use equipment. "Then you are on your own," she said as she faced him again. "I don't know what's living in that tall grass and brush. I don't plan to find out."

He chuckled again. He really was a nice-looking man. It was too bad that she hadn't felt an inkling of interest toward him. "I'm a farmer. I come upon anything that's living in that grass pretty regularly. And I was bitten by a snake a few years ago. It wasn't as bad as I expected—I'm still walking."

With those words, he returned to his truck and what she now noticed was something that looked like a giant mower on a trailer. At the thought that there could possibly be snakes in her yard, she hurried inside and slammed the door shut.

After a morning of stripping wallpaper off the parlor wall, she returned to the parlor to strip something else: the fireplace mantel covered in layers of paint. She hated that she had no way to reimburse George. But maybe she could bake him a sweet treat. He might enjoy that.

Then memories of her last attempts at baking rushed in. Why was it that women were supposed to be good at that? Based on other women she talked to—and the men they baked for—she should have been born with those skills. But all she'd been born with was the ability to add up a stack of numbers in her head better than anybody else she knew. Unfortunately, that wasn't much use in judging the amount of time it took in an oven to get "golden brown" or "burned to a crisp." Knowing numbers would help her run a business well, but didn't help in the kitchen.

Equipment roared to life outside followed by cracking brush as George hacked his way through her yard.

Her time would be better spent working on the fireplace. And her helper would probably be healthier if she didn't bake him anything. She soon kneeled in front of the fireplace, nudging the tool through the cracks and crevices of the design to remove paint. The fireplace was starting to come to life, and that was amazing. But it was one piece in a giant mess.

CJ came into the room as she leaned back to admire her work. "What's going on in the backyard?"

"George offered to do it. Mrs. Brantley sent him."

"That was on my to-do list, but I'm happy to have someone else do it."

"Do you think anyone would mind if I did some basic work like weeding the city park up the street? It's such a mess that it could give guests a bad impression as they come around the bend on the way to my bed and breakfast."

"I haven't lived here long, but I have learned that anyone's help is welcome. If you're unsure, though, contact the mayor."

"Great idea." She fired off a text to Mrs. Brantley.

He pointed at the fireplace. "That's looking good."

She smiled up at him. His broad shoulders were swoon-worthy, but it was really his smile that drew her attention. She might have been interested in *him*. If she had time for men, which she didn't. She could look at him all day, though. Pushing those thoughts away, she replied, "I think it's going to be perfect in here when it's as it should be."

"It looks like there's marble underneath all of that."

"That's what I thought too." She set down her tool and pulled off her gloves as she stood. As soon as she did that, her legs gave way, and CJ reached out to catch her by the elbows. Stomping her feet to get them to work again, she felt burning pins and needles as circulation returned. "Oh. Ouch."

"Are you okay?"

"No. Yes. Legs fell asleep." She shook out one and then the other.

As the pain started to recede, she realized that CJ was still holding onto her. She looked up and into his eyes. He had such pretty eyes. They were brown, but not just any brown. They held flecks of gold. And when he laughed, they seemed to dance with joy.

He wasn't laughing now, though. He was gazing into her eyes too.

They shouldn't do that. Not only did she not want any man in her life, she particularly did not want this man in her life. He had made it abundantly clear that he would not be staying in one place long, while she wanted this to be her forever home. Besides, he worked for her. That just felt icky.

She stepped away, hoping her legs would hold her up. When they did, she breathed a sigh of relief.

CJ let his arms drop to his sides. "I need to run over to my house to get a tool. I'll be right back."

Paige nodded. "Okay." She felt her skin flush from his attention.

They stared at each other for another moment before CJ turned and went out the door.

She put her hand on her too-warm cheek. A ping sounded on her phone, and she found the words, "Anything you want to do on that park is welcome. Thank you!"

Now, she had one more project on her to-do list. But it would make a difference to the way the whole street looked to people who came out here. That would be good. Even though she was the only resident of that street.

CJ went out the door and down the steps toward freedom. Matchmakers were after them. They didn't need to add fuel to the fire. His lovely boss caught his attention more than she should.

He didn't mind escaping George's act of kindness toward

her. Mrs. Brantley had sent him here. There was no question about that. But George had done it because of Paige.

Daisy ran to the gate, reaching it before him.

"I'm not taking a walk."

She danced excitedly around him, and CJ winced. He'd used the W word. "I'm driving."

That didn't diminish her glee.

"Just a minute." He went back inside. "Paige, can I take Daisy with me?"

"What?" she shouted from the parlor.

He stepped into the room. "Do you mind if I take Daisy with me?"

"It's probably a good idea to get her away from the noise. Go ahead."

He grabbed the dog's leash off the kitchen counter. Outside, he clipped it on and led her to his truck. When he opened the door, she stared up at it, then at him.

"That is too tall for you, isn't it?" He picked her up and set her on the seat. "It's a short drive, and be warned that there aren't any treats at my house." As soon as he said "treat," he wondered if he'd made another mistake, but she was so excited that she'd missed it. He couldn't understand how a man who'd grown up around dogs could be so forgetful.

They drove across town to the two-bedroom house he called home. He pulled up, expecting to leave the dog in his truck and run in for the drill he'd left here.

Daisy wanted nothing to do with that plan. When he closed his truck door behind him and started to walk away, high-pitched barking ensued.

Shaking his head, he opened the passenger door. "You win. You want to explore, right?" He set her on the ground. "Stick close to my side. The inside of my house is almost as bad as your mom's house. Maybe worse in places."

He led Daisy into his tiny living room and unclipped her

leash. Everything about his house was tiny. The rent was cheap, though. He paid the utilities every month. And he also renovated the place in his spare time. He hadn't had much of that lately.

CJ grabbed the drill off the kitchen counter and went toward the front door, as Daisy walked to the back. "Let's take you home."

She cocked her head and gave him a look that said, "Not until I've ensured the safety of your backyard." His postage stamp-sized backyard wouldn't keep her busy for long, so he indulged her. Daisy immediately began an inspection, sniffing every square inch, while he sat on the back step. A busy morning meant he deserved a short break.

Once the dog had circled then crisscrossed the yard, he called her. To his surprise, she heeded him. "I have work to do. Maybe your mom's weed cutter will be gone by the time we get back."

Daisy watched out the window as they drove back, giving a bark when they pulled up in front of the pink Victorian. CJ could hear the bush hogging through the closed window. He grabbed the drill and left Daisy in the front yard. George would finish soon. Only time would tell if Paige was interested in him. And that was none of his business.

Work. She had work to do.

The fireplace looked gorgeous. Why someone would ever paint over tiles that pretty, she had no idea. Instead of kneeling again, Paige stepped back to look at what she had accomplished so far. This was one of the first places guests would see when they entered the house, so it had to be finished before opening. She still needed to strip the wallpaper, paint the walls, refinish the floors, get new drapes, and find furniture.

Paige mentally added up an estimate of costs. For the one room. Then she multiplied it with the number of rooms she had to finish before opening.

She sank onto the sofa with a sigh. "I was blindly naïve when I bought this place." It had seemed so easy when she'd seen the photos of the house online. "What have I gotten myself into?"

It felt like there was no end in sight. If she lived here and it was just her house, that would be different. But she couldn't do that. There was no place to get a job to support herself in this town, and she had to open the bed and breakfast soon. Numbers didn't lie. Numbers were the truth. And the numbers said that she had a couple of months to get this finished and occupied with guests or she would be going back to the city.

The sun was low on the horizon when the sound of the equipment died down. Soon, there was another knock at her door. Expecting it to be Farmer George again, she wasn't surprised when he stood on the front step, this time with his ball cap in his hand. He ran his fingers through his hair to smooth it back.

"Your yard's in much better shape now. It's still just weeds, but at least it's weeds you can walk around in without getting, well, *surprised* by anything."

"I am so thankful for that." She wanted to reach out and hug him, but she knew that would give the wrong message. "I'd like to try fixing up the city's lake park. Would you be able to bush hog it sometime?"

"I may as well do it now." He looked up at the sky. "I should have enough daylight. Um." He brushed his cap against his leg, almost nervously. "I wondered if you would want to get pizza some night."

Paige knew she must have a shocked expression on her face. What did she do with this? George was very nice, and he'd just been so sweet to do that awful job for her, but she didn't feel even the tiniest little spark. Should she go on a date with him?

His lack of conversation at Bella's beyond farm activities gave her the answer.

"I'm sorry, but I'm—" She watched the expression on his face as he realized she was going to turn him down, and she leaned forward as though to say something that only he could hear. "Interested in CJ. Shh. Don't tell him."

A flash of disappointment ratcheted up her guilt. "I will not tell him, and I understand. I'm just a little too late."

She nodded gravely. She hated to tell a lie. Ever. But the man had seemed to need to be let down gently.

With a wave, he dropped his cap back on his head and returned to his truck, where she saw the equipment was already loaded again. That hadn't gone too badly. She closed the door and went back into the entryway. Then she noticed CJ standing at the railing on the second story, overlooking her. The expression on his face was one of shock, if she had to guess.

Startled, she put her hand over her mouth. If he thought she was serious . . . "I only said that to break the news to him gently."

"Phew. I wondered." He laughed quietly. "You startled me there for a second."

Her own laughter bubbled up. "This is the trouble a lie gets you into every time."

CJ came down the stairs toward her. "You don't know the half of it."

She narrowed her eyes at him in confusion. "What do you mean?"

"I mean that Mrs. Brantley sent him. You already had one blind date with the man that was set up with Bella. Bella, Cassie, and Mrs. Brantley came here together. They must have tag-teamed on this."

She still didn't have a clue what he was talking about. She shrugged.

"They're playing matchmaker. They sent him over here. And

you just told him that you were interested in me." He pointed his finger at his chest.

As his words and their meaning filtered through her brain, she realized what she'd done. Gasping, she put her hand over her mouth for a moment before saying, "Do you think they're going to change their target for the matchmaking?"

"You haven't seen anything yet. Get ready for a full-on Cupid attack from three determined women."

She could handle that, couldn't she? "That doesn't sound too bad."

He laughed so hard that he sat on the step. "Paige, you're in for the experience of a lifetime. It's a good thing we get along well, because we're going to need to be able to laugh about this."

He was right. They were friends, and that was nice.

"We're in for the wildest, craziest, funniest matchmaking event that either of us has ever seen."

The next morning, when Paige went out the back door onto the small porch, she looked out in amazement at the low field of grass. Well, grass and weeds. She could see hints of where a garden had once been. She stepped out into the yard, grateful that she could now walk through it without concerns, and went toward what seemed to be a structure of some kind.

Roses and other vines had wrapped around it over time. The building turned out to be a shed about the size of an ordinary one-car garage. When she moved some of the vines out of the way, she uncovered a garage door on it, the old-fashioned kind with wooden doors that swung to each side. Whether it had been used only for a buggy, in the days of horses and buggies, or if it had been used for cars, she did not know. Fortunately, there was also a door that she could lock—and unfortunately, it was already locked.

"The key!" She raced into the house and to the drawer where she had found the assortment of keys. She selected those that looked to be the right size for that padlock and hurried out to test them. The second key unlocked it. When she slid the lock off, she wondered if she should have somebody else here with her. What if the building wasn't structurally sound? What if the cool and dark room had turned into a nest of vipers?

She heard whistling, which indicated that CJ had just arrived. Just in time for her needs. She returned to the house at a more sedate pace, but CJ was at the back door before she got there.

"This doesn't look half bad now that it's mowed down. Are you sure you don't want to date the guy? Maybe we could get him to do some other things around the place." The grin that followed softened his words.

"I'm excited to say that I found a shed. Would you like to help me explore it?"

He stepped down off the porch and went in the direction she had pointed. "By the way," he said as they arrived at the shed, "I saw how you completely ignored my comment."

It was her turn to smile back. She was grateful that the matchmakers had never fixed her up with CJ, because he truly did seem to be the only carpenter in town, which meant she would have had to keep working with him after it went badly.

"Ready? Let's open it?" He put his hand over hers. "What if it's just a big empty room?"

"Well," she said slowly. "I'm hoping for something wonderful that will help with the house."

She opened the door and realized that she was going to need a flashlight. The one window on the opposite side was so covered with grime and overgrown with vines that very little light was getting in. She held up her phone and hit the flashlight. CJ did the same, and together, their lights actually illuminated it fairly well.

He stepped inside. "Paige, this actually is a treasure trove for the house."

"What can we sell?"

"Nothing now. But this will help us fix the house up. I see some original doors and some trim pieces. I suspect this gingerbread used to be on the porch. It might be pretty if you'd like to add it."

"I'm all for gingerbread on a porch."

"And there are garden tools."

"Perfect! I want to work on the lake park. I thought Daisy and I could go down there for a little while every morning. She plays, and I weed."

They explored the room further. Something peering out from behind one of the doors CJ liked looked intriguing. "Is that a bicycle?" She pointed to it.

He moved a couple of things. "It looks like two of them—a man's and a woman's bicycle. I think you're going to like the woman's bike."

She stepped around him to see it more clearly. "Why?"

"It's pink."

Paige took the handlebars of what was indeed a pink bicycle from probably fifty years earlier. She started wheeling it outside. "Why don't you grab the men's bike, and we'll see if we have something we can use."

"Not happening. I don't ride bicycles."

His firm tone made her want to know more. Cocking her head to the side, she said, "It sounds like there's a story there."

"Let's just say there was an incident when I was six."

She laughed. It would be so nice if she could find a man she could be as relaxed with as her carpenter.

Outside, she couldn't tell the condition of the bicycle because of the grime on it. CJ seemed to have anticipated that need because, when she turned around, he had the hose out and was turning the spigot on.

"Put down the kickstand and stand back. I'll spray it. Let's see if we can clean this up."

CJ washed it down. Grey and pink became white and pink.

"Do you think the tires will still be good?" She kneeled down. "They're flat right now."

"I honestly have no idea about the longevity of rubber tires. My guess is that heat and humidity destroyed them years ago. But I wouldn't be surprised if there was a tire pump in that shed too." He set down the hose, turned off the water, and went inside again. "Eureka! I found a tire pump and something even better."

He stepped out of the shed with the pump in one hand and an antique tool in the other.

"A hammer? A hammer is better than the tire pump I need?"

He looked fondly at the tool. "This isn't just any hammer. This is a really old hammer. It looks like a handmade piece."

"If you want it, it's yours."

He looked up at her. "Thank you!" He actually seemed to think the gift was special. If it was special to him, then that was fine with her.

They got to work on the tires and . . . air came out as fast as it went in.

"I'd talk to Albert about replacement tires. I wouldn't be surprised if, among all those things in his store, he has bicycle tires tucked in there somewhere."

"That's a good idea." It was just a bicycle, but she'd had fun working with CJ. They made a good team on these projects.

CHAPTER TEN

a phone call from Cassie surprised Paige.

"Are you open for dinner tonight?" Cassie asked.

She'd really rather just sit home with a book and eat frozen pizza, presuming she didn't burn it to a crisp as it heated. But she also wanted to meet people in this town, and to meet people, she needed to get out there. *Please, please, please don't let this be another blind date!*

"Sure. Sort of. I guess I don't have anything special planned."

Cassie ignored her sputtering. "Then I am going to make you the best poppy seed chicken casserole you have ever had, along with country green beans. How does that sound?"

Paige couldn't hold back her laughter. "Since I've never heard of putting poppy seeds on a casserole, and I don't even know what country green beans are, I think you'll be delivering me the absolute finest of those in my memory."

"Now the pressure is on. I have to represent these foods well, don't I?"

Did she hear slight anxiety in Cassie's voice? Cassie always seemed to be confident and in charge.

After a brief hesitation, Cassie continued. "I will see you at five-something? We'll eat about six o'clock. Greg is at my house almost every night for dinner, and he'll be here by then. He has a new deputy to help him out!" With those words, Cassie hung up, leaving Paige to stare at the phone and wonder what the deputy had to do with anything. Maybe it was just Cassie's excitement over a new person in town.

Fortunately, the afternoon passed fairly quickly since she was now removing the horrible wallpaper in what would become her bedroom. A tedious task to some, absolutely. But to her? This was turning her upside-down house into a place that she might be able to call home.

If only she could survive the financial outlay these projects were costing her. She needed an income source, and she needed it in a hurry. Two Hearts didn't offer that. Commuting from Nashville every day—three hours or more when you included traffic—did not sound pleasant. The clock was ticking on her time in Two Hearts.

Paige called Albert, and he did have the tires she needed, so she walked her new bicycle over there, where he helped her put the new tires on and fill them with air. After that, she rode over to Cassie's house, taking a detour up Main Street. The new life here with Bella's bridal shop always gave her hope for her business and the town. She slowed and looked at the bridal dresses in the window display. Would she one day be wearing a wedding dress? It didn't seem likely.

When she arrived at Cassie's yellow house, she started to walk up to the front door, then remembered the lesson that Bella and Cassie had given her. People in Two Hearts went to the back or side doors. Only strangers went to the front door. Unless, of course, you were at Bella's house, where the back door was complicated to get to because there was a fence. Rules on rules. She went up the driveway and around to the back of the house, feeling like a trespasser. Fortunately, when she got there, the screen door was in place but the door itself was wide open, so Cassie saw her approach.

"Come in! Come in! I'm glad to have you here. But I do have to focus on the food for a few minutes more. My future mother-in-law suggested these recipes for tonight, and I want them to come out right."

Paige stepped through the door that Cassie held open for her just as a kitten came around the corner. Crouching, Paige said, "Who are you?"

Cassie glanced over her shoulder to where Paige was looking. "That's Romeo. He's a bit of a scoundrel. But he does seem to be a ladies' man, so he'll probably be your friend in about two seconds." Truer words had never been spoken. He came right over to Paige, rubbed his head on her knee, and meowed. She reached out to pet him, and he immediately started purring.

"I've never had a cat."

Cassie laughed. "Neither had I. We found each other one day in Two Hearts. I didn't know he was mine at first, but that became clear pretty quickly. You have Daisy. I've never had a dog."

"I didn't have pets growing up. We moved too much for that." Paige had missed some things about a normal childhood, but didn't regret it. Military life came with sacrifices, but she and her dad had been a team that worked well together.

"I stayed in one place, but my mother did not allow things like cats and dogs in the house," Cassie said.

Paige continued petting Romeo, who had flopped on to his side and put his chin in the air, which she took as an indication that he wanted his chin rubbed. She seemed to be right since the purring volume increased. "My mom died when I was little, so it was just me and my dad, and he was in the military. I lived in four countries and went to eight different schools."

"That must have made it hard to feel connected, to make friends."

"More than you can imagine. That's why Two Hearts and my house mean so much to me."

"How's that going?"

Paige pasted on what she hoped was a brilliant smile. "Great! Never better!"

Cassie stopped what she was doing, turned, and faced Paige. "That sounded like the biggest lie that's ever been told. Now, why don't you tell me the truth about what's going on?"

Paige looked beyond where Cassie stood to the food she was preparing. Knowing how quickly cooking could get out of hand, she said, "I promise to explain later, but I don't want to distract you from your food prep."

Cassie spun around. "Oh my goodness. You're right. But you aren't getting off without an explanation. Just know that is true. Whether it's tonight or tomorrow, we are talking."

Paige and Cassie chit-chatted while Cassie finished up the meal. The kitchen was soon filled with a delicious scent. Paige wasn't sure what went into a poppy seed casserole, but if it tasted anywhere near as good as it smelled, tonight would involve a great dinner. She was starting to relax and feel like she was making a new friend by the time Greg got home.

He walked in the door with a man who was about thirty and quite handsome in a very clean-cut way. His hair was parted perfectly, his uniform looked fresh, and he stood very straight with his shoulders back. If Paige had to guess, she would say he had recently gotten out of the military.

"Greg, you're here just a few minutes earlier than I expected." Cassie glanced over at Paige, who felt like she was missing part of the conversation.

"It's been a quiet afternoon, and Charlie is catching on quickly. His many years in security have helped. After this week's training, I'm going to be able to let him work on his own, and I can't tell you how happy that makes me."

Cassie stepped over and gave Greg a quick kiss. "I second that emotion. Now you won't be called out in the middle of the night. Most nights, anyway. We'll give you a day or two off, Charlie."

Charlie smiled but never broke his very military-like stance. "I'm glad to have a position in a small town. I wanted something low-key after being in the military."

"Charlie, this is another newcomer to town. Paige has only been here a few weeks."

"Pleased to meet you, ma'am."

Paige had to smile at the use of the word *ma'am*. Coming from a military background, she knew that *sir* or *ma'am* would probably be part of every other sentence.

"Where were you stationed, Charlie?"

He listed several places. She'd lived in one of them also, so she told him so. At his puzzled frown, she added, "Army brat."

Out of the corner of her eye, she caught a look from Cassie to Greg and a very subtle nod. Just when she thought things were going smoothly, she realized this wasn't a casual dinner. It was another fix-up. But at least the man seemed to be nice. Not that the farmer wasn't, but he hadn't been a brilliant conversationalist. Of course, he might have been if she had any knowledge whatsoever of farming.

As Cassie served brownies and coffee to them, Charlie said, "I hope my fiancée likes Two Hearts when she comes to visit. I've been nervous about moving to such a small town and having her hate it. You like it though, Paige, right?"

Paige hid a smile behind her hand. Cassie had paused with a bite of brownie halfway to her mouth and Greg had sat back in his chair abruptly. Apparently, the man's relationship status had never been discussed. It shouldn't have been, of course, in a job interview, and he clearly hadn't been here long enough for him to become friends with anyone.

"Yes, I love it here. The people are very friendly. I moved here from New York City. No matter where she's coming from, it can't get much bigger than that. She's going to have to have the right mindset from the beginning, though. Many things aren't as convenient."

That was certainly the truth when it came to eating. If you couldn't cook, you were on your own. Fortunately, it was a lot harder to burn food in the microwave than in an oven. Now that she'd switched a lot of her cooking to heating frozen meals in that device, at least she hadn't had to go hungry as often or scrape charcoal off of anything. Of course, some things just couldn't be saved, no matter how much scraping you did.

When Cassie stood to take the plates from the table, she said, "Would you like to move into the living room to visit for a while longer?"

Charlie took that moment for a big yawn as he covered his mouth. "I'm sorry, but I don't think I can tonight. Between the moving and learning the ropes of the job, I'm pretty worn out. Can I take a rain check to do that another day?"

Cassie seemed almost relieved.

Paige knew *she* was. Although with the pressure taken off, she'd actually enjoyed the evening.

"And I'd better be on my way, too. I have another early morning of stripping."

All eyes turned to her.

"Wallpaper. Stripping wallpaper off the walls."

She really needed to figure out what she was going to say before she opened her mouth.

~

Paige climbed on her bicycle and headed toward home with a smile on her face. She'd only gotten a block away when something Cassie had said came to mind. She'd mentioned Mrs. Brantley—that she had suggested those recipes for dinner. Bella had said she'd talked over the dinner with Cassie and Mrs. Brantley for what turned out to be a matchmaking attempt.

Her name kept popping up. Everyone in town knew she was an amazing planner. And Paige could tell that she was the mayor this town had needed for years. Was Mrs. Brantley the instigator of these blind dates? No matter what, Cassie and Bella seemed to be willing parties.

Paige rode along for a while longer, watching the houses pass by, and then the town more or less ending as she grew closer to the lake. She really wanted to be friends with Cassie and Bella. They were close in age. They had similar backgrounds as newcomers to town and people who used to live in cities. She thought that she could relate well to them—at least at first, as she found her footing here in Two Hearts. She'd just have to be wary about invitations for a while. And she'd be extra careful around Mrs. Brantley.

How did you avoid a woman who was so incredibly nice, though? *And* the mayor of the town?

CHAPTER ELEVEN

*P*aige crouched in front of the freshly weeded patch of daisies, hoping that the dog would come over to see what she was looking at. Daisy had a curious streak. Instead of sitting in front of the daisies, though, she sat behind them, peering through. Paige hoped she would stay there long enough to get the pictures, because this was as cute as it got.

She stood slowly and stepped backward, glancing over her shoulder occasionally so she didn't fall. Miracle of miracles: Daisy stayed put. Paige had taken about ten photos before the dog was distracted.

As she was about to turn off her camera, a tiny butterfly landed on Daisy's upturned nose, catching the dog off guard. By the time Daisy rushed off to chase her tiny target, Paige had managed to snap enough photos that she strongly suspected would win a photo contest if she entered.

With that task complete, she knew she had to get back to wallpaper. Why, oh, why had people in times past not only thought that garishly colored floral patterns on their walls were attractive, but that they should put layers on top of layers? How much ugly could one wall stand?

As she walked into the house, she knew she was going to have to take a break soon from that wallpaper removal task to check out the photos on her computer. Then she would order some prints. She could put one in her bedroom on her dresser. When she had one. She enjoyed taking pictures of people, but maybe she could start a sideline with dogs if they were as cooperative as Daisy.

Daisy whooshed past her, racing into the house.

Or maybe they would be more cooperative than Daisy.

~

A few days later, Paige sat at her kitchen table flipping through the photos of Daisy that had arrived. They were so cute that she wanted to show everyone and shout about her photography. Maybe even ask someone if they wanted to have their dog's photo taken.

CJ shouted from what sounded like upstairs, where he'd been all morning. "Paige? If you're there, could you give me a hand? Please!" There was a sense of urgency in CJ's tone that he didn't normally have. Paige dropped the photos and hurried out of the room, following his voice when he called again. "Help!"

She found him with his left hand clutching a curtain rod, his right foot barely touching a ladder and his left foot dangling in mid-air. An assortment of tools underneath him would not make for a soft landing.

She ran over to him.

"I'm so glad you were home. I'm too experienced to have done this, but I reached over to grab a loose piece of plaster and slipped. If it hadn't been for this curtain rod . . ."

She moved a circular saw, shop vac, and power screwdriver from beneath him. All things she could now name because of recent research. "Now, lift your foot off the ladder."

He didn't move.

"I need to slide the ladder underneath you."

She heard him suck in his breath. "Let's give it a shot. But act quickly."

He grabbed the curtain rod, and she pulled the ladder under him and guided his feet onto the step. When the solid metal was beneath his boots, he leaned against the wall and relaxed. "I was envisioning a broken arm if I hit the shop vac or saw wrong. Never again will tools be anywhere near me when I'm on a ladder."

"Now you have a better idea of how I felt in the butler's pantry. At least you didn't cut yourself, because then everybody looks at you like you're stupid when they find out."

He chuckled as he took the steps slowly and reached the floor. "Paige, no one would ever think you were stupid."

Her job had always been her place to shine. He was talking about her outside of work and numbers, so that had to be—hands down—the best compliment she had ever been paid.

"I could do with a break right about now. Is there anything edible in the sweets realm?" The hesitation in his voice made her smile.

"I grabbed some scones at Dinah's when Daisy and I took our long walk this morning." She'd also had breakfast there because she couldn't face another day that began with either burned toast, rubber eggs, or both. She could switch to cold cereal, but that felt too much like she was giving up. She was not a quitter. She put a scone on a plate for each of them—today's flavor being pumpkin spice—and made coffee for CJ and tea for herself using her single-serving drink maker.

CJ took a sip of his coffee and sighed. "I am so glad that you realized these premeasured pods could turn out good coffee even if it was against your DNA to use them." He grimaced. "I shouldn't have said that."

"When you're right, you're right." She probably did need to embrace premade things more.

CJ quickly scarfed down the scone and reached into the bag for the last one. She'd been hoping to save that for an afternoon snack, but she wasn't going to stop him. He'd worked hard all day. He set it on his plate and then glanced to his left. "What's this?" He brushed the crumbs off his hands and rubbed them on his pants, presumably to make sure they were clean, even though the pants no longer were.

She followed his gaze and saw the stack of her photos of Daisy. With a gulp, she set down the half of her scone that still remained. "Um. Those are pictures of Daisy that I took last week."

He picked up the prints and started sorting through them.

"These are good. Not like a snapshot. More like a portrait, if that makes any sense." He reached the bottom of them. "How did I not know you did this?"

"What?" Paige said through her panic. Photography was her private joy. She'd only shared it with family and friends in the past. Sure, she'd taken some shots of the burned not-brownie, but that hadn't yet been shared.

"That you took such amazing photos. I saw you with the camera, but I expected you to get results like *I* would. Have you taken any of the house? We could probably use those for advertising when you're ready to go."

His use of the "we" puzzled her, but he seemed to have become part of the project, hadn't he? "I've always taken pictures of people and now Daisy. I could probably do the house, though." She did have the equipment for it. But not as much passion. It was her house, but she'd rather be taking a picture of something living as opposed to a piece of wood.

He picked up the prints again and flipped through them. "This one"—he tapped her favorite—"could win an award. The way that the light is coming in. You captured Daisy so well. And the butterfly. Did you stage that somehow with a paper butterfly?"

"Serendipity. It just happened. And you know how much Daisy loves to chase butterflies."

He chuckled. Setting down the stack, he turned toward her. "Have you done portraits of people? It sounds like you have."

She nodded, but then realized he was focused on his scone again. "Yes, I have done quite a few portraits." And won several awards for them, but she wasn't going to say that.

"My mother has been bugging me to send her a photo of me. I snapped one on my phone, and she immediately replied that she wanted a real portrait to put up on her wall with her other kids' and that wouldn't do." He rolled his eyes toward the ceiling. "The wall by the stairs is covered with family pictures. I have five siblings, so that's given her plenty to post there, and now that some of them are giving her grandchildren, the wall is becoming more and more full. She hasn't had anything from me since high school, and that apparently means that I have failed her." With a chuckle, he took a sip of his coffee.

CJ wanted *her* to take his picture. He was handsome beyond any man she'd ever met—broad shoulders, red beard, brown eyes—but could she take a photo of him? She'd probably be so nervous that she'd use the wrong settings. Besides, she'd rarely taken photos of anyone who wasn't a close friend or family member.

He leaned back in his chair and focused on her. "Paige, I can almost see the wheels turning in your mind. You're trying to figure out a way to back out of this, aren't you?"

She gasped.

"I guess that would be a yes." He carried his now-empty cup and plate to the sink. "You would like my mother. She's kind and very friendly. But she's also quite insistent. I need your help."

"You haven't known me long, and you've already figured out how I work. That's a little scary, CJ."

He chuckled. "I've learned to be a people watcher because of all those siblings. And my parents came from large families, so I have cousins. So many cousins. It helps to be able to read people well." He turned to face her and leaned back against the counter. "But seriously, will you take photos of me so that I can make my mother happy?"

When he worded it that way, there was nothing she could do but agree. "Yes. We want mothers to be happy."

"Maybe other people in Two Hearts would like to have photos taken, too."

Paige jumped to her feet, knocking over her tea. She quickly pulled the prints out of the path of the flowing liquid, then ran to the kitchen counter to get a roll of paper towels.

"Sorry!" CJ held up his hands in surrender. "I didn't mean to upset you."

She wiped the tea from the table. "This is kind of a secret. My hobby."

He picked up her salt and pepper shakers so she could wipe under them. "Well, start with me. And don't worry about it. For now, I guess we are just two people who are trying to save a house and turn it into a bed and breakfast."

He was right, but again, it seemed like it was *their* project more than hers, which felt strange.

"I have an idea," CJ said. "Why don't you work with me upstairs in that one room? Let's get everything in a single room done and then move on to another one. I feel like we have bits and pieces that aren't adding up to what you need."

That was because long conversations were harder for her to do. She had to focus so much on her words that she might not pay enough attention to the work. Numbers, yes; people . . . sometimes. But CJ seemed to get her and understand what she needed. Maybe spending more time with him would be okay.

CHAPTER TWELVE

*A*fter their snack, Paige grabbed her wallpaper steamer and headed upstairs with CJ. When she'd removed one section of it—gleefully discovering only paint under it and not another layer—she sat back on her heels and admired her work.

Then she noticed the lack of noise. "It's very quiet."

CJ looked over his shoulder from the ladder to answer her. "That's the nice thing about being out here on the lake."

Paige stood. "No. I mean, it's *quiet*. Daisy hasn't made a sound recently."

"Maybe she's sleeping."

Paige hurried to the front door with CJ behind her. "Even then, when she's outside, she'll wake up just to bark at a squirrel and then go back to sleep."

She stepped out the open door. "The yard is empty. Daisy!" When there was no answering bark, Paige raced down the steps and to the side of the house. "Not here!" she called to CJ, who had gone the other direction. Paige called to Daisy as she walked the perimeter of the yard.

"Or here," CJ said from the opposite side of the house.

They met in front of the steps.

"She's gone." Paige stared at the empty front yard. "I've got to find her." That dog had become part of her family. Had become her whole family.

She ran into her house to get her car keys and stopped in the entryway. Where had she left her purse? Kitchen table. As she grabbed it, she noticed Daisy's food bowls. That dog loved to eat. Tucking the box of dog treats under her arm, she hurried to the door, pulling out her keys on the way.

When she returned, CJ was walking around the yard, looking at the fence.

"What are you doing?"

"Finding the way she got out."

"She must have used the gate somehow, even though it's closed now," Paige said. "I thought I latched it earlier, but I guess it didn't catch. When Daisy pushed it open and went out, it must have slammed closed and locked behind her."

He crouched beside the ancient fence on the left side of her yard. "No. It's my fault." He swung a faded board from side to side. Still with a single nail connected at the top, it hung straight until pushed. He stood and brushed off his hands.

"We need to stop blaming ourselves. We don't know how she got out." She dangled her car keys. "Right now, I just want to find her, and I hope she didn't go too far. The highway's over there." She gestured with the keys to her right. "People are usually slow driving through town, but..."

Paige started toward the gate. Then she stopped. "I've seen stories about a dog that traveled miles to get home to its family. You don't think she'd take off for New York, do you?"

"From what you've said, she wasn't happy there. You were the only good thing in her life."

"I hope you're right."

"Call me if you find her. Let's drive and cover the town. I'll take the areas closest to my house." She pictured everything nearby. Paige turned around. "The lake! Can corgis swim?"

"I have no idea, but let's not think the worst." He pulled her in for a hug. "Don't worry," he muttered against her hair.

Paige closed her eyes and drank in the comfort.

He stepped back. "I'll cover the rest of the town. I'm much more familiar with it than you are."

In her car, Paige went up one street, turned, and went down the next, weaving her way through her side of Two Hearts. As loudly as she could, she yelled the dog's name out the window, waited a few seconds for her reply, and then called again when none came.

When she circled back toward home, she stopped at the overgrown lake park and got out. Daisy loved coming here on walks.

No answering woof came to any of her calls. Well, no answering woof that belonged to Daisy. Quite a few dogs had barked a reply when she'd driven by. Pulling out her phone, she considered her options.

"I've covered every street," she said once she had CJ on the line. "I can't find her."

"I think it's time to call in an expert."

"An expert in finding lost dogs?" She didn't know that existed.

"An expert in many things."

Paige knew who he meant: Mrs. Brantley.

He must have sensed her reluctance because he added, "Hear me out. I realize that she made you nervous with her matchmaking attempts, but she truly is the best when it comes to organizing anything."

"Fine." *I'll do whatever it takes to find Daisy.*

"I'll call her. Let's meet on Main Street over by Bella's wedding dress shop."

A few minutes later, Paige pulled to the curb in front of the store window filled with all things bridal. CJ parked behind her. She met him on the sidewalk.

Dashing at tears on her cheeks, she waited for Mrs. Brantley to arrive.

"I told Mrs. Brantley where we would be, and she said that was a great meeting spot." As he finished his sentence, first one car and then another drove up the road and parked. Soon, a line of cars waited to find a place on the side of the road. Men and women on foot walked swiftly toward them from the north and south. By the time Mrs. Brantley arrived, dozens of people had gathered.

CJ put his arm around Paige. A tiny voice in her brain wanted to ask what he thought he was doing, but she enjoyed the warmth and comfort.

Dinah and Michelle from the restaurant; Bella and Cassie; Randi, the real estate agent; a few people she'd seen in church, including the minister; Albert; and a couple dozen more she didn't recognize crowded onto the sidewalk.

In a low voice, she asked, "Are they all here to help me?"

"Paige, it's a small town. You need help. They're here to do that."

Mrs. Brantley clapped her hands together to get everyone's attention. "Many of you have met Paige, but for those of you who haven't, she bought the old Samuelson house on the lake and is fixing it up."

A murmur went through the crowd, and people looked at each other. Paige saw more than a few raised eyebrows, probably because the house seemed to have everything broken. Including the fence.

Mrs. Brantley asked, "Paige, do you have a photo of Daisy?"

Paige pulled out her phone. "I do. But for those of you who know dog breeds, she's a Welsh corgi, so she's tan on top and cream on her belly. Her legs may be small, but they can move quickly. Don't worry about her biting. Daisy doesn't have a mean bone in her body."

She handed her phone to Mrs. Brantley, who held it up for nearby people to see and then passed it around the group.

"Everyone, get out there and find this dog."

Paige remembered the box of doggie snacks. "Wait!" She ran to her car and pulled it out. "Let me give you treats in case you need to lure her in." She moved through the crowd, thanking people as she gave one or two to each.

As people fanned out, Mrs. Brantley turned to her and CJ. "You need to take a deep breath and relax. We are going to find Daisy."

Tears filled her eyes again. She couldn't lose this dog. What would she do without Daisy? She stepped away from CJ, immediately missing his warmth.

CJ reached out and caught her by the elbow. "Ride with me. I'll man the wheel; you call out the window."

Mrs. Brantley said, "I was about to suggest the same thing. I don't think you should be driving, Paige."

Wiping at her eyes to clear them, Paige realized that Mrs. Brantley was right. She shouldn't do that if she couldn't see.

Rolling through town, she lost track of where they were, but they often passed townspeople calling Daisy's name. Paige called her so many times that her voice cracked.

"We're near my place," CJ said. "Let's stop and get something to drink. You're going to wear your voice out if we don't."

Paige swallowed and realized how dry her throat had become. "Thank you."

She'd wondered where CJ lived and was surprised when they pulled up the driveway of a charming small cottage. She had envisioned a place that was a little less cute and a lot more bachelor-like. The house was freshly painted white with light-blue shutters and a navy-blue front door. The brick walkway was neat, the yard perfectly mowed and trimmed. It was a very domestic image for a man she knew didn't stay in one place long.

He put his truck in park. "I'm sure you're wondering about the house."

Did he know her that well?

"When I arrived in town, I stopped at the hardware store first, as I do in most towns. Albert gave me options of places he knew of to rent. They included this one. Aside from paying the monthly utilities while I'm here, I get free rent if, in my spare time, I fix it up. The family would like to sell the house now that the town seems to be coming into a little more prosperity. It had sat empty for years."

If she'd seen this pristine care of his home when she'd met CJ, she wouldn't have hesitated to hire him. It looked like something out of a small-town-life magazine.

"We'll have to use the front door instead of the friendlier back door because of some construction that's blocking that entrance." It was still amusing that the use of a front door had to be explained in this small Southern town.

As they went up the walk, she thought about the places they'd driven and wondered if they needed to circle back and try again. Halfway to his front door, she noticed a tan lump on his porch. He must have had a package delivered.

Then she realized what it was. Running toward his house, she cried, "Daisy!"

CJ said, "What?" Then he saw the dog. "She came here?"

Paige sat on the step and pulled Daisy onto her lap, the corgi licking her face and arms anywhere she could. Laughing, Paige said, "But how did she know where you lived?"

"She's a very smart dog. I forgot a tool the day George worked on the back yard. I brought her with me when I came to get it. That was one time, a week ago, and we didn't stay."

"The little scamp must have escaped and run off to explore. Then she realized she was lost."

They stepped inside the house. Daisy raced ahead but returned to Paige's side, as though she needed to make sure her owner was still there, before heading off again to check out the house. Maybe she would stay closer to home from now on.

CJ's place was a mix of charming and under construction.

"I'm surprised you're willing to work on my house all day and then come home to more of the same."

A much-too-cute, lopsided grin appeared. "Your house has occasionally been uncontrolled chaos. Besides, this is what I do. I don't see the mess here so much as I see a project that needs to be done. But I'm on the home stretch."

She saw a kitchen in complete disarray. *Kitchen* wasn't even the right word for an area with a refrigerator and a single rough cabinet with a sink. The stove and some cabinets were clumped together in what must be the dining room.

"It's no wonder you're willing to try food at my place if this is where you have to cook."

CJ chuckled. "It has been a while since I was able to use this kitchen. I was planning to finish it up right about the time I started working on your house. About a week of solid effort on it will take care of it. Take care of the house, really. Everything else is almost finished." He gestured toward a small loveseat that was the only living room furniture. "Please have a seat."

When she did, she sank into the well-worn cushion. Maybe he would sit next to her and put his arm around her as he'd done earlier.

He continued across the room. "I took down this wall to make it an open space. I thought a buyer might want that in a house this small." He reached the fridge, opened it, and took out a pitcher of what looked like iced tea.

"Have you been in the South long enough that you're drinking tea all day?"

He sheepishly said, "It isn't just tea. It's sweet tea. I actually discovered it when I was in Texas for about six months. There's something about a tall glass of tea on a hot day that cools you down." He poured two glasses.

Daisy jumped up next to Paige.

"Daisy, get down from here."

CJ said, "Don't worry about her. The furniture is quite old."

Sitting next to her obviously wasn't a high priority for him.

The dog nosed Paige's pocket. "Ah, that's why you're here. You smell the dog treats I put in there." Paige took one out. Daisy gently grabbed it with her teeth, then jumped to the floor to enjoy it.

CJ sat next to Paige on the couch, scooting as far to the other side as he could, but the small loveseat dipped in the middle, tugging them together. He cleared his throat. "The family cleared out most furniture years ago but left behind a few things like a refrigerator, a dresser, a small table outside that has seen better days but gives me a place to eat, and this couch."

That was apparently his way of explaining why the two of them were shoulder to shoulder on a small piece of furniture.

This probably wasn't the best time for Paige to remember how much she'd enjoyed having his arm around her. Maybe if she leaned his direction, he would do that again. No. She couldn't be interested in him. She pushed farther away, or at least tried to. He was a man on the move, and she was a woman with a disaster of a house who might not be able to stay. The two of them could win an award for Least Likely to Have a Relationship in Two Hearts.

CJ sprang to his feet, taking his warmth with him. "I just realized that we haven't told Mrs. Brantley to call off the search."

He grabbed his phone and called. Paige could hear the happy sounds coming through it when he said they'd found Daisy. From what CJ said, it sounded like plans were being made for something.

"Okay. I'll tell her." He ended the call. "I've gotten the impression that you don't enjoy crowds, but Mrs. Brantley thought everyone would like to meet Daisy. She also said that it was probably a good idea—and I have to agree—for everyone to know what she looks like in case she gets out again."

"Then I guess we'd better go." As much as Paige did not want to dive into a large group, this town was filled with the most kind and loving people she'd ever met. "Daisy." The dog looked up. "Are you ready to meet new fans? Because everyone is going to love you." She reached down and rubbed the dog between the ears.

Seeming to understand, Daisy said, "Woof," and ran to the door.

The three of them arrived at what looked like a party in the park with people she recognized from Main Street a few hours ago. How someone had managed to pull this together so quickly baffled her. There were several trays of sandwiches, jugs of tea, and—if she wasn't mistaken—pies from Dinah's. The chocolate cream pie had the same decorative touches as the slice she'd had last week.

Everyone came over to say how glad they were that Daisy had been found. Quite a few crouched down to say hello to the little dog, who lapped up the attention. Before the end of the afternoon, Paige had an open invitation to dinner with several families. And Daisy had a play date scheduled with Mrs. Brantley's dog, Cookie, because they'd gotten along so well as they'd run around the park.

All in all, it had turned out to be a good day. If only she wasn't far more aware of her contractor than she had been this morning. Glancing over at CJ, she wondered what she should do about that.

Then she realized Mrs. Brantley was watching her.

The last thing she wanted was to bring on more matchmaking, especially with a man she had to spend so much time with already. She needed to keep this all business in order to keep her heart intact.

CHAPTER THIRTEEN

*P*aige was out walking Daisy, so CJ tackled cutting a piece of plywood, throwing sawdust in the air. He'd clean up the mess before they returned, so the dog wouldn't get in it. He and Paige had managed well working together yesterday afternoon and this morning in the broken-window room. Paige had continued her task of stripping wallpaper, while he'd made repairs. Daisy had happily curled up in the corner chewing on the bone Paige had insisted on stopping at the grocery store to buy last night on the way home.

As he worked, he thought about what he'd have for lunch— hopefully something Paige hadn't made. That reminded him of Michelle at Dinah's Place and his recent narrow escape with matchmaking. It had been a huge fail. He hoped that meant they wouldn't try again. He didn't know why the matchmakers had focused their attention on him in the first place. It wasn't as though he was the only single man in town. Besides, he hadn't decided if he was staying in town.

Once he and Paige had realized what was going on, it had been an entertaining diversion and nowhere near as challenging as he'd expected.

When his phone rang with an unknown number but the local area code, he answered.

"CJ? This is Bella Bennett. No! Walker." She laughed. "It has been such a short time since I decided to use Micah's last name that I still get it wrong sometimes."

"What can I help you with today, Bella?"

"I need several shelves for my living room wall. They shouldn't be too difficult to put together. Of course, I have absolutely no idea how to do that." She laughed again. Bella was a happy person in general, but not usually bubbling over with laughter.

"I could come over today and take a look at it if you're able to be there."

Words rushed out of her. "I can be here any time you want to be here, CJ."

They agreed on his going over right away.

That was weird. He put his tools in his truck and drove toward the Walker house. When he arrived, Bella seemed fairly normal—but not quite—as she let him in the house and explained her project. He was soon in the backyard, cutting wood that she'd already bought for her shelves.

"CJ?" Bella stood in the open screen door to their back porch. "I need to go back to my shop now. Do you have everything that you need?"

He glanced around. "I do. I'll give you a call when they're done. If you can come back, we can get these hung today."

Bella looked at the wooden floor of the porch and scuffed her foot on it. "I think I can get away this afternoon. If you could stay here through lunchtime."

He knew that this job would not take anywhere close to that number of hours. "I'll be done before then."

"Oh, no!" Her eyes widened, and a shocked expression crossed her face. "I mean, I'm sure there's something that we can do to keep you busy longer. I know you'd like a bigger paycheck." She laughed. Sort of.

CJ looked around. "I could do a fresh coat of paint on the screen door."

Bella stepped out and checked it. "It is starting to look a little shabby, isn't it?" This time, her voice didn't have any of the odd qualities. "That sounds like a great plan. Thank you for noticing." She returned to the house, and a few minutes later, he heard her car start and drive away.

When noon came, he realized he was getting hungry and hadn't thought to pack a lunch. But why would he when he'd expected this to be a very simple project of a few shelves? And he hadn't known Bella would already have the supplies waiting for him.

As he stood and stretched, his stomach rumbled. Brushing off his hands, he started for the side gate so he could get lunch, but as he reached it, the gate began to open. Randi stood on the other side, staring at him.

"Mrs. Brantley called and said you were working on something at Bella's house and asked if I would bring you lunch." Her tone rose at the end, almost forming a question.

"That's nice of you."

"It is, isn't it?" She grinned. "The weird thing—well, the weirder thing—is that she said I should get something to eat, too, and that she would pay for all of it."

Dread sank down his spine. More matchmaking. Maybe he should have realized before that he was being set up today. How had he not?

He waved her in. "Let's go sit on the back porch. If you don't mind the slight smell of paint. I just redid their screen door."

"Doesn't bother me. Remember that in addition to being a real estate agent, I also own the motel. I've done almost every kind of work on the cottages that you can imagine, including painting the inside and outside of them many times."

Once they were seated, Randi handed him a paper bag from Dinah's. Inside, he found a roast beef sandwich he knew would be made with the delicious meat Dinah baked herself, potato salad, and a piece of chocolate pie. "This looks great, Randi."

"Don't give me any credit for the selection. Emmaline Brantley placed the order. Michelle had an odd grin on her face when she handed the two bags to me." She pulled out a sandwich, which looked more like a vegetarian special. Then a package of chips. "Do you have any idea why?"

CJ choked on his first bite. Coughing, he reached for the bottle of water that had also been provided. "I know you wondered why you were sent here today." At her nod, he continued. "It seems that a few of the ladies—notably Mrs. Brantley, Bella, and I believe Cassie—are indulging themselves in some matchmaking."

Randi's eyes widened, and then they twinkled with glee. "Now it all makes sense. Why do people do that?" She shook her head and took another bite of her sandwich.

He wasn't sure if he should be happy she wasn't interested or slightly insulted. "They haven't succeeded either time with me."

Randi chuckled. "Wait! I shouldn't be so amused. They've pulled me into this." She opened her chips and popped one in her mouth.

"I think you'll be fine as long as you tell them that you're not interested. Make that very clear."

Randi rolled her eyes, then she took a bite of her sandwich. "Definitely not."

His ego suffered a direct hit.

As she realized what she'd said, Randi waved her hand in front of herself and said, "Not that you aren't attractive and a good male specimen. It's just that you aren't my type." She shrugged and took another bite of her sandwich.

Yep. Definitely feeling some stab wounds.

"And what is your type, Randi? Not that I'm interested, but I am curious at this point since I've clearly missed the mark on every characteristic."

She laughed. "You know, I'm not exactly sure. But I've always been sure that I'd know it when I saw it. You're handsome, and that's good. You're nice. You're a hard worker." She studied him harder, and he started to get nervous. Was she changing her mind about the matchmaking efforts? "But we don't have any chemistry. Do you know what I mean?"

He did. Once again, he thought of Paige. They certainly didn't have any relationship together, though, except maybe a growing friendship. "Since this is a second attempt at me, I seem to be the focus, and you're just the person they're trying out for me this time. Any suggestions on how to get this to stop?"

She chewed thoughtfully, then took a sip of her water. "It seems to me that the only way to get them off the scent would be to find someone they thought you were having a relationship with. You know—if they thought you were interested in a specific woman, maybe they'd leave you alone."

"Then I'm in trouble. Because I don't want to date anyone right now."

"You know, that may be the thing I sense about you more than anything. You just aren't interested." After a few moments of silence, she added, "Are you planning on staying in Two Hearts, CJ?"

Randi's direct approach startled him. Most people in this town gently skirted issues. Other than Mrs. Brantley. She took things head on, which was why she was going to make an amazing mayor for Two Hearts. "I haven't decided."

She set down the potato chip she'd been about to put in her mouth. "I haven't said I was sorry yet, CJ. I know that you were looking at that house on the lake, but I thought you were just *looking*, not seriously interested. When the offer came through from Paige—and it was a great offer—I didn't even think to see if you wanted to bid too."

He certainly did regret not getting it, but that wasn't her fault. "I waited too long to decide. It's a hundred percent on me."

Randi crumpled up her empty bag of chips and threw it in the sack that had once contained their meal. Standing, she smiled and said, "I enjoyed our free lunch." As she started for the exit, she glanced over her shoulder and said, "Oh, and if you do meet a nice, new, handsome man in town, send him my way."

He laughed outright. Why wasn't he interested in either Michelle or Randi? They were both great women.

When she'd left, he thought about her advice. Before he got wind of another matchmaking attempt, he might have to think of his own way to convince the matchmakers that he didn't need their help.

~

An insect circling around Paige made her lean back from her coming-to-life garden to figure out if it was friend or foe. It turned out to be a fly, but that meant she was looking up as a car pulled in front of her house. A car she recognized as belonging to Mrs. Brantley.

Paige crouched down in the taller plants. What could she want here? Bent over, she ran toward the front door, pushed through it, and stepped behind the door to peer outside.

No more matchmaking, please!

Mrs. Brantley stood as she got out of her car. Smiling, she made her way toward Paige's gate.

A voice near her ear said, "Can I ask what you're doing?"

Paige jumped, bumping her head against CJ's face.

"Ouch!" He reached up and rubbed his nose.

"Sorry. But shh. I don't want her to know I'm home." Paige motioned with her thumb toward the front of the house.

He peered around her. "Mrs. Brantley? You're afraid of Emmaline Brantley?" he asked incredulously.

Paige put her hand on her racing heart.

CJ stepped toward the door's opening and raised his hand as though he was about to wave. Paige grabbed him by the shoulders and yanked him back.

"Please! I don't think I can deal with any more."

"But she's nice. What happened?"

Humiliation rose up inside her. "She's still playing matchmaker with me. I thought I could take it, but—"

CJ chucked. "I've been on the receiving end of more of that myself."

Relief rushed through her. "I thought she had turned her attention toward me."

He asked, "Are you sure she was the one involved?"

Was she? "It was at Bella's house, but she mentioned that Mrs. Brantley suggested the idea. The mayor is a really good organizer."

"And she's going to be on your doorstep in ten seconds."

Paige glanced out the door. Mrs. Brantley had reached the porch's first step. Pausing for a moment, she checked out the flower bed Paige had been working on and gave a nod of approval.

CJ whispered in her ear, "I have an idea. Maybe it will get us out of their matchmaking attempts."

When he put his arm around her shoulder and pulled her against his side, Paige tried to move away.

Under his breath, CJ said, "Go with me on this. If we want to stop the matchmakers, we may need to take a bold step. Are you with me?"

She nodded.

"Paige?"

The doorbell rang.

He hadn't been looking at her, so he couldn't see her nod. "Yes." She could barely hear her answer, but he must have because he swung the door open wide and said, "It's nice to have you stop by our place."

Mrs. Brantley took a step backward.

"I'm here so much that it feels like mine, too. Doesn't it, Paige?" He rubbed his hand on her shoulder.

Instead of flinching as she would have expected, warmth rolled through her, and she wanted to lean into his touch.

With a long glance at the hand on her shoulder, Mrs. Brantley said, "I'm glad to see the two of you getting along well."

"Oh, we are, aren't we, Paigie?"

It took every fiber of her being to not roll her eyes at the pet name. No one beyond her grandmother had ever called her Paigie. "Where are my manners? Please come inside." Paige stepped back to allow Mrs. Brantley to enter, and CJ dropped his hand from her shoulder. She immediately missed having it there.

"Tea?"

"That would be lovely, dear. But first, I'd like to see what you've achieved so far."

Paige could spend all day talking about her house, so her heart lifted. "In here, I've been working on the fireplace, both the tiles and mantel."

When they stepped into the room, Mrs. Brantley put her hands on her face and stopped. "That's beautiful! I remember it being orange, a poor choice for a fireplace no matter the era. Getting all of that off must have taken a lot of work."

"Hours." Paige rubbed her finger through the carving on the fireplace mantel, which had been hidden. "I can't imagine why anyone would do that?"

"It's easy to understand. It wasn't one person's taste, so they painted it. The next person wanted to freshen up the paint, and there you go." She turned to see the rest of the room. "Now you just need to get more furniture."

"Yes. I know that." She could hear despondency in her voice. "I'm going to have to live with it for now."

CJ touched her shoulder again, and it felt like pure comfort.

Mrs. Brantley added, "Renovating can be expensive."

"Yes, it can."

"Have you decided whether or not you're staying here?"

"I need to stretch the money. Right now, I don't have a source of income. But I certainly have plenty of ways to spend my money. If I can hang on long enough for this to become a bed and breakfast . . ."

Mrs. Brantley's gaze went from her to her carpenter. "And you, CJ?"

After a moment's pause, he said, "For now."

Mrs. Brantley pursed her lips. "I can't get a commitment out of either of you."

At least this conversation had absolutely nothing to do with matchmaking. Maybe CJ had the right idea earlier with his subtle—or maybe not-so-subtle—attention toward her.

"I can get you that tea now, Mrs. Brantley."

"If you have a sweet treat, too, that would be lovely."

Nothing she'd want to eat. Thankfully, this morning's charcoal smell had aired out.

CJ stepped in. "I don't think there are any baked goods in the house. Right, Paige?" His eyes danced with laughter.

"Not right now."

"No one bakes like you, Paige." With a grin, he said to her guest, "Mrs. Brantley, her baked goods disappear from the pan almost as she pulls it out of the oven. Paige can't keep them in the house." Chuckling, he led them into the kitchen.

CHAPTER FOURTEEN

a fter Mrs. Brantley had left, CJ pointed toward the parlor. "Let's sit down and figure this out."

"We could do that at the kitchen table. We might be more comfortable there."

CJ gently nudged her in the middle of her back. "Please? I have come to think of that table as the place where burned offerings are presented. It's a place of sacrifice. My stomach's sacrifice."

Paige stopped, turned around to face him, and he slammed into her. Nose to nose, they were so close she could feel his breath on her face.

He reached up and tucked her hair behind her ear. "Aren't you going to make a snarky comment?"

Paige stared up into his eyes. Was she? He was looking into her eyes, too. The mood shifted.

The hand that was still near her ear rested on her cheek. "Paige—"

She took a step backward. "Um." Then she remembered what he'd said right before she'd stopped. "My cooking isn't always bad." She had come to the point, though, where she wanted to have an attractive kitchen, but knew it wasn't going to be getting much use. With a sigh, she added, "Yeah, I guess it is."

He followed her lead. "Have you thought about taking lessons?"

She laughed as she headed for the couch. "I have watched many videos. They didn't help."

"No. I meant, have you tried to have someone teach you one on one? Maybe that's how you learn."

She shrugged. "It's a thought. If you find anyone who would do that, let me know."

"I've heard that Mrs. Brantley taught Cassie to cook."

Mrs. Brantley was a wonderful cook. If she could help her . . . No, that wouldn't work. The less time she spent with the matchmaker-in-chief, the better.

CJ sat at the opposite end of the couch instead of beside her. "Of course, she's the one who is setting us up. Is that the conclusion you reached?"

"Yes. She always seems to be involved. And Cassie and Bella mentioned her name with those blind date dinners."

"My dinner was at Mrs. Brantley's house. It was Michelle from the diner, and she had to leave—Mrs. Brantley, not Michelle—during the middle of the meal. That left us alone."

"At least that didn't happen to me. What did you do?"

"We had a nice dinner. And that was it. I've known Michelle since the day I pulled into town and stopped at Dinah's for a cup of coffee. She seems to be the girl that all the guys see as a friend."

"Maybe the matchmakers backed away from you. You've lived here for a while, but that was the only attempt."

CJ laughed. "That would be nice. But they didn't. One day, Bella called with a simple job she needed done. While I was working on it, Randi stopped by with lunch for me from the diner."

"My real estate agent?"

"She also owns the only motel in town."

So, that nice woman who had sold her the house also owned the one business that would be Paige's competition. Randi probably wouldn't be happy about that.

"Randi and I chatted, and then she left. I have a feeling that wasn't what Mrs. Brantley had intended, since she'd ordered my lunch and paid for it, then told Randi to get a meal for herself and have Dinah charge it to her, too. And Mrs. Brantley took care with the order. She knows I love chocolate, so chocolate pie was in the bag."

Paige and CJ had never talked specifically about foods they liked or didn't like, but chocolate was near and dear to her heart. She'd thought in the past—imagined, really—that her right man would show up on her doorstep with some truffles the first time they went out. Sometimes she'd pictured a heart-shaped box, but she wouldn't be that picky. Chocolate was chocolate, after all.

CJ reached over and nudged her arm. "Do you have any ideas about what we should do?"

"You said you had an idea and then you . . ." She hesitated to even say it, but she had to. "Put your arm around me. Was that your only idea?"

"That was what immediately came to mind. Throw her off the scent." He paused for a moment, then said, "That might be the best plan, though. What do you think, Paige?"

"About what?"

"About us pretending to be dating so that the matchmakers will stop trying to fix us up."

He had certainly seen a lot more in his actions than she had. Sure, she'd liked it, but . . . "CJ, I'm not sure—"

"I know I'm probably not your type, but it might work. Unless you have a better idea."

Not her type? He was handsome, nice, hardworking. And he

made her heart race. "I don't want to lie, though. One lie leads to another, and you're soon caught up in a web that's so tangled, you can't fight your way through it."

"What if we don't go all out and say we're dating, just give off signals that we are?"

She couldn't see any problems with that. And she certainly didn't object to spending time with CJ away from here. "That sounds okay."

He put his arm out along the back of the couch, almost reaching her. "We will have to fix one thing, though. You're afraid of me. We won't look like we're dating or even considering dating if you're jumpy when I'm nearby."

"I'm not afraid of you. Not in the way that you mean. I'm just nervous around men." There. She'd said it. She swallowed. She admitted softly, "I haven't dated very much." *Barely at all.* When had there been time with school and then work?

He was silent for a moment. When he didn't say anything, Paige turned to him. He was watching her with a serious expression on his face. "I think we're going to need to do this, or no one will buy into our having any sort of relationship. At least not beyond carpenter and homeowner."

"*This?*" Before she had time to figure out what he meant, or even come up with possibilities, he'd scooted over next to her. He leaned forward, put his hands gently on either side of her face, and slowly lowered his head toward hers. Her heart must have figured out that he was going to kiss her before her brain did, because it started beating so rapidly that it threatened to pound out of her chest.

When his lips touched hers, they were feather light. He brushed his lips over hers. And as he started to move away all too soon, Paige reached up and put her arms around him, tugging him closer.

He moved forward, pressing his lips against hers more firmly. All too soon, he moved away again.

~

CJ leaned back and gazed into Paige's eyes. What had just happened? He had meant to give her a light kiss, one that would make them maybe—he had thought in his stupidity—act more like they were actually dating. When Paige had pulled him toward her, though, he had gone willingly.

Paige's face flamed bright red. "I'm so sorry, CJ! I don't know what came over me!"

"Everything's fine." He took her hand in his. "Don't worry. And look on the upside." *I enjoyed it more than I thought I would. Enough that I'd like to kiss you again.*

"Which is?" Paige asked after a few seconds' hesitation.

Ignoring his thoughts, he said, "We'll probably look more like we're dating."

Tears welled up in her eyes. "But we aren't dating. Not really." She muttered under her breath what sounded like, "No one would ever date me."

"Paige, have you ever had a boyfriend?"

She shook her head.

"Dated?"

"Define 'date.'"

CJ leaned back on the couch, still holding her hand in his. He liked the feel of it there. "'Date' as in two people going out together with a possibility of something romantic happening, either then or in the future."

"In that case, no."

"No? You have never been on a date? You must be about thirty?"

"Thirty-one. And counting. I really want to get my life pulled together soon."

"I think buying a house and fixing it up in a town almost halfway across the country from where you were counts as being bold and moving forward."

"But never a real date." She punctuated each word as she tapped her finger on his thigh. "Not unless somebody fixes me up. Oh, and then it goes really badly almost every time. Do you know the first date that they sent me on here? A farmer. He only talked about farming and wanted to eat his dessert. He was a nice man, but . . ."

"Yeah, and he bush hogged your yard."

"And down at the lake park when I asked him to after that."

CJ chuckled in spite of himself. "How did you get him to do that? I wondered what happened down there. I thought maybe Mrs. Brantley had gotten the city moving on it."

"I think she has too many other projects. It seemed such a shame that it was overgrown, so I asked him to take care of it, and he did."

Paige was actually kind of funny when she got going. "And the other date here?"

"He has a girlfriend. They forgot to ask him about his love life in advance."

CJ laughed. "The new man in the sheriff's office."

"Correct. Deputy Charlie. Again, a lovely man. But incredibly unavailable."

"We're going to figure this matchmaking thing out. You and I will work together. We're here all day together doing things with the house, so it's only natural that it'll seem as though we're dating. I'll put my arm around you, maybe kiss your cheek. No major public displays of affection."

"Deal." Paige put her hand out to shake his.

A handshake wasn't exactly what he expected to seal what should be a romantic arrangement. But he reached his hand out. "Deal."

CHAPTER FIFTEEN

"*I*'m sorry you can't come with me this time, but I'm getting lunch for CJ and me at Dinah's."

Barking ensued, and Daisy danced around Paige. Did the dog understand her?

"I won't be gone too long. We can go out together later."

Daisy sat and focused on Paige. Just as she decided the dog had calmed, Daisy leaped in the air and tried to nab a hovering butterfly in that spot. Nope, not listening. Bug watching.

Paige watched Daisy dash across the lawn as she chased her butterfly, thankfully not catching it.

"So, you're sure you don't want to go for a bike ride today? I'm understanding you correctly, right?"

When the dog didn't look up from her pursuit, Paige chuckled and headed down the path to the bicycle that was leaning against the fence. Daisy would be perfectly fine alone in the front yard.

She pointed her bike toward Dinah's Place, then took a right turn instead. It was time for her to explore the town and see more of her new home. Two Hearts was small enough that every unfamiliar road must somehow eventually connect to one she knew. When she reached the highway, her thought was proven correct.

With a left turn, she headed toward town on what became Main Street, and slowed as she approached the buildings that had once been part of a bustling town. Wedding Bella stood out because of the bright pots of flowers and the fresh new sign hanging in front. As she neared that shop, she noticed that the one car parked in front of it had the driver's door open, and a woman sat sideways on the seat with her feet on the ground. She had guessed it was a woman, based on the purple sneakers she could see. Paige slowed her bicycle and then stopped, got off, and walked over to find out if everything was all right.

It clearly was not. The woman pressed her hands over her face as she sobbed, and tears ran down her cheeks.

"Are you okay?" Obviously, the dumbest question anyone had asked at any point in history. "Can I help you in some way?"

"Dress . . . a mess." She gulped again. "Help."

Paige looked around. This might be more than she could handle. No one else was in sight.

The woman stood, and Paige took a step backward. When the sobber reached for her car as her legs wobbled, Paige dashed forward to steady her. The woman pointed toward Bella's. "Thank you for helping." She punctuated the end of her sentence with yet another sob.

"You need help going into Wedding Bella?"

She nodded vigorously. "Wedding dress." She pointed to a mound in a clothing carrier in her back seat.

Paige opened the car's back door and gathered up the garment in her hands. It was surprisingly heavy. What did they put in these things? She held out her elbow toward the woman and said, "If you hold on to me, we can go inside. Do you think that will work?"

She gripped Paige's arm with surprising vigor. With her still sobbing and taking hesitant steps forward, they made their way over to the Bella's entrance, where Paige tried to shift her load so she could open the door. Between the woman's grip on one arm and the voluminous garment bag over the other, she couldn't grab the door properly. Giving up, she knocked, and Bella hurried over.

Bella looked from Paige to the woman, and her jaw dropped. "Can I help you?" At least Paige didn't feel as bad about asking the obvious when Bella had done the same thing.

"Wedding dress. Ruined!"

Bella stepped up to the woman and took her other arm. "I understand. Let's get you inside, and we'll see what we can do to help."

Paige supported the woman into the store and over to a chair. When she finally released her and stepped back, Paige breathed a sigh of relief. This situation was completely outside her comfort zone.

With her client settled, Bella reached for the dress carrier Paige held. She hung it up on a hook, unzipped the carrier, and peeled it off.

Both Bella and Paige gasped.

"That's . . . colorful, isn't it?" Bella examined the dress from all sides. Bright streaks of pink and red slashed across the fabric from the sweetheart neckline to the lace-trimmed train. No part of it had been left unscathed.

"Four-year-old niece." Tears kept flowing down the woman's face. How had she managed to drive here? "Lipstick."

"I'm Bella." She held out her hand.

"Nikki." The woman sniffed.

Paige patted Nikki on the shoulder. "You two have this under control, so I'll be on my way." She took a step backward. "It was a pleasure meeting you." As Paige started to turn, Nikki reached out and grabbed her lower arm with a vice-like grip.

"Please don't go. I know I just met you, but I need to be

surrounded by people who understand right now. And you seem to understand." Nikki looked up at her with pleading eyes.

Paige inwardly sighed. There was no way she could turn this woman down. "Sure. If Bella doesn't mind, I'm happy to stay." She looked over at Bella, who exhaled with what seemed like relief. Paige would have thought she'd been through all kinds of situations like this, including those involving hysterical, weepy brides. But maybe you never did quite get used to that.

"Can . . . Can you save the dress, Bella?" Nikki's tears had slowed. Paige looked up at Bella, who one by one lifted the layers of chiffon in the skirt, each streaked with color. Even as someone who had only dabbled in sewing, Paige could tell there wasn't much that could be done.

Bella inhaled, put her shoulders back, and turned around to face her customer with a smile. "Nikki, I am sorry, but if this is lipstick as you've said—"

"It is."

Bella still had that smile on her face—and Nikki could probably tell it was forced—but she cheerfully continued. "Then I can't save it. If it had been in one area, I might have been able to camouflage it."

Nikki's face screwed up into a grimace, and the tears started running down her cheeks again. With a hiccup, she said, "I knew you'd say that. I hoped if I drove all the way out here that you would be able to help. Carly says you're a miracle worker." She gasped for air.

Bella stopped moving. "Carly sent you?"

Nikki nodded. "We're friends. She said you're the best."

Paige might be new to town, but even she knew that Bella had designed a wedding dress for country music star Carly Daniels. She'd read about that wedding before she'd moved here, and Michelle had told her about Cassie and Bella's role in it during one of her first visits to Dinah's Place.

Bella's eyes widened as she stared at Nikki. Then she swung back toward the dress and walked around it again. Shaking her head, she said, "I'm sorry I can't save *this* dress. Carly is a dream client, and I loved working with her, but—" She held up her hand as Nikki let out a wail. "I'm going to offer you the same thing that I would offer any bride at this moment. We're going to have to start from scratch and make a brand-new dress."

Nikki kept crying. "You can't!" she said between sobs. "There isn't enough time!"

Bella gave her a steady stare. "I've been able to pull off miracles in the past. How much time do we have?"

Nikki swiped at her tears on her cheeks. "Everyone I asked said they needed months. Or I was going to have to buy a ready-to-wear dress off the rack. My wedding is going to be on all the media sites. I need something special and unique." She seemed to get her strength back and stood. "I thank you for looking at it. I guess I'm just going to have to move my wedding date. Three weeks isn't going to cut it."

She turned toward the door and had taken two steps when Bella called out, "Three weeks? We can do that!"

Her statement held such assurance that Nikki swung back around and stared at her, open-mouthed. "You can get me a new dress in three weeks?"

"I won't *get* anything."

Nikki's face dropped again.

"I make custom wedding dresses, Nikki. We can make you the dress you want in that amount of time. There'll be a slight upcharge for the rush."

Nikki raced at Bella and scooped her into a tight hug. Paige was just glad she hadn't slowed down as she'd passed her to do the same. Then she turned, zoomed in on Paige, and grabbed her just as strongly.

Stepping back, Nikki raised her hands and waved them in

the air. "Thank you! Thank you! I can't believe this. No wonder Carly raves about you." Wiping her still-damp cheeks, she added, "Can we get started on it today?"

The transformation in Nikki was so surprising that Bella chuckled, and Paige held back a laugh.

"We *have* to get started today." Glancing over at Paige, Bella said, "I think it's safe for you to leave now. We've got the situation under control."

Nikki looped her arm around Paige's. "I'd love to have both of you give me your opinions. I know Bella's the expert, but I feel like I need some additional girl input. Would you mind, Paige?"

Could she stick around? It was either staying here or getting a fast bite to eat before heading home and diving into more renovations. "I don't have any big plans for the day." She was only going to work on the fireplace and follow that with trying to cook something, but why add a burned smell to the air of the house again this soon? She'd keep it fresh and clean for 24 hours. At least as fresh as paint stripper had made it.

"Then let's get started." Bella stood in front of the wedding gown and glanced between it and Nikki several times before speaking again. "Do you love everything about this dress? We're starting from scratch, so it can be anything you want it to be. Within reason." She held up a hand. "We may not have time to cover it completely with sequins or something like that."

Nikki laughed. "Please," she said emphatically. "No sequins. I know there's a cliché assumption that everyone in my profession wants to be enrobed in sequins from their neck to their ankles, but that isn't me."

"Then why don't we all sit down, and you can tell us about your personal style and your venue? We'll go from there."

Paige took the chair that Bella indicated, and the three of them talked about the wedding. Well, the other two women talked while Paige stared in amazement. She'd had no idea up until this moment that there was so much involved in a wedding dress. Didn't people just stand in front of a minister, her in a beautiful dress and him in a tuxedo or suit, say "I do," and then walk out of the church as Mr. and Mrs.? Apparently not.

A few minutes into the design process of Nikki describing her dream dress and Bella sketching, Nikki relaxed. Paige wasn't even sure if she realized it.

Moments later, the bride-to-be shouted, "That's it! That's my dress."

Bella looked up from her sketchpad and smiled at her customer. "This doesn't actually look like the gown you brought me—even minus the colorful additions. Are you sure this is what you're interested in this time?"

Nikki studied the drawing in Bella's hands. "This is what I said I wanted when I went shopping for my original dress. I tried on quite a few, and I decided that the one I bought was right. But now I wonder." Sadness washed over her.

Bella said, "Don't worry. I have samples we can combine into more or less this style. Do you want to try?"

Smiling again, Nikki said, "Absolutely. And thank you. With so little time, I know I won't be able to change anything when it's finished." Tucking her long blonde hair behind her ears, she added, "I'm not usually an emotional mess."

A few minutes later, Nikki stood in front of the mirror in a mishmash of pinned-together pieces that actually looked remarkably like the drawing Bella had made. When Paige heard her sniffle and saw her wipe at her wet eyes, she thought she was having a meltdown because it was completely wrong.

Bella held out a box of tissues. "Is this your wedding gown?"

Nikki nodded her head vigorously. "I don't know how you did this. You saw into my soul, and you pulled out the dress of my dreams. Thank you!" She took a tissue. "But are you sure you can get this done in three weeks?"

"I am. You'll need to come out to Two Hearts for a couple of fittings, but that should be it."

"I'll do whatever you say. I just want to have this nightmare over and to marry my man."

CHAPTER SIXTEEN

"Who's the groom? Someone famous?" Bella asked as she filled out some paperwork on her tablet.

That seemed like an odd question to ask, but maybe Bella had a lot of celebrity clients.

Nikki waved her hand in the air to dismiss the thought. "He's actually just a regular guy. He was the contractor for the house I had built. I stopped by a few times, and we got to talking, and the next thing you knew, we were at dinner together—and the conversation was even better then. I can't wait to marry him."

Bella checked her watch with barely a glance. Paige noticed it, but Nikki didn't. She must have another customer coming in. That was further suggested when she said, "Let's get you out of this outfit and on your way back to Nashville."

Nikki returned a few minutes later, dressed in her own clothes. Fluffing her hair with her hands as she stepped through the doorway, she said, "I barely noticed this town when I pulled in, but your shop is so cute. Do either of you have time to show me around before I have to drive back to the city?"

Bella's eyes popped wide, and she turned to Paige with a pleading expression.

"I can take you around town," Paige offered. She knew Bella wanted to be polite to Nikki. Then she realized she didn't know much about the town herself.

Once Bella knew her customer was taken care of, she stepped away and began working on something at the cash register stand.

"That sounds wonderful." Nikki's hand flew to her mouth. "Although, now that I'm not sobbing uncontrollably, I realize that I interrupted you. What were you on your way to do?"

"I was on my way to get lunch at Dinah's."

"Then let's go there."

Dinah's Place was a small-town restaurant. Something about this woman said she was used to the finest places in the country —if not the world. "It's simple dining with a lot of homey foods."

"Is there anything special about it? Or any reason I shouldn't go there?" Nikki said with some hesitation.

"Absolutely not. Dinah's Place is amazing."

As they stepped out the door with a last glance behind them to wave to Bella, Paige realized she had left her bike out front.

"Bella," she called out before the door had had a chance to close. She blocked it with her foot. "My bicycle is here. Do you mind if I leave it?"

"Why don't you wheel it around to the back? Then you know nothing will happen to it."

The trust here was unfamiliar to Paige.

Nikki seemed to agree. "That wouldn't be the answer I'd receive in Nashville."

"Or Berlin. Los Angeles. Or Manhattan," Paige said. "I've lived or worked in all of those places and more. That's one reason I chose a small town." They went outside. When Paige reached her bicycle, she added, "Please wait here for just a sec, and I'll be right back." She pedaled off around the corner before her guest had a chance to reply.

They were soon walking past closed shops. "The town looks abandoned."

"It's coming back to life, though. Bella opened her shop. And Cassie has a wedding planning business. It's my understanding that it all started when Cassie was a runaway bride and ended up in this town."

"Now that sounds like a story I want to hear."

"I don't know details. She ran away to romance. She's marrying the town's sheriff." When they were beyond the main street's shop section, Paige pointed ahead of them. "Dinah's Place is just past the church."

Nearing the small, freshly painted white building, Nikki squealed with delight. "This chapel is adorable. I see stained glass windows. So charming."

"It has old-fashioned wooden pews inside. When sunlight shines through the stained glass, it's especially beautiful."

A couple of minutes later, they went up the steps to Dinah's Place. When Paige opened the door, a wonderful scent she couldn't quite put her finger on wafted through the door.

Nikki said, "Chicken soup."

Michelle walked over to greet them. "Almost correct. Today, we have chicken and dumplings. A favorite here. Just the two of you?" She glanced from Paige to Nikki. Then her eyes narrowed as she considered the other woman. Michelle gestured toward two unoccupied tables, so they went that direction and sat. When she returned with menus, she focused on Nikki. "You look familiar."

"I hear that a lot," Nikki answered.

"She's here to see Bella."

Michelle lit up. "You're getting married?"

Maybe Paige shouldn't have mentioned that.

Nikki didn't seem concerned, though. "I am. Bella is making my dress."

"Are you getting married here? Carly Daniels did not long ago." The excitement radiated off of her.

"As charming as this town is, I'm not. My wedding has been planned for a year. I did hear that Carly's wedding went well."

Michelle sighed dreamily. "It was so beautiful. And the reception? Absolutely gorgeous." As they gave their drink orders—sweet tea for both of them—the waitress seemed half focused on their words, with the rest of her attention on Nikki. She stared at the other woman, then shook her head and walked away.

Nikki glanced over at Paige and shrugged.

"Are you someone famous I should know?"

Nikki laughed happily. "I don't think there's anyone you *should* know. I'm just a much happier bride-to-be. That can be my identity for today." Abruptly, she asked, "What's good here?"

Paige picked up the plastic-covered menu in front of her and scanned the options. "I tend to get whatever the special is. It's never steered me wrong, but that makes me unable to advise you about many of these options."

Michelle returned with their beverages and placed them on the table, giving Nikki another hard stare before she straightened and became her usual self. "Have you decided what you'd like? Or do you need more time?"

Paige spoke up. "What's the special?"

Michelle slapped the side of her head. "I didn't even tell you, did I? What have I been thinking?" Her gaze flickered over to Nikki and then back. "It's meatloaf, broccoli casserole, and mashed potatoes with gravy."

"Sold!" Paige held her menu out toward Michelle, and the woman took it and tucked it behind her notepad.

"I think I'd like the chicken and dumplings." Nikki pursed

her lips as she studied the menu. "Should I get a salad or something too? Or will that be enough?"

Paige and Michelle said at the same time, "Leave room for pie."

Laughing, Paige added, "Dinah makes the best pie you've ever eaten."

"That sounds wonderful to me. I may watch my figure most days, but this isn't one of them."

They settled into the usual new-acquaintance conversation about the weather.

Then Nikki changed the subject. "What brought you to Two Hearts?"

"I'd been saving for a house for years. I saw a news story about Carly's wedding and checked out the town online. To my amazement, real estate was inexpensive. I'd been hoping for my own place in Brooklyn, one of New York City's boroughs. To live there, I was looking at several years or more before buying." *And that much time in a job I hated,* she added silently. "I made an offer on a beautiful Victorian home, sight unseen, quit my job, and moved here three weeks ago." Paige took a fortifying sip of her iced tea. It sounded crazy every time she said that.

"Wow! I thought I'd done some wild things in my life, but I think you might have beaten me on that." Nikki took a sip of her own drink. "Dinah makes a good glass of sweet tea."

Paige was glad the attention had shifted away from her.

"So, was the move a good decision?"

Or not. "I think so. The house . . . It was perhaps more needy than I had anticipated from the photos. The real estate agent had told me that it was an old house that needed some love and care, but I hadn't realized it was in need of quite that much affection."

"Ouch. Is it getting fixed up? I guess I should ask: Is it livable?"

"It was always livable. But it hadn't been loved in probably fifty years. Two or three decades at least."

"The whole town feels that way. But Carly had only good things to say about her wedding here." Nikki grew silent as her expression turned dreamy. Maybe an idea had come to her for her own wedding. Before Paige could pursue the question of what that might be, their food arrived.

"Oh my goodness. This smells heavenly," Nikki exclaimed, and waved the steaming scent toward herself. She took a bite of the meal and sighed. "Oh my. I do love Southern country food."

Paige tasted her own lunch. True to form, it was excellent. She debated what to ask or talk about with Nikki. They weren't really friends, but they were getting along as friends. The eternal problem of an introvert was that she wasn't sure what to say. She decided to go ahead and just talk. "Where are you from originally?"

Nikki held up a hand to say *just a moment* as she finished her bite. "I'm originally from a small town in Minnesota. One I doubt you've ever heard of."

"I would imagine your doubts are correct. I've never been to that state."

"I enjoy being in Nashville. It might be nice someday not to travel as much as I do for work, but for right now, it's fun. And it's putting the food on the table."

When they'd finished their meal, they each ordered pie—Paige choosing pumpkin caramel and Nikki choosing pecan.

"If I'm going to go for the calories, I'm going to go for them big. I think I'll need a walk after this, though, to burn them off." She chuckled. "So, tell me about this house of yours. Is it being worked on?"

"I have a carpenter who's there now. And I'm doing everything I can myself."

Their pie arrived, along with the cup of coffee Nikki had ordered, and her new friend wasted no time in trying her dessert. "Mmm." When she'd swallowed, she asked, "You enjoy do-it-yourself?"

Did she? She pictured what she'd done so far. "I actually enjoy seeing the finished work. The wall without old, peeling wallpaper." Paige tried her pie. The autumn flavors of pumpkin and caramel melted on her tongue. "Try this one next time."

Nikki grinned. "I will need a next time at Dinah's Place."

Paige thought about her house as they quietly ate their desserts. "I had saved what I believed was plenty of money, but it turned out that everything cost more than I expected, including the broken window I hadn't known was there."

"Ooh. If you needed to replace a window, you must have had some water damage?"

"Surprisingly little. The problem is mostly neglect. The original features have been hidden under paint or just completely covered up. But she'll be a beauty when she's done."

Nikki sipped her coffee. "As I mentioned earlier at Bella's, my fiancé works in construction. He's wrapping up a couple of houses in Nashville right now. He's promised me that we'll be able to go on our honeymoon with no deadlines looming and no calls from panicking subcontractors on the jobsite."

"Sounds like that happens often."

Nikki scoffed. "So often. But sometimes, work just follows you."

She glanced over at Michelle, who was now busy at the counter. The waitress handed Sheriff Greg, Cassie's husband-to-be, a bag and a thermos. That reminded her that she needed to get lunch for CJ.

"Just a sec." Paige hurried up to the counter, and Michelle took down the order, promising to bring it to their table. Even with that moment away, she finished her pie before Nikki did. "That pumpkin caramel was amazing."

"Mine was good too, but I may have to try that one if it's still on the menu when I'm here again."

Paige looked around the small restaurant. Most of the people here were familiar now. Some she'd met before Daisy ran away, others because of that. "There's something special about this little town. It makes you feel like you want to stay longer, doesn't it?"

"It's charming." After using the ladies' room, Nikki reappeared with fresh makeup, and the difference was quite startling. When Michelle glanced their way, Nikki pulled out sunglasses and put them on, before confidently striding over to the table.

Michelle arrived with the check and CJ's order, all of which Nikki paid for immediately without giving Paige a chance. "You have been more than kind this morning. This is my privilege."

Paige wasn't going to argue with her. The more she saved, the more she could put into the house.

As they walked toward the door, Nikki said, "I thought about what you said. About it being charming here. Can you show me more of the town?"

"Well, there isn't too much more to see. At least not too much that I know about."

Paige opened the door, and the two of them went out and down the steps. When they reached the bottom, Nikki said, "Then show me the part of the town that you know. Did I hear something about a lake when you were talking to Bella?"

"You did. My house is on the lake, and not too far. Although it is a little further than what we've already walked. Are you sure?"

"I am so sure. I think I just need some quiet time and a walk with a new friend today. And I probably am going to need a gallon of tea to replace all the liquid that I cried out. I may have to stop here for a to-go cup later," Nikki said with a rueful smile.

Paige gestured to their left. "Let's go this way."

The two chatted as they walked through the streets and down in the direction of the lake.

Nikki motioned to a house with an overgrown yard. "It's a real mix here of houses. Some are taken care of and some look all but abandoned."

"That startled me at first. I wondered if I'd made a mistake in moving to Two Hearts. I've had to keep reminding myself that I'm here because the house was affordable. It wouldn't have been so cheap if it hadn't been in this condition. Even in Two Hearts. The bonus is that the people in town are wonderful. And Nashville is out there. It's only an hour and a half away, so if I do get an urge to go to a city, I can do that pretty easily."

"I couldn't come to Carly's wedding because I had . . ." Nikki hesitated for a moment, and Paige wondered why. "Other commitments that couldn't be moved to another date. Is this the direction of her wedding or the reception, by chance?"

"The wedding was in that little church that we passed."

"Oh, that's right."

"And the reception was on a farm outside of town. I haven't been there yet. But I've been told about it multiple times." The road curved toward home, and Paige caught a hint of water glistening. "We're here."

"At the lake?" Nikki stopped and looked around carefully. "I don't see one."

"Sure." Paige pointed. "There. Through the trees."

Nikki shielded her eyes with her hand. "Oh, I see it now."

Paige could picture a charming park on the shore of a lake. "I want to restore this to its former beauty. It must have been pretty years ago. When . . . someone I know bush hogged my yard, I asked him if he could do the park here too."

Nikki raised an eyebrow. "A man?"

"Yes, but just an acquaintance."

Nikki seemed poised to ask more about the man, so Paige

plowed on. "I had hoped that alone would make it usable. It did not. And everything he cut is already starting to grow back."

"Your idea was good. But it's going to take a lot more than that. Maybe the town can hire a company to come in and fix it up."

"There isn't money for anything like that. I know they just restored a park in the other direction from Dinah's Place."

Nikki took a few steps toward the park and leaned one way, then the other, and crouched. "I'd like to see it if it's fixed up again. In fact, I'd come out here to help if they ever did a work day."

Paige really couldn't see this woman, with the perfectly manicured nails and her hair just right, digging in on a job like that.

Almost as if she had read her mind, Nikki added, "Don't let my appearance fool you. I grew up on a farm. We did everything. Some things that you don't even want to know about."

Paige grinned. "In that case, I'll make sure Bella contacts you if that happens. My house is just up the street."

After a few steps, Nikki stopped and put her hands on her hips as she scanned the street. Then her jaw dropped. She cleared her throat, probably as she considered what she was looking at. That had to be it, because the woman hadn't been silent since Paige had met her.

"I know it doesn't look good."

"Honey, it's far beyond not looking good. It looks like somebody put out a do-not-disturb sign on this road a long time ago. There isn't one of them that I'd even want to go near."

Paige swallowed. "I know. It surprised me too." Maybe they should just turn around and go back to town.

"Show me your house. I still want to see it. You have a vision for it, and I want to know what that is."

They started forward and, as they walked by each of the old

homes, Paige had to admit that they weren't inviting. She had tried to block that out since the first morning.

As they continued, Paige's nerves flared to life. It felt personal to show someone a work in progress. She had spent so many hours slaving over removing paint from the tiles around the fireplace downstairs, stripping wallpaper, and fixing up the butler's pantry. Not to mention the initial cleaning that she'd had to do in the bathrooms and kitchen. But nothing was done. Her nerves ratcheted up as they continued past the houses.

They stopped in front of hers.

"This must be your place, because it's actually charming."

"Do you think so?" Paige felt like a proud parent.

"I can tell that there's some love going into it. It's massive for a single person, though."

Did Paige dare share her dream with someone else? She took a deep breath. "I'm starting a bed and breakfast."

To her surprise, Nikki nodded slowly as she looked at it. "How many bedrooms?"

"Six."

"That sounds perfect. I can see that she used to be beautiful, but she's had some bad years."

Paige sighed, this time more despondently. "I know." Could she risk inviting Nikki inside? She certainly couldn't have her sit down at the table for a cup of tea or coffee and a brownie. And the current lack of furniture would stand out.

"Let's go inside."

Paige opened the gate. Daisy raced over, barking at the top of her lungs. Instead of running away, Nikki laughed. "She's wagging her tail, so I'm guessing this is okay."

"It is. I haven't seen her be mean to anyone. But then, we haven't been together too long."

Nikki turned toward her. "What's not too long?"

"Three weeks and four days."

Paige kneeled down to scratch Daisy behind her ears the way she liked it. "But she's a good girl, aren't you?"

Nikki kneeled beside her. Loving the double attention, Daisy quickly rolled on to her back to get belly rubs from one of them. She must have figured that she had a better chance with two humans.

With another laugh, Nikki rubbed her belly. "Corgis are adorable. We had a lot of dogs on the farm growing up, but none of this breed." Nikki stood. Glancing around, she said, "I can tell that you've made progress already, just from the front. I assume it looked the same as the other homes and yards on the street."

"Exactly. Well, let me change that: It was really bad, but the real estate agent had mowed the grass and weeds in the front yard."

"We'll be back soon, little one," Nikki said.

Miraculously, the dog went back to playing.

When they arrived at the porch, Paige motioned Nikki to the left. "Stay over here. The right side still seems unstable, even with CJ's patch on one part of it." At Nikki's questioning glance, she added, "The wood is rotten over there."

Nikki did a quick jog to the left and followed behind Paige to the door, gingerly testing each step before putting her weight on it. That was probably a good idea.

"Is that you, sweetie?" CJ called from the direction of the kitchen. He stopped in the doorway with a hammer in his hand. "Oh, I heard two voices and thought you were here with—"

"Nope," Paige interrupted.

Nikki gave her a long look. "Is he your—"

"No!" both Paige and CJ yelled.

Nikki stepped back. "Whoa!"

Paige's face turned hot, and even CJ shuffled his feet nervously.

Paige needed to explain this in a way that didn't embarrass

her further, if that was possible. She'd reached a new embarrassment high this time.

CJ rescued her. "There are matchmakers working to fix each of us up. We found that if we pretend—"

Nikki laughed. "Say no more. You're hiding from matchmakers by pretending to be together." She stared at CJ a moment too long. "Are you sure you don't want him for yourself, Paige?"

CJ laughed. Walking toward the two of them, he said, "While I appreciate that, I'm planning to head out of town soon. Not that Paige isn't great."

Great. That sounded like something a handsome man would call her. Not pretty. Not girlfriend-worthy. *Great.*

CJ's gaze narrowed. The hammer slipped in his hand, but he caught it before it fell. "Nikki Lane?"

"You know her?" A beautiful woman and CJ?

Without breaking his stare toward Nikki, he said, "Everyone knows Nikki Lane. She has a song right now at the top of the charts."

Nikki gave a girlish laugh. "It's number one today."

Paige stared at the woman she'd come to think of as possibly a new friend, and her heart leaped into her throat. "I'm so sorry. I don't follow country music, but I should have known who you were."

"I was thrilled that you didn't know. You treated me as a normal person. Like a friend. And I'd like to be your friend." She paused for a moment. Was the star a little unsure of herself? "If you don't mind."

Paige's embarrassment faded. "I would love that. I just moved here, and I don't have friends yet. Wait! You don't live here."

Nikki laughed. "No, but I'm in Nashville. We can do lunch."

"I never say no to lunch, especially with a friend," Paige said.

CJ smirked. "Especially if it means she doesn't have to cook."

"Honey, I agree with that. If I can get out of cooking, I will almost every time. Now, show me this house of yours. I love the original details."

CJ continued staring but grinned. "She's a beauty."

"Paige or the house?" Nikki raised an eyebrow.

CJ became flustered. "I was talking about the house, but—"

Nikki laughed. "Sorry to put you on the spot. Paige's beauty is obvious. You're going to have to show me the hidden potential in this place, though."

Paige had never been showered with so many compliments, and this one from Nikki caught her off guard. "Thank you. Follow me." Upstairs, and away from CJ, she continued, "It still needs so much work. Since we're alone, I'll say that I get overwhelmed sometimes."

"She's still a little rough around the edges, but I know she'll be beautiful when you're done."

Paige felt a smile, and then it widened. "You're right. I get so caught up in the details that I forget to look at the house as a whole. When you're here next time . . . Never mind." Nikki would want to try on her dress and leave. Paige didn't want to impose.

"I'd like to have lunch again and see what you've accomplished here."

She did think they *could* be friends. "We'll plan on it."

As they wrapped up the tour of the second floor, Nikki said, "Are you sure you and your hottie carpenter aren't dating?"

Paige sputtered. "Definitely not. We're friends. Sort of."

"Huh. I thought the look he gave you said 'more than friends.'" She shrugged. "Maybe a different Two Hearts man will win your heart."

Maybe. *If* she stayed.

CHAPTER SEVENTEEN

*W*hen they came out of the house, Daisy ran over again. She followed them up to the gate as though she thought she'd get to go along.

"Do you take her for walks?"

"As often as I can. Not as often as she would like, because that would be most of the day. She may have short legs, but they're mighty."

"Why don't you bring her along, then?"

Paige ran back to the house and grabbed Daisy's leash. The dog had run off on her favorite pursuit: butterflies. When Paige called her over, the dog hesitated, but must have chosen the walk over all else.

She snapped on her leash. "I would be upset about you and your butterfly obsession if you had any chance of catching one. Fortunately, they just burn off some of your excess energy— your *very abundant* energy—and you cause no harm."

To Nikki, she said, "I took a photo of her with a butterfly on her nose. So cute!"

"She is adorable."

The three of them walked back to town—with Daisy being

surprisingly well-behaved. Paige said goodbye to her new friend, who climbed into her car and drove off with a promise to be back. As the car disappeared down the road, Paige realized she had a problem.

She'd ridden her bike here. Daisy couldn't be trusted to stay beside the bike and not dive under the wheels. But it had a big basket. Paige peered in the front window of the bridal shop and found it empty. Thankfully. She stepped inside with Daisy next to her and called out, "Bella?"

Bella appeared from a backroom. When she saw that it was Paige, she hurried forward and lunged at her for a hug. "I can't thank you enough for staying while Nikki was here. She was so upset, and it's often hard to calm a bride down who's that far gone. But she relaxed with your help, and she was able to focus on what she wanted for a new dress. If she hadn't been able to today, it never would have been done in time for her wedding."

Paige felt a smile begin and grow. "She's very nice. We had lunch, then we walked down to the lake because I'd mentioned it earlier, and I showed her my house." She paused for a second as she felt heat rising in her face once again when she remembered who Nikki was. "Bella, I didn't know she was famous. You should have told me."

Bella laughed. "I get a lot of famous clients. I've gotten so used to it that I don't pay attention. I didn't recognize her because she was ugly-crying. When she said her name and I looked closer, I realized that I knew who she was, and that's why she's talked to Carly, I'm sure. It was probably best that you didn't know because you treated her like a regular person, and that seems to be something they don't get a lot of."

Paige had to admit that was true. Daisy's low bark reminded her why she was here. Paige looked down at her dog. "Thank you for our reminder that you're waiting for your bike ride. Bella, do you have anything like a blanket that I can put in the basket so I can ride home with Daisy? I can bring it back later."

Bella tapped her mouth with her finger as she pondered. "Just a second." She raced away and around a corner. Then Paige heard heels tapping up on what must be stairs. Until earlier today, she'd never even been in here. She'd only peered through the window and wondered if one day she might be able to get a dress from Bella. That wasn't likely to happen, though. She tended to end up with male buddies like CJ. Some women attracted men who wanted relationships. Some attracted men who wanted to have pizza and strip paint.

Bella was hurrying back down the stairs, if the tap-tap-tapping was any indication. She appeared with a fluffy wad of fabric in her arms. "I don't even know why I kept this. It's a dress that got ruined in water." As she handed it to Paige, a dreamy expression came on her face. After a sigh, she said, "But if that hadn't occurred, I don't think I would have found Micah and married him. That was the best thing to ever happen to me." Bella handed her the dress.

"Are you sure this is okay?" She could tell that at one point it had been a gorgeous dress.

Bella laughed. "More than okay. I need to get it out of here. You're doing me a favor. And remember, you don't know when a good thing is going to happen. Sometimes it doesn't even look that way when it does."

Paige left, and with Daisy beside her they went to the back of the store. She filled the basket with the dress and hefted Daisy into it, where the dog made a happy nest. What would people think if they saw a wedding dress billowing out as she rode down the street? Paige found some of Nikki's songs to play on the way, and then they started back. She liked the sound of them. Before long, she was humming along and tapping her fingers on the handlebars.

At home, she walked the bike through the gate and closed it behind her and Daisy. CJ hurried over and lifted the dog to the ground.

"How do you know Nikki Lane?" He still looked a little dumbfounded when he asked that.

This must be what Bella was talking about. She wasn't sure CJ would ever be able to treat Nikki as a regular person.

"I just met her. She's very nice. We had lunch together at Dinah's."

"Lunch?"

She watched Daisy play, while they talked. "She's just a person, CJ."

He shook himself off. "I guess you're right. But I've spent a lot of hours listening to that woman sing. She has a gorgeous voice. I was surprised you didn't know who she was."

"I played some of her songs on my ride back. She's good."

CJ laughed. "Of course, she's good. She's been on the top for a while. I didn't ask, but she said something about ugly-crying?" He said the last part with complete confusion.

Paige laughed. "That's what women call crying so much that your face is screwed up, it's splotchy, and you look bad. It's an ugly cry."

"That makes sense. But I can't imagine her ever looking anything approaching ugly."

"She went into the bathroom at Dinah's and put on makeup. She appeared to be a completely different person when she came out. But she was wearing sunglasses, and that's probably what saved her from being spotted by Michelle."

"Michelle does love country music. I know that Cassie hired her to work at Carly's wedding, and that she was thrilled about that. She must have mentioned it a hundred times in the diner that next week." CJ sighed and glanced over his shoulder. "I guess it's time to get back to work, then."

Paige laughed. "I guess it is. I need to have that tattooed on my forehead backwards so that every time I look at the mirror, I remember." She went into the house with him beside her, then to the front parlor's doorway and stopped. "I'm definitely ready to move on to something else for a while. Instead of working here, I think I'll go back to stripping upstairs." She went that direction, laughing. "I have to be careful who I say that around."

CJ surprised her again with his voice right behind her. The man moved softly for someone his size. "If it were me, I would finish this job no matter how tired you are of it. Then every time you walk into that room, you'll admire your work instead of thinking that you've got to get back to it. Speaking as someone who does this kind of work for a living, that's the better way."

Paige leaned against the side of the stair rail. "I like that idea. I just needed a nudge in the right direction."

"I'm happy to nudge you any time you want." He went silent. "That may not have come out quite as I'd meant it to."

Paige laughed. "Probably not. But I'll take it in the spirit it was intended."

Near the top of the stairs, he said, "Would you like to get an early dinner at Dinah's tomorrow? To add to our appearance of dating."

This caught her more off guard than entertaining a music star had. "I guess so. Are you sure we should take it that far?"

"We're either in or out. We've both had two match-ups."

"Good point. Dinner at Dinah's works for me."

CHAPTER EIGHTEEN

*C*J stared at the clothes hanging in his closet. Jeans and t-shirts had been his weekday uniform since moving here. A date required something better.

Except it wasn't a date. It just had to look like one.

Would he get to kiss her again? He wanted to. But he also needed to keep their relationship platonic.

That didn't seem to be going well.

He chose khaki pants and a navy-blue polo shirt. While combing his hair in the bathroom mirror, he wondered if he should shave off his beard. It had been a couple of years since he'd been clean-shaven. He tossed his comb on the counter and marched out of the room. Acting like a love-sick teenager over a fake date was ridiculous.

He stopped at the grocery store for something to bring when he arrived. Even though this wasn't a real date, she would need to be able to tell people about it. Chocolate seemed like a natural first date gift, and the small store had a surprisingly good assortment. He chose the most date-worthy box they had, paid for it, and went to Paige's house.

As he approached her door, he wondered if he should go

right in after a quick knock, as he had been doing every day, or if he should wait for her to answer his knock. Paige took the decision away from him because she opened the door while he crossed the porch.

She was even prettier than normal and that was saying something. He stopped on the step. "You look great."

"You too."

When he offered the gift to Paige, she gasped. "A heart-shaped box of chocolates? Thank you!"

She stared at it as though she couldn't believe her eyes. Maybe he should have brought flowers instead. Shifting on his feet, he said, "I thought this would add a nice touch if anyone asked."

"I appreciate it. And I'll be sure to mention it to Bella or Cassie when I see them again." She turned toward the inside of the house. "Daisy!"

The dog barreled out the door and danced around his legs. "Have you been a good girl?" She flopped over for a belly rub. Laughing, he crouched down and obliged.

"Daisy can play in the yard while we're gone." She locked the door. "We'd better hurry. It's strange not having any restaurants that are open at a normal dinnertime."

"I know. Neither the grocery store or Dinah's stay open late, so I have to figure my dinner out early. Or get pizza about a half hour from here in Sweetly."

"I haven't been to the pizza parlor yet."

He held out his hand to her. "We have to look like a couple." When she put her hand in his, warmth spread through him. "Maybe we can have pizza sometime soon."

"No one will be there to observe us, so it wouldn't help solidify our dating status."

Right. None of this was real. He needed to get that through his head.

Hand-in-hand, they walked down the path. When she

directed them toward her small car, he pulled them to a stop.

"We're going in my truck."

"I thought we could take my car."

He chuckled. "I don't fit in small cars. I'm not sure how you fit in this one."

"I needed to save money. I tried several compacts that were cramped and finally found this one, which I like. But you're probably right that you wouldn't fit." Grinning, she added, "We'd have to squeeze you in sideways."

He tugged her in the direction of his truck. "This fake date is uncomfortable enough without that." He had to keep mentioning their dating status, that they weren't a couple, because their relationship felt more real every day.

They parked on the street in front of Dinah's. Word would spread like wildfire after this meal. He doubted anyone would play matchmaker with either of them, but there were also expectations of how a dating couple should look and act. "We should go inside." CJ tapped on the steering wheel.

She pointedly checked her watch. "This isn't helping. Dinah's only open for another hour."

He opened his door. "I'm avoiding going inside without even realizing it. Let's get moving."

Climbing the stairs toward the door, Paige asked, "What if no one we know is there? Will this all be for nothing?"

Not a chance. "It's a small town, Paige."

After years in cities, the meaning of that hadn't completely sunk in. "Everyone will know within the hour that we've been here together."

"Exactly. It's unlikely that an hour will pass with no one we know coming here." He put his hand on the small of her back as they entered, and it felt right.

Michelle seated them at a table for two next to the wall. She leaned closer as she handed them menus. "This is the most private table in here." She glanced over her shoulder. "Not that anything is private in this place."

CJ whispered, "She believes we're a couple. And the other diners are watching us."

Paige did a quick—and more or less subtle—check of the room. "People have stopped eating to focus on the two of us." She held the menu in front of her face.

Michelle returned to take their orders, and both he and Paige chose the special. He hoped he'd like it when it came, because he hadn't been able to focus on the waitress's words.

When she'd left, CJ drummed his fingers on the table. "We're not selling the idea of us as a couple. We're just sitting here."

"It does look more like a bad date, doesn't it?" She grinned, and that helped him relax.

"Let's try small talk. I'm an only child, but you have brothers and sisters, don't you?"

He held up one hand. "Five sisters. No brothers."

"Whoa. That must have been interesting."

"You can't imagine what it was like having five females, six with my mother, telling me how to dress or do a million other things." He cocked his head to the side. "Not that I don't love them. I would do anything for them. But . . ."

"That's why you're on the road. You don't want to find roots because then you have structure and rules to follow."

Was that true? "I thought you were an accountant, not a psychiatrist."

"I'm a woman."

She definitely was that. Their dinners arrived. He was relieved to find fried chicken, mashed potatoes, and fried okra. His mood lifted, he continued their questioning. "What was it like growing up in the military?"

"I can hop on a plane at a moment's notice. Packing a suitcase—or everything I own—is easy. I both like and dislike meeting new people. I know it has to be done, but I also know I won't be in one place long."

"I have been avoiding permanence."

"And I crave it."

"I know your mother died when you were a child. What about your father?"

"We were a team when I was a kid. He remarried a few years ago. I miss him being my whole life, but it's right that he has new interests. We still talk, but he's stationed in Japan right now and the time difference is brutal. I see myself as on my own."

He had too many people in his life. She didn't have enough, especially other women.

Dinah came to their table. "I'm sure you want pie." She leveled a gaze at them that said she expected that.

Paige answered before he could. "Of course."

"We only have a few slices left this close to closing and no chocolate."

Paige startled him with her next words. "That's okay. CJ brought me a beautiful heart-shaped box of chocolates. I'll share those with him. After pie."

Dinah whipped around toward him, and heat shot into his face. "Nice touch, CJ." A woman coming through the door, thankfully, distracted her. She gestured to Michelle to take care of her, then went back to dessert. "Pecan, lemon meringue, or cherry?"

Paige called dibs on the cherry.

"I'll have the lemon. It's hard to go wrong with that. And . . . I may want the pecan for breakfast."

Dinah patted his shoulder. "I do love a man who starts his day with pie. I won't even charge you for it. That's on its way, along with coffee for you, CJ, and tea for you, Paige."

Paige grinned. "If she wasn't a decade older than you, she might have been your match. Unlimited pie for life."

"That sounds like a good deal. And no one is nicer than Dinah."

Michelle tidied up the restaurant, wiping down tables as guests left. Some to-go orders were picked up, but without more customers coming and going, he began to wonder if Paige had been right earlier. Other than a few people he didn't know well, only Dinah and Michelle had seen them, so this meal together might not be enough to establish them as a couple.

Bella walked in the door, heading for the cash register. Michelle hurried over and took her payment.

CJ reached for Paige's hand.

When Bella turned back to the door, she spotted the two of them and her mouth dropped open. Quickly regaining her composure, she assessed the situation. Waving at them, she hurried out the door with a glance over her shoulder toward them as she exited.

"Mission accomplished." He let go of Paige's hand and sat back in his chair. He dropped his voice. "The matchmakers will be called off. The two of us can return to boss and employee most of the time."

"That's great." Her voice didn't carry the enthusiasm he would have expected.

"Let's eat pie and enjoy the rest of the evening."

She perked up. "There's nothing better than pie with a friend."

Was he just a friend?

CHAPTER NINETEEN

The sound of the wonderful old-fashioned doorbell ringing brought Paige down off of her ladder and over to the window to see who was outside. A luxury car parked at the side of the road near her fence didn't look familiar. Hurrying downstairs, she almost tripped, caught the railing just in time to spare herself incredible pain, and got to the door as the person rang the bell one more time. As she opened it, CJ called from the top of the stairs, "Honeybunch, do we have visitors?"

Nikki's startled face greeted her as the door fully opened.

"Come inside. And it's not what you think."

The music star's high laugh brought a smile to Paige's face. "For a second, I wondered what I'd interrupted. Are you two still playing the dodge-the-matchmaker game?"

"Let's say that it has been blissfully silent on the matchmaking front ever since we started doing this."

"Public displays of affection?"

CJ had come down the stairs while they'd been talking. "Paige won't let me do public displays of affection. Will you, honeybunch?" He kissed her cheek.

Paige rolled her eyes. "He never stops."

When he turned toward Nikki, he stopped and stared. Even though he knew who she was, he still got starstruck when he saw her.

"It's good to see you again, CJ."

He nodded. After blinking a few times and seeming to come to his senses, he said, "I'd better get back to work. The clock is ticking."

When he'd gone upstairs, Nikki asked Paige, "Do you have a deadline you're working toward? It sounds like you're in a hurry."

"Every day this isn't a bed and breakfast is a day I'm losing money. I thought I had plenty for the remodel."

Nikki patted her arm. "I'm sure everything will be okay. Do you have any other skills you could use in the interim?"

Paige thought of her photography one more time. But that would be as hard to earn money at as a bed and breakfast in a town that was barely waking up from a long slumber. "Not really."

"Since that wasn't a hard no, I'll take it as a maybe. You'll have to tell me all about it soon." She checked the watch on her wrist. "Right now, I have to get over to Bella's, and you need to come with me."

Paige pointed at her chest.

"Of course. I need your input on the dress."

"Don't you have family and friends that you want to help with that?"

Nikki started for the door. "I did that with the first dress. I never saw so many different opinions—strong opinions—in a single room. I am not going down that road again."

Paige started to follow her, then shouted over her shoulder, "CJ, I'll be back soon."

They settled into Nikki's car. There was something to be said for a high-priced vehicle. This was the most comfortable car seat she had ever been in. Parking was, as usual, too easy in front of Bella's. It was hard to imagine a day when cars would have been lined up and down the street. Maybe again someday.

This time, Bella and another woman greeted them. "Nikki, welcome back. And Paige." Bella had a questioning look in her eyes.

"Nikki insisted that she needed a second opinion and that keeping family and friends out of it was her best option after her last dress shopping experience."

"Say no more. I have sat in on any number of family dress shopping appointments that have gone awry. Wonderful people who are usually kind and loving are often very opinionated about wedding dress design."

Nikki went toward the seating area after Bella motioned them in that direction. "My mother wanted a ball gown. Nothing else would do. My sister wanted a mermaid. Don't even get me started on what my grandmother and my great-aunt wanted. Let's just say I was going to be very covered. Head to toe would have been their preference. Oh, and my best friend from childhood that I flew up here especially for the appointment wanted to see me in a sexy dress that rivaled those that I've worn on the stage. None of those was what I wanted. I'm sure you know they exist, Bella, but I was surprised to find see-through wedding dresses."

Bella grinned. "I do know they're available, but I've never made one. I think I will always advise that there is a piece of fabric behind the sheer area. There are some brides, though, that are quite happy with a lot of skin showing." She gestured toward the woman with her, who had stayed silent. "This is my assistant, April. She's part of this appointment today because she is in charge of the fabrication of the dress. She will oversee many of the steps after today."

"It's a pleasure to meet you, Miss Lane."

"Nikki. Please."

They got to work on the dress. As they fitted it to Nikki's form, Paige watched from the chair she'd sat in the other day. Everything was going quite nicely until Nikki dropped a bomb.

"So, I noticed that Paige and CJ might be an item."

What hole could she crawl into? She tried to speak, but no words would come out.

"I've seen the two of them together." Bella turned toward Paige with a pin in her hand. "Are you two dating?"

How could she get out of this and not dig a worse situation for herself? "We're friends."

That might have been the dumbest answer she'd ever given. They had spent time building the story of the two of them, and she had just blown it in a sentence.

Bella went back to her work but said, "I've noticed a few things that indicate otherwise." She tucked another pin into Nikki's dress-to-be.

Okay. She could continue with denial, or she could say something that indicated they actually were dating. She opened her mouth again to speak, but nothing came out. This was not a good moment.

Nikki saved her. "I have heard the words 'honeybunch' and 'sweetie' directed toward her, and I witnessed a kiss."

Bella frowned. But then she seemed to realize she was doing it and smiled. "That's great, Paige. He's a good guy. Has he decided to stay here, then?"

There was the eternal question with CJ. Of course, Paige wasn't a lot more stable herself, was she? "Maybe," she squeaked out in a throaty voice she barely recognized as her own. Clearing her throat, she added, "He hasn't decided what he's going to do yet."

She was spared from any further conversation because April stepped over and started inspecting the bride in her now-pinned pattern dress. "Miss Lane—I mean, Nikki—how does it feel? Is it comfortable to wear? Can you breathe easily?"

Nikki took a deep breath and wiggled her hips. It all looked like some sort of choreographed dance move. "It feels wonderful. Not the prettiest thing I've ever seen, though." Nikki stared at herself in the mirror in the pinned muslin dress.

Bella smiled. "Just wait. A week from today, when you come back for your first fitting, you're going to be amazed."

"Honey, if you can make a beautiful dress from this in a week, you will be nothing short of a miracle worker. I'll buy all of you lunch at Dinah's."

"April, pencil that in our schedule. We're going to need time to go up to Dinah's with Nikki, because she is going to love her dress."

Nikki laughed. "I do love a woman with a positive attitude."

CHAPTER TWENTY

*C*J went back to the kitchen and continued removing the cabinet doors. He'd told Paige that he would have her do it, but she had a long list already. She could take over the project once he'd prepared the job for her.

His whole life had begun to revolve around Paige. He wanted to spend every minute with her. At first, she'd seemed so closed off, but now that he'd gotten to know her more, he saw that she was warm and bubbly and funny.

Pushing thoughts of his boss out of his mind, he got to work. It would be helpful to have a kitchen with this much storage, but that meant he had to renovate a lot of cabinets. All the screws and the hinges had been painted over and over and over again. He hoped they'd clean up well—and that they were pretty to start with underneath the paint—but right now, he just needed to get this project rolling.

Once the new counters were in and the cabinets were stripped and painted properly, this could be an attractive kitchen. One thing Paige was right about, though, was that the job did seem overwhelming at times. And that was saying a lot, coming from someone who had spent a good deal of his career in remodeling.

A couple of hours later, CJ heard Paige shuffling around in the butler's pantry. He figured he had another twenty or thirty minutes tops until he had the rest of the doors down. He'd labeled them according to the location they had to return to and stacked them, but he had left the kitchen still functional.

Paige's footsteps toward him grew louder.

At least it would be functional for someone who could manage to make anything in the kitchen that was worth eating.

She came through the doorway. "I was thinking of testing a new recipe this afternoon."

CJ turned away as he closed his eyes in horror. What would happen this time?

"There must be something that I can cook. Don't you think?"

That was a loaded question if he'd ever heard one.

"At least I hope there is."

The despair in her voice made him turn around, ready to reassure her, but he wasn't sure how. "I still think you need lessons. Maybe there's something you could cook well, but you haven't come upon it yet."

"Maybe." She didn't sound convinced.

When CJ finished with the kitchen for the day, he moved upstairs to work on her room, commenting, "You deserve a nice place." She knew *her guests* needed that. But she also craved a place with order in the middle of the chaos her house had become, so she hadn't stopped him.

The beginning of her day had been spent sorting out the dishes and glassware in the butler's pantry. Those pieces would give charm to the breakfasts she served. Unless her skills amped up, a pretty distraction might be needed.

CJ called her. "Paige, I need to talk to you about something."

After carefully setting a plate on the counter, she rushed out and found him at the top of the stairs.

"I want you to see this." He turned and went down the hall.

She headed upstairs, hoping there wasn't some new disaster that had befallen this money pit of a project. Instead of a crisis, she found CJ staring out a window that overlooked the backyard, a yard that had the same view it had since George had cut the tall growth near the house. The far back of the property remained a tangle of branches and brush, with the corner of the shed peeking out in between.

"I don't see any problems."

"Where's the lake?" He tapped on the window. "This is a house on a lake, right?"

"Yes," she said slowly. The thought that she had one more project all but overwhelmed her. "CJ, I just can't take on anything else."

"No." He put his hand on her shoulder—something she found quite comforting. "I'm wondering if we could get together a work party from the town to come help. They fixed up the city park as a team, and before that, the church."

"Absolutely not." The strength in her words surprised her. "I am not going to be an object of pity that the town needs to help. I'm going to figure out how to do this on my own."

"Things don't always work like that in a small town. In a small town, people help other people. You helped Nikki when she needed you."

"But I would have done that in a city."

"Better example: How about when George bush hogged your yard? What about that? He even went down the street and took care of the park when you asked him to."

"That's because Mrs. Brantley sent him to me. She was playing matchmaker."

"Well, what about the times you were invited over for dinner?"

Instead of annoyance now, Paige was getting amused. "Matchmaker."

"Oh, I forgot about that. And—"

Paige held up a hand to stop him. "There's no reason to go on. Anything that anybody has done since I got here was because of matchmaking."

"Yes and no. Admit it. In the city, does a matchmaker send someone over to mow your yard?"

"They might if someone told them to, but I see your point." After a moment of thought, Paige said, "I appreciate what everyone has done, but I don't want to ask people to help me with my yard. When we finish the inside of the house, we can do it." She'd do what she could to be sure guests saw her bed and breakfast in a positive light when they arrived. That included her front yard . . . and maybe the lake park. *If* she could find the time, she needed to make it pretty too.

A call from Nikki surprised her. Her new friend leaped into the conversation. "Can you meet me in that park down the street from you tomorrow morning? At about ten?"

"Sure, but—"

"I'll see you then." She stared at the silent phone. The singer blazed through life. She did it with a smile, making others want to play along. Paige would definitely be there.

She spent the rest of the morning working on the kitchen cupboard doors CJ had taken down. He had shown her how to sand them down to prepare them for being painted again. She'd paint them a pretty color that added brightness to the room, but also would wear well in a busy bed and breakfast's kitchen.

When she turned off the sander a short time later, she heard C.J. calling. He must have timed that for a quiet moment.

"Paige? I have a question, if you could come upstairs for a minute."

She took off her protective eye covering, set it to the side, and went upstairs. Back in her room, she said, "I hope it isn't another mention of the back yard."

"Nope. I think I may have found something interesting."

Paige stopped in her tracks and stared at the wall, which was now down to studs instead of covered with plaster as it had been that morning. Her budget couldn't take many more hits. "What happened, CJ?!"

"I knew I was going to have to do this when I saw all the plaster damage. Don't panic. It's possible that it had damage because someone didn't do a great job of covering this up."

Paige stepped closer. Now that she wasn't shocked by the destruction, she realized that wall studs outlined the shape of a doorway.

"Would you like to have a door leading from your bedroom to an office?"

"I love that idea!" She examined the wall with growing excitement. "And what if part of that room became a master bath and walk-in closet?"

He stared at it and, after a moment, frowned. "You're talking about quite a bit of added expense. Putting a door here is easy. That storage shed has a lot of old materials in it, and I wouldn't be surprised if we actually found the door that belongs here in there. But when plumbing and electric come into the mix, you're adding to the scope of the project."

Her glee diminished. "Then let's push the door through for now. Could I add the bathroom and closet later?"

"Let's check it out and see what we find." The two of them hurried to the hallway and around to the other room. It wasn't the smallest bedroom, but it wasn't overly large either. She hated to lose a possible guest room, but if this house was also going to work as her home, she was going to need a private space.

"It wouldn't take much to divide it and put in a closet. It's the bathroom that's the big deal. What if we put up a wall here?" He made a slicing motion with his hand in the center of the room. "To the left will be the closet, and eventually, a bathroom. I know plumbing from another bathroom is on the other side of the wall, so it's easier and less expensive to put it there. To the right will be your office, since that gets you the window."

She could see his vision. "Let's do that. Then the bathroom I'm using now could eventually be given to the bedroom on the other side."

He nodded. "I'll get to work on this. Do you want to help me take the wall down? Destroying things is actually kind of fun." His boyish grin surprised her.

When he handed her a sledgehammer, her arms dropped with the weight.

"Swing it. Hit it with all your might right there." He took a pencil from his pocket and made an X on the wall. Then he moved to the other side of the room, probably because he wasn't sure about how her wielding the tool would go.

She did as instructed, swinging it over her head to get power behind the blow and striking the plaster with force. The sledgehammer crashed into the plaster, the momentum jerking the heavy tool out of her hands as it vanished through the new hole. "Oh my gosh! What have I done?"

CJ laughed so hard he leaned against the wall.

"Did I hurt the house?"

Grinning, he said, "I didn't hear glass breaking or other sounds of destruction, so we're probably fine."

She smiled back. "My one use of a sledgehammer will be memorable."

"I have never, in all my years of construction work, seen anyone do anything even close to that." He shook his head. "I'm going to go get it. Let's see if I can't knock down some more of this. Unless you want to try again? Sledgehammer throwing might become a new sport."

"I'm good. I'll just watch you do that."

He returned with the tool, easily carrying it. "It landed on your bed, so nothing was damaged. But you may have some plaster dust to shake off the covers." He raised the sledgehammer. "Stand back."

She did as he asked, and he swung it—making short work of the doorway through to the other room. When it was open, she could see how great it would look. She would be able to move from personal time to business easily without running into her guests. And her desk would have a view of the lake. Eventually.

If only she could find a quicker way to earn income in Two Hearts. But wasn't that the problem of a dying town in the first place?

CHAPTER TWENTY-ONE

*P*aige approached the lake park with CJ to her right and Daisy on a leash to her left. The dog happily zigzagged between them and the side of the road, checking all scents.

When they arrived at the park itself, Paige looked out at it. "Thank you for taking a walk with me after working all day."

He put his arm around her waist. No one could see them now, so he didn't need to do that. She liked it, so she didn't comment. "Even I can use quiet time after hours of sawing and hammering."

That made sense. "Nikki asked me to meet her here tomorrow, but I can't figure out why. It's hard to imagine this as somewhere people would want to be."

"I know what you mean. But the city park downtown transformed quickly from an overgrown area with a forgotten bandstand buried under weeds to a pretty and popular spot with a restored bandstand."

Paige said, "I've ridden my bike around that park. Are you telling me it used to look this bad?"

"Close to it. This park has been completely neglected for

decades, though. The downtown one had a corner or two maintained. Barely. But people did use it some." He waved to the mess in front of them. "No one has been brave enough to have a picnic here for a really long time. Not in our lifetime."

"I wish it could be brought to life."

"It would take a lot more effort than just you having it mowed."

She sighed. "I know. But you already know I'm a dreamer. I want to come down here to make improvements, but I never have extra time." Paige closed her eyes as she set the scene in front of her. "There are a few picnic tables here. If they can be salvaged, we could paint them."

"But not pink," CJ said firmly.

"What is it with you and pink? My house is quite pretty. And the picnic tables in the other park are—"

"Feminine and pretty." CJ said the words with disdain.

"I like to think that I am feminine."

"And you're pretty."

Her heart did a little flip.

He didn't seem to realize the effect his words had had on her, because he continued speaking. "It would take a crew coming through here to get rid of all the weeds, to mulch, and to make sure the dock is safe. Which I highly doubt."

"Dock?" Paige held her hand over her eyes to shield them from the sun. "I don't see anything like that."

"You can't from here. I may have walked through here—in a moment that could either be called foolhardy or brave—to get to the lake."

She really wasn't sure which one it was. "That was before the grass was cut, right?"

His expression told her she was right.

"Foolhardy," she said. "Do you know how many snakes could be hiding in there?"

"I can't be afraid of those things. I crawl in and out of

basements and attics and all kinds of places. I just have to trust that, if something happens, I will be fine and/or I will get the care I need in time."

His determined expression told her he meant that. She wished she could move forward so bravely.

Daisy tugged on her leash, wanting them to keep going.

"I may have to come up here every night when I'm done working, just to pull out a few weeds," Paige said. "It seems such a shame for it to be this way." They continued on their way. "Nikki was surprised at it too. Maybe we could attract more people to Two Hearts if we had places they could enjoy, like the lake."

"Listen to you! You sound like you've decided to make Two Hearts your home."

Had she? It didn't really matter, so she wouldn't put too much energy into that thought. She was going to have to support herself, and if this house couldn't work as a bed and breakfast, she was going to be in trouble.

This park was a key component to her success.

CJ started back toward Paige's house. "Restoring this park can wait until your business is up and running."

She grabbed his arm to still him. "I'd like to fix up the city's lake park *before* I open."

He swiveled around to face her. "Are you serious? We have talked about not having enough time to work on your yard, and now you want to take on the city park? I don't need to remind you that it's as much of a mess as your own backyard."

"I think it will help me and my business if it's prettier nearby. Admit it, CJ: When you come around the corner and the first thing you see is that park, you don't get a good feeling about what's up the street. Next, you notice a row of run-down houses. In the midst of it, there's mine. I wouldn't blame someone for hitting the brakes and doing a U-turn to go back to where they came from."

What she said made sense, as much as he hated the idea. "So, you're willing to have the town help with the park?"

She hesitated for a few seconds, and he knew she was deciding if she could somehow do it on her own. Her small efforts were barely noticeable. "We are going to need help." She didn't say anything else for a minute or two. They just stood there together. It was what CJ considered "companionable silence," something he hadn't experienced much of in the past.

When she did speak, she said, "I'm going to have to get together with Mrs. Brantley. Most of it is manual labor. For now, if there aren't salvageable picnic tables, we'll do without them. It would be better to have a so-so park where everything's safe than an attractive park where you can get hurt."

"I'm sure there's some sort of business truth in there. Should I call her?"

The strain on Paige's face said everything. When he was about to offer to take it on, she surprised him. "No, I'm going to do it, and I will get this done." After a pause, she added, "In a day or two."

He grinned. "Chicken?"

She leveled her gaze at him. "No. I'm . . . considering my words." When he kept smiling at her, she added, "Carefully."

He didn't know why Mrs. Brantley unnerved her so much. Then again, he didn't want to purposefully spend time with the mayor until she got over her focus on him and Paige. She'd been quiet toward them recently, so maybe she already had.

Paige put her shoulders back. "It's my town, my street, and my business." CJ barely heard her next words. "For now."

~

Paige got up early the next morning and went down to the park after a cup of tea but before breakfast. She left Daisy behind to keep her out of trouble. The unhappy dog barked her disappointment, but at least there weren't neighbors who could be disturbed.

The expanse of weeds and brush made her want to go back to her house, but no one had ever called her a quitter. She pulled on garden gloves and got to work pulling weeds. Fifteen minutes later, she stood. One small area looked better.

A hungry rabbit could have done as much. Turning, she headed toward home. She'd have to call Mrs. Brantley.

After a breakfast of coffee and scones CJ had picked up at Dinah's she went to the park to meet Nikki. A large SUV pulled up soon after she arrived, not the sporty car that Paige had seen Nikki drive in the past. Her new friend stepped out of the passenger's seat, and a man about the same age came out of the driver's side. The ruggedly handsome man walked over and put his arm over the music star's shoulders. He must be her fiancé. Then a third person climbed out of the vehicle, this time someone more about Paige's dad's age, maybe a few years older than that. Could he be someone from Nikki's family, or maybe the fiancé's?

"Paige! It's so good to see you. Thank you for meeting us here." In her charming way, Nikki ambled over and stood, looking, as she often did, as though she was ready for a photoshoot or a music video. If Paige hadn't seen Nikki in the midst of an incredibly ugly, ugly cry, she wouldn't have thought that this woman could look anything but stunning.

"I brought Griff here because I'm trying to talk him into one of my crazy ideas."

A low rumble of a laugh sounded from the man.

"Paige, this is my fiancé, Griffin. And this dapper gentleman in the suit is James, my wedding photographer."

It seemed very strange to be bringing a photographer out to a derelict park in a small town. What did Nikki have planned?

"Oh, honey, your face can be so transparent. You're thinking I've completely lost my marbles."

Paige opened her mouth to argue that point, but then she changed her mind. "I'm going to let you explain before I pass judgment on your mental state."

Nikki laughed. "Wise idea. That charming church in town would be a great site for the wedding. Carly showed me all her photos. They were beautiful. But then the question became where to have the reception. I've never been someone who's interested in a farm or a barn or anything like that. But I do love being outdoors. And I especially love being near water."

Nikki turned to face the lake—at least what she could see of the lake with everything overgrown between them and the water.

Paige tried to process what she'd said. "Are you telling me that you're moving your wedding from a big fancy church in Nashville and a park there to Two Hearts?" Even she heard the incredulous note to her voice. She hoped it wasn't insulting to Nikki.

The other woman smiled. "I grew up in a small town. If there was anything there for me to go back to, I would have this wedding there. There isn't. My family has moved on, and now it's just dirt, and not very nice dirt. But Two Hearts is different. Each time I come here, I like it a little more."

Griff, who had remained silent until that moment, said, "Nikki, this is a completely overgrown park. It's past its prime. In fact, it's been so many years, it can't even find its prime anymore."

Nikki patted him on the arm. "But what could it be?" She gestured toward the lake. "Tell me what you see."

Paige had to smile. It was the same thing CJ had told her just the night before. The small, cleared patch was barely noticeable. It needed more than one person trying to fit it in between her morning cup of tea and a long list of home improvement projects.

"I see overgrown grass—so much grass that I'm not walking through it. I see brush so thick that I don't think a deer could find its way through there. I see picnic tables that would probably collapse to the ground if I tried to sit on them. And in the distance, I see a little hint of brown on the water, so my guess is that I also see a dock that is incredibly deadly to anyone who dares to step on it."

Instead of appearing daunted by her fiancé's words, Nikki grinned. "I see the same thing, Griff. But then, I look a second time and I think, 'Wow! This is beautiful.' The grass is taken care of. There are flowers set up for the wedding. There's a tent in case the weather turns bad. Brand-new picnic tables, if need be, and they're painted the same cute pink as at that park downtown. And the dock is wonderful. It has some canoes tied up to it, and the guests can go out and paddle around if they want. We'll even give them life jackets to make it safe."

Paige liked Nikki's vision. It was so similar to her own. But the amount of work she'd managed to find time to do on it had barely made a difference in one small corner. It had felt like she was doing something important at the time, but it was going to take her a year to do anything that really mattered here. "Nikki, I want it to be what you're picturing, but—"

Nikki kept grinning. "All it's going to take is a little labor. I'm willing to chip in. I know Griff is willing to chip in."

He shook his head for a moment. Then he turned and pulled his fiancée into the air in a hug, swinging her around. "If you see that, we can make it happen." He set her down on the ground and gave her a quick kiss.

Nikki turned toward her photographer. "What do you think of the setting, James?"

"I only know what's here now, because that's what I would

capture if I held up the camera lens. But the way you talk about it leads me to believe that this could turn into a fabulous place for a wedding. I can imagine photos of the two of you in front of the water. And assuming it's a sunny day, it would be sparkling behind you. It could be truly beautiful."

"Then I guess we'd better figure out how to clean up a park an hour and a half from the city."

Paige didn't want to volunteer the people in the town, but she knew they had done work together before to fix something up. Maybe they'd be willing to step up one more time to work on the park. Mrs. Brantley would be the one to ask, though. "I think we'd have to go through the mayor. We need to have some kind of approval and get this organized." She pulled her phone out of her pocket and held it up. "Give me a moment to call to see if we could set up a meeting right now since you're here."

"That would be awesome."

Paige moved far enough away that she didn't think anybody would hear her talking. When Mrs. Brantley answered, she said, "I have an idea to propose. And I'm new enough to Two Hearts that I'm not sure if this is a good thing or a bad thing."

"Give me all the facts. We'll figure it out together."

Paige relayed all the information she knew. When she finished, Mrs. Brantley said, "They're here right now?"

"Yes, ma'am. We're at the city park at the lake."

Paige heard scuffling sounds. "Why don't you bring them over to my house? We don't have a beautiful office for the mayor, but I'm putting some cookies in the oven. And I'll get some coffee going, along with hot water for you."

They ended the call, and Paige returned to the group. "I was able to get us in right away. Let's head over there."

"What's your mayor like? Is he stern or open to new ideas?"

"Our mayor is Emmaline Brantley."

Nikki smiled gleefully. "A woman mayor. I love that."

"And she is open to any idea that helps bring business to her town. She's only been in office a short time, but even before it was an official vote, she was doing great things for Two Hearts. People have told me all kinds of stories. I understand that it all began with Carly's wedding. That's when the town started to turn around."

Paige climbed into the back seat next to James, the photographer. She wanted to pepper him with questions about wedding photography. Someday, she'd get the chance to photograph weddings and do portraits. But some dreams were just meant to be kept to the side while you kept going forward with life and pursued other dreams.

They arrived at Mrs. Brantley's a few minutes later. She greeted them at the back door and cordially introduced herself, not flinching at all when she found out that Nikki was one of her guests. And then James stepped up to her. She started to speak but sputtered, and her cheeks turned a rosy pink. She held out her hand tentatively. "Emmaline Brantley."

He too seemed mesmerized, as he hesitated for a moment before taking her hand. "James Lyons. I am their photographer."

Paige waited for them to be invited inside, as always happened, but Mrs. Brantley just stared at James. Paige considered him for the first time to see what someone Mrs. Brantley's age might find appealing about him. Then the spell broke, and Mrs. Brantley held the screen door open. "Everyone, please come inside. Can I get you some coffee or tea? Maybe a cupcake?"

Yes, Mrs. Brantley was back to herself, but she had made Paige see the photographer in a different light. She'd seen a spark between them.

～

Cassie met them over at Mrs. Brantley's. They sat in the living room—Nikki and her fiancé on a small sofa; Mrs. Brantley,

Cassie, and Greg on a larger one; and Paige and CJ on chairs that had been brought in from the kitchen.

Cassie furiously scribbled in a notebook on her lap. "This is going to be a tight one. But I have done weddings on a shorter timeline. I had one day for Bella."

Nikki and Paige both looked up.

Nikki said, "One day?"

"It was complicated. But, yes, just one day. It was a lovely ceremony in Micah's backyard. We had a cake. We had everything. But you have vendors already set up for Nashville. Don't you just want to have them shift over here, Nikki? You don't have to use me as your wedding planner just because you're holding the ceremony in Two Hearts. Or I could work with your people."

She waved away that idea. "I haven't been overly happy with the process. I feel like they've given me the wedding that they believe a country music star should have. But I didn't feel as listened to as I would have liked. I prefer a natural setting and things that are simple. Peaceful. That isn't the wedding they have planned. So I think I'm just going to pay everybody what they're owed, tell them thank you very much, and start over.

Cassie looked down at her notebook. "What did you think of the flowers that had been done for you?"

Nikki thought about that for a moment. "She was the one person who really listened to me. In spite of what the wedding planner wanted, she gave me charming bouquets tied with ribbon, and the flowers looked more like wildflowers as opposed to carefully sculpted bouquets of white roses and greenery." She shuddered. Paige had to assume that meant that the planner had been pushing for the white roses that Nikki did not want.

"In that case, let's just ask them to bring the flowers out here. I can get with her and figure out the logistics and any needs that have changed. If that's okay with you, of course."

"I'll contact my friend and fabulous baker Simone for the wedding cake. She did Carly's cake. And I've been using an amazing caterer from a high-end Nashville restaurant for some weddings. I think they'd both be great for you. Does that all sound okay?"

"More than okay. My last concert for six months is tomorrow. After that, I'm off. If you have any questions from Sunday on, you just let me know."

"A six-month honeymoon?"

Nikki reached over and took her fiancé's hand, giving it a squeeze. "Not so much a honeymoon as time to spend with each other. I'm so tired of traveling this country in a bus and not really knowing anybody except the people on that bus. Sure, they become like family, but what about any real family? And what about just traveling for the pleasure of seeing somewhere new? Staying in one place for a week or two and feeling like you belong there." She sighed.

"That sounds heavenly," Paige said.

"Besides, if I get bored, I can always find something to do. And if I can't take time off like this after working hard for years, what's the point?"

Paige looked at the future in front of her. A bed and breakfast was going to take every moment of every day for years. But that was the path that she had chosen, and that was what she was going to do. It didn't seem as easy now, though, as it had when she'd thought of it.

Cassie stood. "Then I think I have everything we need for now. The plan is to get the park cleaned up."

"I am on that task," Mrs. Brantley said.

"And I want to pay the city for being able to use the park. If I do that now, would that help?"

Mrs. Brantley looked tongue-tied—an uncommon situation. Then Paige realized that she was probably trying to decide if she should take the money or just consider it free publicity for the city to have the wedding here. It would probably be promoted in many magazines and online. "It would be lovely if we could have it now. Then maybe CJ would have time to make some new picnic tables. That's, of course, if that's the amount that you would like to give us."

"You just tell me how much. I'm looking forward to being here in two weeks."

CHAPTER TWENTY-TWO

*P*aige got up early on park cleanup day. She needed to get in an hour of wallpaper removal on her house and another attempt at making breakfast before they went up the street. CJ would be here soon, and she hoped to have a plate of scrambled eggs and bacon waiting for him when he arrived.

A half hour later, CJ tapped on the front door before opening it and coming inside. She peered out through the kitchen doorway. "Is a good smell coming from here?"

Was it? She glanced back at the stove that she had walked away from. "Just a sec."

She stirred the eggs, thrilled to find that nothing had burned and that they actually looked . . . edible. CJ slowly entered the kitchen, almost as though he was afraid something was going to hit him. He moved to stand beside her at the stove.

"I recognize that. Scrambled eggs."

She had successfully made scrambled eggs. She pulled them off the burner and stared at them happily. And then, an acrid smell tickled her nose.

"Oh, no!" She opened the oven door to find smoking bacon.

"The eggs look good." CJ thankfully chose to focus on the positive.

"But I wanted to make bacon *and* eggs. Not just one of them."

She took the smoking pan out and set it on top of the stove. Then CJ's arms wrapped around her, and he pulled her in for a hug. "Don't worry. The eggs are pretty. We can have toast too. Do you have bread?"

She sank into his embrace. His warmth moved over her like a blanket. It was so nice to have a friend. She leaned back to look at him, and he looked down at her at the same moment.

They sprang apart.

Paige turned off the oven. "Let me get the bread and put it in the toaster."

"I'll do it!" CJ hurried over to take care of the task. Probably because he remembered recent toast incinerations. They sat down at the table, and she took a bite of the eggs. "These are good. I made something you can actually eat."

"You made other things that could be consumed. It's just that you wouldn't want to." He winced. "I shouldn't have said that."

CJ's words caught her off guard. Instead of being upset, she laughed. "There's so much truth in that. I'm excited about getting started on the park."

CJ picked up a slice of bacon. "You've already made a good start on it."

"Barely a dent."

CJ slathered butter on his toast. "But without you, I don't think Nikki would have given it a second glance. You made sure the grass was mowed. You weeded that one bed. And because of you, the roses can now be seen. Before, they were hidden, and you might catch a glimpse of yellow now and then."

What he said was true. She so wanted this part of town to be beautiful.

"I wonder if I'll ever get neighbors."

"If Cassie and Bella can attract other wedding professionals, and the wedding business in this town grows, I'm sure that people will start moving here. Look at you! If you hadn't seen the story about Carly's wedding, you never would have known Two Hearts existed. It wouldn't even have been a dot on the map because it's such a tiny dot."

At the park, they met Mrs. Brantley, Greg, Micah, George the farmer, and others, including a team of teenagers apparently led by a boy named Justin. Paige stepped into CJ's shadow to avoid George, but he seemed oblivious to the situation and completely uninterested in her. He was just a nice guy.

Mrs. Brantley clapped her hands together to get everyone's attention. "Okay. Let's get started on this. I need some volunteers to start pulling the vines off of the trees and off of . . . Well, everything, really."

Hands went up in the group.

"And I need others to start weeding anything you think needs it and digging up anything you think shouldn't be there. But please check with me or Micah's grandmother"—she pointed to a woman about her age—"to make sure that it isn't actually something we want to keep. Once we get to the picnic tables, we can evaluate from there. CJ, I'm putting you in charge of that."

With that done, she stopped and looked around as though she expected the work to begin, and everyone split apart, not wanting to disappoint the new mayor. She must have been amazing as a mom with young kids. Paige continued her work on what she knew must have been vibrant beds of yellow roses. She heard joking and laughter and grunting as people tugged on vines. A pile to the front of the park grew larger and larger and larger as the hours passed.

Finally, she heard Mrs. Brantley say, "Look!" You could now see through to the lake itself. When she'd bought a house on a lake, this was the view she had hoped for. If she ever had the time and money to take care of the overgrowth on her own property, then she could get somewhere. That was just one more thing that really should be done before she even tried to rent out rooms to people. They would want to see the lake from their lake house rooms.

CJ was working on the other side of the park from her. Every once in a while, she glanced up. She told herself just to check on his progress. It was not in any way because she just liked to look at him.

A cry of alarm went up. She turned from her task and found CJ with Michelle from the diner in his arms.

Her heart crashed to her feet.

He braced Michelle with one arm on each of hers and stepped back.

Mrs. Brantley came over to see what was going on. Turning to face the workers, she raised her voice. "Everyone, there's a stone-circled fire pit here. Michelle would have taken a header into it if CJ hadn't noticed her falling and grabbed her at the last second. Keep your eyes open, because if there's one hazard, there are probably others."

Paige stood and shook out her legs, which were tingling from being in a crouching position for so long. CJ might not be interested in Michelle after all. *Thank goodness*, her heart whispered. That same heart had a lot to answer for. She might not be staying in Two Hearts. He seemed to have plans to leave, too. *He's just a friend.* Friends couldn't break your heart.

When the sun started to go down around dinnertime, they were a haggard bunch. The park had been taken from a mess to something with a glimmer of hope. CJ had pronounced the picnic tables salvageable. The dock had been disassembled because sitting in water for decades apparently did wood no good.

Bella came over to talk to her. "Today went surprisingly well. I only have a hundred or so scratches and scrapes on me." She chuckled. And yet she was just as cute as ever. Bella had a pixieish look about her. Paige had only seen her in impossibly high heels at work, but now she had on jeans and a ball cap and seemed down to earth.

"I've talked my husband into helping me paint the picnic tables one day this week. I thought we could do them in teal. Nikki said she loves that color and that she's using shades of aqua for her wedding."

For a moment, Paige was disappointed that she wasn't going to be able to do that job, and then relieved. She had enough work happening at her house up the street.

"That will be beautiful. And it'll be different from the pink in the other park."

Bella chuckled. "I have taken so much grief from the men in town for those pink tables. Especially from Micah."

"You did them?"

"They needed to be painted. I do weddings, right? Pink is pretty."

Paige chuckled and sat down on one of the picnic table benches. "That is so funny. I wondered how on earth they'd gotten pink picnic tables in a city park. They're usually that—"

"Ugly brown, right?" She sat down next to Paige. "I thought a park with an upcoming wedding should be nicer than that. I think men will complain less about teal."

"I hope so. I think most people do expect that brown color, but I don't get it. That shade never really looks like trees or woods."

Bella raised her hand for a high five, and Paige slapped her hand against it. "That's it exactly. You live in a pink house. Are you going to keep it that color?" Paige could tell she would love it if she did.

"I like it. But my carpenter tells me that I should replace it with something else."

Bella looked from her to CJ and back. "Is he going to have a say in paint color choice?"

She knew what Bella was really asking. "I'm not sure." And she may be running out of time to figure it out.

CHAPTER TWENTY-THREE

"Hey, CJ, would you like to have lunch?"

Silence greeted her.

"CJ?"

He appeared at the railing at the top of the stairs. "I can just grab a snack." After a moment, he added with more excitement, "Or are you planning to go to Dinah's?"

She'd hurried to the grocery store last night after their park cleanup, and arrived minutes before they were ready to close. "I bought some sliced cheese, lunch meat, and bread. I'm actually quite competent with sandwiches. I won't cause damage to my home or to another person."

In spite of the simplicity of the task she'd outlined, he only stared at her. He finally said, after a sigh worthy of a man going to the gallows, "I'm willing to give it a try. I would have thought measuring coffee and water and putting those into a machine would be simple, too." He shook his head with mock sadness. "But that didn't go well, did it?"

Somehow, she just wasn't the person to follow directions. She needed tasks where she could do them her way. Cooking didn't seem to work best like that. "Okay. Give me ten minutes."

She had the sandwiches ready on paper plates when CJ came into the kitchen. "Why don't you get the cold drink that you want out of the fridge and let's go outside?" She started for the front of the house.

"We can sit on the back porch. The sun's there now."

She glanced to the front and the back and saw that he was right. "No wonder I was so hungry. I hadn't realized it was so late in the day."

"That's because you were interested in what you were working on. There's nothing quite like stripping wallpaper to make you lose track of time."

She laughed as she grabbed her plate and drink.

It would be obvious which was the front and which was the back of the house, even if all someone saw was a photo. The front porch was much more elaborate with the gingerbread, corbels, and other details. It was quite beautiful in a Victorian way. The back porch was much simpler, but at least it had an overhang to prevent the elements from hitting you if you wanted to be out there. As they sat on the wooden porch with their legs dangling over, she looked around. "This would be nice screened in. If and when I can see the lake, I bet that would be wonderful for me and my guests."

CJ took a bite of his sandwich and didn't say anything.

"Don't you agree?"

He swallowed his food and took a sip of the soda that he'd taken out of the fridge. "All I see are dollar signs. It's not just a matter of closing this porch in. We have to repair it first."

Paige settled back to eat her lunch. Then she remembered the other part of it. "Oh, I forgot the chips." She ran inside and came back out with a bag, and poured some on each of their plates. "It's a gorgeous day."

"I have to agree. Fall is my favorite time of year in Tennessee. It's actually my favorite time of year anywhere."

"I always enjoyed spring because it was new life emerging after the frozen cold of winter."

"You traveled a lot with your dad. Weren't you ever somewhere warm in the winter?"

"You would think so, wouldn't you, considering the number of places we lived in? But, other than a very short stint in Okinawa—I believe it was three months on a special assignment—we ended up in places with cold winters. Germany and Colorado, to name a couple. It snows where my dad's stationed now."

She took another bite of her sandwich. She had managed to put mustard, mayo, and some sliced meat and cheese between two pieces of bread to produce something palatable. That was a nice change. When she finished, she brushed off her hands and leaned over to more closely inspect the porch. "This actually looks like it's in pretty decent shape to me."

"It's better than the front porch, but this side of the house gets a lot of shade, so it's also going to have more deterioration. I think if we put pressure on some of those boards, they'd give way. Like right there." He pointed at the porch floor behind her.

Paige braced her hands, lifted up, and sat down hard. "It's fine." A loud crack sounded. She scrambled to jump to the ground, but couldn't move fast enough as she felt the boards beneath her collapse. When she stopped moving, her arms and knees were in the air with her bottom hanging down below into who-knew-what underneath the porch. "CJ! Please get me out of here in a hurry. There are probably bugs and snakes and all kinds of creepy things living under a dark porch."

Laughing, he stood, reached for her hands, and tugged. She barely moved. "Your backside is tightly wedged in there." He put his hands under her knees and around her back, hefting her up out of the hole. Still cradling her, he stepped down into the backyard. "Are you okay?"

Paige gulped then nodded.

He shifted her weight in his arms and brought her closer to his chest.

When she looked up at him again, she realized that he was focused on her—and not just her, but her lips. As he lowered his face to hers, she reached upward. When their lips met, a sizzle traveled all the way through her body. Judging from his heartbeat, he felt the same. Much too quickly, he released her legs, had her standing upright, and was stepping back.

"Anyway, that's the way a gallant knight rescues a damsel stuck in her castle." He turned and went into the house without another word.

Up until that moment, she'd kept putting him in the friend category, even though she knew better.

His instant regret told her he wanted things to stay like that.

"That's too bad," she muttered. Complications in her life, she did not need. Maybe they could both pretend that had never happened. She could try. But, even after CJ had temporarily covered it up as he had on the front porch, the hole in the decking would remind her every time she stepped out the back door.

CHAPTER TWENTY-FOUR

*W*hen Bella called and asked if she'd like to meet with her and Cassie for a girls' lunch that day, Paige's first instinct was to scream "No!" at the top of her lungs. The last meals they'd had together had been blatant matchmaking attempts. But that was before she and CJ had acted as though they were dating. Maybe they'd leave her alone now.

Besides, she badly needed friends in town. Nikki was great, but she not only didn't live here, she was on the road a lot. Paige could envision long chats with a girlfriend when one of them had a problem, or even just sharing fun things that happened.

She didn't know how two women in the wedding industry had a Saturday off, but she'd take it. "I would love that."

"I'm doing an easy dinner of salads with lots of toppings. It's what Micah calls girly food, so I tend to save it for girly times."

Paige laughed, feeling much lighter. No matchmaking.

"If you could stop at the store and get some rolls or biscuits, that would be great. Cassie is going to pick up a dessert from her future mother-in-law. We've both been busy with weddings, and I know you have been working hard on your house, so we're making it easy on everyone."

"Busy" was the understatement of the century. With the arrangements set up, Paige found CJ and told him her plans.

"You'll be gone for hours?" He sounded happy.

"I guess so. It's lunch with Cassie and Bella. She said she's serving girly salads she doesn't feed to Micah. I think I'm safe from matchmaking."

"I do actually like a salad. But if Bella considers that girly food, you're in the clear." He kept smiling like this was the best news he'd had in days.

∼

CJ watched Paige drive off. Then he grabbed his phone and made some calls. "Greg, she's out of here. Your plan with Cassie worked."

"I'll call Micah. See you in a few minutes."

Before long, those two descended on Paige's house. More specifically, into her backyard.

"This is worse than I imagined." Greg stared at the wall of overgrown brush that stood between them and the lake.

"I know. And I want to have a fire pit there." He pointed to a spot near the brush. "Why do you think I asked you guys over here to help?"

"But how long did you say that we have? This is going to take us a week!" Micah shook his head as he stared at the yard.

Greg answered. "We have a couple of hours. She's having lunch with Cassie and Bella."

The men trudged through the cut-but-growing-back weeds to the thicket.

Up close, the task appeared even more daunting. The guys were right. CJ knew that, but he wanted to—no, he *needed* to—

have this done in case he decided to leave Two Hearts. Paige had to have a lake view.

"CJ, we need more time than we originally planned. I'm texting Cassie to see if I can get this extended somehow." He stepped away for a few minutes and returned. "Good news! Cassie just added watching a romantic comedy movie after lunch. I think that should get us a solid four hours."

CJ handed him a pair of clippers. "Everyone! We're going to have to hustle on this. I'm sorry. But I really want to surprise Paige with a view when she comes back."

CJ wiped the sweat from his brow. They had made progress in the hour they'd worked, but could they finish in time?

Greg seemed to be wondering that, too. "This took decades to grow. Maybe if we find a way through and work from the lake side, she won't know what we've been doing and we can wrap it up later?

"Good plan. Let's switch to doing that. I'll just tell her I spent some time working in the yard when she notices the clipped brush." He frowned. "But if we could finish this tonight, I would love that."

Micah shook his head. "You've got it bad."

CJ jerked his head back and looked at his friend. "What do you mean? I just want to do something nice for Paige."

Micah chuckled. "That's how it starts."

CJ stared at him. "Do you think I shouldn't do this?" Maybe he was on the wrong path. Micah was newly married, so he should know how women thought.

"I'm not saying you shouldn't do it." Micah grinned. "I'm just saying—and this is coming from someone who took a long time to figure out his own life—that you need to look inside yourself to understand *why* you're doing it."

"To be nice?" It seemed pretty straightforward to CJ. Paige was a nice person, so he wanted to be nice back. That was a whole lot of nice in one place, but that was just how he felt about her.

Greg slapped CJ's back and said, "Join the club, buddy."

With grins on their faces, Micah and Greg went to tackle the brush from the other side. CJ got to work building the fire pit that he knew she would love, but he wasn't sure how to keep it a secret. As time passed, he realized he'd taken on an overwhelming task with the whole backyard project. They had about a half hour left, by his calculations, and they probably needed another two.

Greg emerged from the brush with Micah behind him. "Great news! Cassie contacted me. She and Bella came up with the idea of taking Paige over to the big box store in Sweetly to get her a housewarming gift. The way those women shop, I think you might have bought yourself another hour and a half to two. Maybe longer when you consider the drive." He held up his phone. "And I called three other guys to help."

CJ let out a whoop and did a fist pump. "Then let's get this done. I may drop from exhaustion tonight, but we're going to finish it."

The new recruits soon arrived. After another hour, CJ could see the water through the brush, and soon after that, there was a clear corridor that widened by the minute. He and George, the farmer who had been on that blind date with Paige, moved the fire pit's stones into place. He framed the fire pit with three benches he'd made for it.

Greg raced over to them. "Paige is getting ready to leave Bella's house. We've got maybe five minutes to get out of here."

CJ called out. "Everyone, grab your tools, if you brought them yourself. If they're from the shed, please put them back. Hurry!"

The men raced about and hurried around the side of the house to their vehicles. He heard doors slamming and vehicles starting. Then barely a minute of silence before another car door closed. The men had gotten away in time. At least, he hoped they had.

CJ sat down on the back step, tired but really pleased with the day's work. He could now see out to the water. He wanted to get the remainder of the brush behind the shed cleared, but it already looked fabulous. The problem was Daisy's inquisitive nature, so until he put up some sort of fence between here and the lake, she was going to have to stay in the front yard. That wasn't exactly a hardship, because that's where she'd been hanging out.

He hoped Paige liked what he'd done for her. He was looking forward to seeing her face light up with joy. He felt a little tug near his heart. The words and expressions of Micah and Greg came rushing back. Did he have a problem here? Had the man on the move fallen completely head over heels for the woman who might not be staying? He might be in bigger trouble than he'd ever been in before.

And that was saying a lot.

Paige had enjoyed her day more than she'd expected. Hours later than she'd initially planned, she pulled up to her house. A vehicle drove away as she did, and it looked like Micah at the wheel. Maybe CJ had brought the guys over to help her out. A room or two that had been painted would be a treat.

A glowing light behind her house made her wonder what was going on. Instead of walking around the side of the building at night, she went through it. When she peered out the window over the kitchen sink, she could see what looked like a fire pit with a fire blazing in it. CJ appeared from the shadows and walked across the porch.

She pulled the door open as he neared it. "I asked Bella to let me know when you would be on your way. I have a little surprise for you." He reached out his hand for her.

She looked at it for a moment, knowing that by taking it, there was going to be a shift in their relationship. This time it wasn't for show. She felt her hand settle into his, and he squeezed it gently as she walked down the steps beside him. "There wasn't a fire pit, CJ. You must have been busy. How did you do this?"

"There were a lot of us here today."

As they neared the fire pit, she saw that it had been built of a circle of stones, probably some of those that had been sitting on the property and had been a trip hazard, and there were benches facing it that CJ must have made. They were from logs cut in half, with feet underneath them. The biggest surprise when she got there wasn't any of that. It was that she could see the lake sparkling by the light of the campfire.

She gasped.

He leaned closer. "Do you like your surprise?"

Looking out at the lake with the blazing fire adding warmth to this fall night, she couldn't imagine anything better. "It's the best surprise I've ever had."

"I'm glad." She could hear the pride in his voice. "It was no small amount of work in one afternoon and evening."

"I can imagine that. It must be beautiful in daylight."

He chuckled. "I haven't seen the whole thing in daylight yet. It was twilight by the time we got through the brush to the lake. It'll need a little more work, but—"

Still holding onto his hand, she rubbed her thumb over his. "It's beautiful. Even if there was never any more than this, I could be content." She knew those words were true. Standing here with CJ at her house in little Two Hearts, Tennessee, she felt truly settled and happy.

He motioned toward the bench in front of them. "I made

these out of that tree that had fallen in the back of the yard. It's gorgeous white oak, so it will last nicely."

"Then let's sit down." He started to pull his hand away, but she held onto it tightly. "I think there's room for both of us on one of the benches, don't you?"

He hesitated for just a second, as though she was asking something more than she really had been. Maybe she was. Paige leaned back and looked up at the stars. "Until I moved here, I had only seen bright stars like this a few times. Those moments stand out to me because both were with my dad. Once was in Germany when we'd escaped city lights on an overnight trip. Another time was when he was stationed in the Philippines. Again, we'd gone somewhere away from the base, and it was truly dark." She sighed and closed her eyes. "Everything is beautiful, CJ. Thank you."

They sat in silence, and the firelight flickered over the water. As the wood burned down, she lost track of time, but she didn't care. If she could capture a moment in time and hold it in her heart forever, it would be this one.

The light dimmed as the fire burned itself out.

"CJ." She turned to him. As she did, she realized how closely they were actually sitting—too close, and not close enough.

He reached up and put his hand on her cheek, rubbing it gently. That was another thing she'd remember about this moment and CJ.

Electricity sparked between them. He said, "Paige . . ."

And then he leaned in slowly, giving her time to back away if she wanted to, but she didn't. The kiss was sweet and grew in intensity.

"Thank you," she said when they broke apart.

CJ replied, "For what?"

"Perfection. This night is absolutely perfect."

He chuckled low in his throat, and she could almost feel the vibration of it through her. "Then I'd better put out the fire and go home. I don't want to mess with perfection."

He leaned in for one more too short kiss, then stood up. Because of the darkness—and because her attention had been focused elsewhere—she hadn't noticed the bucket of water CJ reached for to extinguish what was left of the fire. She already missed its warmth and CJ being beside her.

Maybe, just maybe, they could have a future together. She'd have to see how everything went in the next couple of weeks.

CHAPTER TWENTY-FIVE

*W*hen they stepped through the back door to her house, Paige felt wrapped in a glow from their evening. She flipped the switch on the kitchen light. It came on, flickered for a second, and then went off, as did every other light.

"CJ, what just happened?"

"My guess is that you blew a circuit. That's occurred a few times when I've been sawing and using other pieces of equipment. It's an older house, and I'm sure the wiring is not to current code. Let me see what I can do." With his phone as a flashlight, he went to the door that Paige knew led to a side room that held the water heater, the vacuum cleaner, and apparently also the electric panel. It wasn't something she had ever searched for. The power popped back on just a few seconds later.

"I got it!" CJ shouted. "I had a spare fuse I bought last time this happened."

When he stepped out, she said, "You never mentioned that there was a problem with the electrical." *Please, please tell me there's no real problem with the electrical.*

He shrugged. "A fuse blew occasionally, and I fixed it. I've had to do that in old houses before. Tomorrow morning, though, let's check the basement and attic, where we should find wiring that isn't hidden behind plastered walls. I have basic knowledge of most parts of construction, so I should be able to see what we're dealing with. We can get an expert to look at it if we need to." He turned off his phone's light. "It's time for me to head home. I'll see you bright and early."

He left Paige wondering how she'd been so blessed to have him helping her.

~

CJ returned as promised the next morning, and Paige had scones for them from Dinah's.

He reached for his cup of coffee after finishing his first scone. "You know, you don't need to buy these every time. That's going to add up. I could grab some toast at home. Or we could do that here."

She liked the sound of them sharing meals. "It has been fun to go over there every morning and see what she's got going. And I'm starting to learn some of the people in town because they're regulars." As soon as they finished, she stood. "I had nightmares of being electrocuted last night. I woke up this morning picturing my hair standing straight up."

He pushed back his chair and stood too. "I don't *think* that's the situation."

Somehow, she did not feel assured.

He pointed to the back door. "Do you want to go outside to the basement access to check under the house first or up to the attic?"

Paige headed for the stairs in the living room. "I'll take upstairs every time. I opened the hatch to the basement once, saw the mass of cobwebs, and closed it. If I never went down there again, it would be okay." She didn't add that she hadn't even tried the attic door after that experience, but at least it was above ground.

With Daisy on their heels, they went up the stairs to the end of the hall, and CJ opened the door to the attic. About ten steps led into near darkness. Paige flipped a light switch to her right and was surprised to find a clear path.

"You've been up here?"

"I checked the roof before starting any work, and was surprised not to see any leaks."

She followed up to the attic. A wide expanse under the eaves had old steamer trunks and furniture she'd need to sort through, and an assortment of toys and other things from the last century. She'd come back sometime. Maybe wearing a head-to-toe protective suit.

CJ pointed up. "You can see the wiring here."

Paige leaned back and looked at the underside of the roof. "There are ceramic-looking pieces between them spacing them out." She pointed.

CJ sucked in a breath and grimaced. That didn't seem positive.

"Okay. What does this mean? It just looks like wires to me, but apparently it says something more to you."

"It means that the wiring—at least up here—is really old. Very, *very* old."

"So is the house." Was old wiring somehow worse than old boards?

"We'll see when the electrician can come out and take a peek."

With that, they went to work for the day—him upstairs, and Paige focused on finishing up some of the details in the kitchen, which was finally almost done. At least he hadn't suggested a trip to the basement.

The doorbell rang a while later. When she answered, an

older man with black hair stood there.

"I'm Herb, the electrician."

"I'm Paige, the owner of this house. Let me get my carpenter. Just a second." She ran upstairs to find CJ, and he followed her back to the door.

"And this is CJ."

The men shook hands. "I've heard good things about you, CJ. And Miss Paige, welcome to Two Hearts."

Everybody knew everyone, and that made her feel warm and fuzzy inside.

They went up into the attic and then outside to the basement access. The men went into it, but she chose to wait on the porch. The electrician wrapped up the tour with the inside electrical panel and said, "Oh my!"

CJ glanced over at Paige and shrugged. That didn't bode well for any of the finances that she had set aside or the plans she had for using them.

"Tomorrow, I can give you a detailed estimate of the work to be done. Or I can give you a broad figure right now. We'll need to do a formal bid if you decide to go ahead with it, though."

"Tell me now. I didn't sleep well last night wondering, so I might as well find out."

The electrician quoted a figure that left her stunned.

"That much!" The zeros at the end boggled her mind.

"Is it unsafe?" CJ stepped around the electrician and put his arm around Paige's shoulders. She appreciated the comfort.

"I'm sorry to say that there is a fire danger. You have old wiring. It's exposed, it's been chewed on by rodents or squirrels at some point, and that's just what I can see. There's more hidden in the walls. It will all need to be replaced."

Paige took a deep breath. Most of her savings would be gone. She probably couldn't finish the renovations and open the bed and breakfast. Her dream of owning a business had ended with his words. But she could save the house, and hadn't that been her goal once she'd seen it? "Then let's get this done."

CJ turned to face her. "Paige, are you sure?"

She gave a single nod, so focused on the cost of this that she couldn't speak.

CJ rubbed her upper arm. "Is there anything I can do to save money on the project, Hank? Maybe prepare areas for your work?"

The other man pursed his lips as he considered it. "I can give you a list of pre-work that will help. Let's talk it over."

Since her carpenter wasn't an electrician, she didn't think it would save much, but he was sweet to offer.

She nodded again and left them, feeling more defeated than she'd ever been.

CJ got started on the work Hank had outlined. It was the least he could do for her. He just wished he could do more. She had dreamed of this. When he'd gone downstairs right after Herb had left, Paige had been standing in the living room, staring forlornly at her fireplace. She'd put so much time and hard work into it, and it looked like she was going to have to walk away. He didn't want that to happen.

His phone rang, and he picked it up after noticing the caller.

"Mark! How's your project in Alaska going?"

"I've got a bit of a situation here. I didn't mention it earlier, but my wife is expecting a baby."

"That's great! When is she due?"

"Not for a few months, but she's told me that I have to be within driving distance in case she needs me. Being a clueless father-to-be, I didn't see that coming. It's our second baby, so I thought I could be at an out-of-town job until closer to the due date."

"Just from the little I know about Alaska, 'within driving distance' could be an issue in much of the state."

"Exactly. I had been out on that jobsite with no road for hundreds of miles. She has told me there's no way I'm going there again, at least not any time soon." After a short pause, he added, "And I can't really blame her. She didn't get into this situation alone."

CJ chuckled. "No, she didn't."

Mark cleared his throat. "Did you give any more thought to that job?"

The days were getting shorter here as fall approached, but it must already be wintry in Alaska. "As long as it doesn't involve being in the middle of nowhere in an Alaskan winter, you're on."

Silence greeted him.

"You want me to be in the middle of nowhere in a frozen wilderness, don't you, Mark?"

"I really do. I trust you. I'm not sure who else to ask. I committed to doing this job. It may take the rest of the winter, but my homeowners expect their new home to be ready in May."

"So, they want you to build it in the winter, but they don't want to have anything to do with being there in the winter?"

"That pretty much sums it up. It is a gorgeous location in the summertime. Excellent fishing, and the views of the mountains are spectacular. What do you say? Are you so entrenched in your small town that you don't want to go anywhere else?"

He didn't want to be anywhere but at Paige's side. But if she had failed, she'd probably be heading back to New York City. He knew he didn't belong in a big city.

"It pays very well. The homeowners know that it's remote, and they didn't want second-rate work. They've given me a premium over the top of normal rates to make sure they had quality."

"How much extra money?" Maybe he could go there and give Paige the money so she could have her dream. Friends helped friends, and they were friends, weren't they?

Mark named a figure that had CJ standing up straight. "How many weeks? A month?"

"Honestly, it would be at least a month, maybe two. Or more. Of course, there's the weather too. You have to be able to have a plane land," Mark said.

He'd be gone for a while. If he could help her, though, it would be worth it. But what if she was gone by the time he got back?

Then he realized that, no matter what, this house was not going to sell in the condition it was in. It had sat on the market for decades, and the houses on either side of it were still empty. "I'll do it."

"Thank you! We may have to name the baby after you."

CJ laughed at that. "You don't even want to know what my actual name is. What drove me to use my initials. Let's just say that for some odd reason, my five sisters got easy-to-spell-and-pronounce names like Emily and Caroline. As the only boy, they honored me with my first name from one great-grandfather and my middle name from another, and neither one is easy to figure out."

Laughing, Mark said, "CJ it is." With the decision made, Mark gave him details about the plane ticket he would buy and the accommodations when he arrived. Now, all CJ had to do was break it to Paige. That wasn't going to be easy.

He went back to work on the list he'd been given. He'd help Paige every way he could. A little voice asked him, *Why do you care so much?*

~

Paige sat down at her dining room table with her list of work to be done and the figures for the money she'd spent, and the money she had allocated to future projects. The list had been the bare minimum of making this a place that visitors, including brides around their wedding days, would want to stay. No matter how many times she added the numbers, the results were the same. She wouldn't be able to make it into a bed and breakfast. The electrical issues had just shattered her dream.

CJ stopped in the entryway to the kitchen. "I'm done for the day. I'm heading out a bit early to help Greg with something over at Cassie's place. Do you need me to do anything before I go?"

"No. I'll see you in the morning." Paige used her best upbeat tone of voice. CJ hesitated as though he knew it was fake, but she watched him check his watch before she said, "We can talk then."

"Paige, I need to tell you something." His voice sounded serious, so she pulled herself away from her spreadsheet.

"What's wrong?"

"There's no good way to tell you this. I was offered a job in Alaska, and I accepted it."

Panic slammed into her chest. "You're leaving?" she whispered.

"Not yet. Don't worry. I can stay to help for a while. And tonight or anytime, if you need me, you can call. You know that, right? You can call me anytime."

The two of them had been working together. At least, she thought they were.

After he left—with a reminder to call him if she needed anything, Paige toured her house to take it all in. The bedrooms were all almost bare of wallpaper. The house was starting to look as it would, eventually. The plan had focused on preparing it for guests before, and now she wasn't sure what to do. She crossed her bedroom to what would have been her office, closet, future bathroom. There wasn't money to devote to any of this. She was probably going to have to sell the house. But to who? It had been empty during her lifetime.

Sitting on the floor in the doorway between the two rooms, she added up what needed to be done in here. If she'd been working, it wouldn't be as big of a deal. But she had put all her hopes and dreams into making a living with this house. It wasn't as though there were lots of jobs in Two Hearts.

She liked to think that one day she could get a job taking photos somewhere, but that was about as unlikely today as . . . her moving from New York City to Two Hearts, Tennessee.

One tear became a flood. What was she going to do? She didn't want to return to her old job. A job in Nashville would put food on the table, but the commute wouldn't be pleasant. She'd have to move closer. Daisy trotted across the room and snuggled next to her. And she'd need a dog-friendly rental now.

Two Hearts had captured her heart.

CJ had too.

Taking that job in Alaska was the stupidest thing he'd ever done. Sure, he'd had good intentions, but from the expression on Paige's face, he knew nothing could make it okay with her. She depended on him, and he'd let her down. He didn't think telling her about the money would fix things.

He decided to call Mark to see if the situation had changed.

Mark answered enthusiastically. "Hey buddy, looking forward to seeing you up here soon. And my wife is thrilled. I was in deep trouble, and you saved me."

This wasn't going how CJ had hoped. "How much work has been done?"

"Everything is on track. I had one carpenter out there for a while. I wish he could stay longer, but he lives in Texas, and he has another job. I don't blame him. It's hard to live remotely." After a pause, he added, "Maybe I shouldn't have said it that way."

CJ chuckled. "I've never minded being in the wilderness. I guess it's a good thing I accepted the job. You hadn't been able to find anybody else. Am I right?" CJ held his breath as he waited for Mark to say, "No, there are three great candidates, and I could go with any of them."

"I am so grateful to you. I asked everyone I knew, and you were the only one who had availability."

"Okay. I'll see you soon." CJ hung up after a promise to spend the first night in Alaska at their house in Palmer. He really wanted to see his friend and meet his new wife, but more than that, he wanted to be wherever Paige was.

CJ picked up his phone and called every skilled carpenter he had in his contacts. After a fruitless two and a half hours, he set down his phone, admitting defeat. No matter what, it looked like he was on his way to Alaska.

CHAPTER TWENTY-SIX

*P*aige had a hard time focusing the next day. Even the bright, sunny morning in the park couldn't defeat her cloud of gloom.

Nikki wanted her to be part of the planning committee for her rapidly approaching wedding, so she had no choice but to do her best for her. CJ was madly trying to finish up work before he left, so he wasn't distracting her.

Not that she'd ever minded his presence.

Or his arm around her.

Or his kisses.

The group sat at one of the recently painted picnic tables, discussing the upcoming wedding.

"I envision the bride and groom over by the water. There." James pointed to a clump of trees.

Both Nikki and Cassie agreed.

As they discussed it, Paige reached down and rubbed Daisy behind the ears. Her dog had finally settled down after racing around for the last half hour and seemed to have all the play out of her. Cookie was panting and lying on the ground by Mrs. Brantley.

A few minutes later, Cassie glanced around the group. "I think we can say we're done, can't we?" To Nikki she added, "This is going to be an amazing wedding." She said it with such conviction that Paige believed it, so Nikki must be thrilled.

That was proven when Nikki said, "I believe you are right. I'm so glad I moved the wedding here."

Everything seemed to be in place. Paige would be a guest, but didn't have a role to play like Cassie, Bella, and James. Just being invited surprised her, though. A couple of months ago, if someone had said she would be going to a big country music star's wedding, she would have laughed. Or cried. No one like her did something like that.

And yet here she was, hanging out with this star who was becoming a good friend. She was a real person even though she was a musician and well-known.

Cassie climbed off the teal bench. "If you have any questions, Nikki, please don't hesitate to contact me. That goes for you too, James and Bella. I have been working behind the scenes, as you know, to make sure all the other pieces fall into place, and I'm happy to say they are."

Everyone else stood, something that was rather awkward to do with a picnic table bench. Finally, with them upright, and the dogs back on their feet, the group started for their cars. A squirrel chattered from a tree to their left, and both dogs perked up and looked that way.

Laughing, Mrs. Brantley said, "I think they're so exhausted that they aren't even going to chase a squirrel." She led the group back to the cars, in charge as she naturally was with everything.

Halfway there, the squirrel got bold. It ran from the tree on one side of the park to the other side, zigzagging between them. Daisy and Cookie, who had been exhausted earlier, came to life and surged toward their bushy-tailed prey, leaving everyone stumbling to get out of the way.

The squirrel did a U-turn, probably because it didn't feel safe now—and rightfully so. When the dogs spun around after it, Paige almost hit the ground. She caught herself in time and reached out to grab Cassie to prevent her from falling. The others were too far away, and before she knew what was happening, James did what could be best called a somersault as he went over the top of one dog. The dogs were moving so fast that they were already over by the tree and barking at the squirrel by the time James hit the ground.

Where he was very still.

"Oh, no!" Nikki raced over to her friend. Kneeling beside him, she said, "James, are you okay?" She leaned over his face. "He's breathing." Then she put her hand on his neck. "And his pulse seems okay." She looked over her shoulder at the rest of them. "I made sure everyone in my band took emergency medicine classes, just in case. You never know what's going to happen at a concert or with fans."

Cassie was on the phone. "Greg, the dogs tripped Nikki's photographer at the park, and he's unconscious. Okay. Will do." She raced to her car, got something out of the trunk, and came back with what turned out to be a blanket. "Greg says to keep him warm to prevent shock, and that he's calling an ambulance. It's just that we're in the middle of nowhere, so the ambulance is going to take a while." She pulled the blanket up higher on James. "It's a good thing Greg put an emergency kit for me in the car. I thought he was just being overprotective."

Paige watched from the sidelines as James lay there for a minute and finally opened his eyes and blinked. Thank goodness! She let out a long breath.

"James . . ." Nikki leaned closer to him. "Are you okay?"

He tried to nod and winced. "I think I'm just bruised. I have a vague memory of flying through the air."

Mrs. Brantley knelt next to him. "I am so sorry, James! The dogs seemed to be fine, and then—a squirrel."

He murmured, barely at a level Paige could hear, "Not the dogs' fault. *Squirrels.*" He said the last with a deep sigh. Paige had a feeling he'd been around a lot of dogs.

Sirens blaring, Greg arrived with Daniel, the closest thing Two Hearts had to a doctor. They raced over, and Daniel examined James.

Daniel stood. "I don't believe anything is broken. I suspect a mild concussion and a sprain in his right hand and his left ankle. I must say that it could have been worse. But I am going to wait for X-rays from the hospital before I say this is done and diagnosed."

Another siren approached them. This time, an ambulance.

"I don't need to go to a hospital." James looked around as though trying to find someone who'd listen to him. His gaze stopped on Nikki. "Tell them I don't need to go to the hospital."

She kneeled beside her friend again. "There is no way I would let you go home without being thoroughly checked out. But don't worry; I'll be there beside you the whole time."

"I'm going too," Mrs. Brantley said.

Cassie agreed. "I think we'll all be there."

Paige nodded.

Only Bella said, "I'm really sorry, and I want everyone to update me every time that you learn something, but I've got to get back to working on this dress for Nikki."

James said, "Not a problem, my dear. I want Nikki to be beautiful. Not that she's ever anything less."

Nikki chuckled. "Always a charmer."

James tried to sit up. "I'm fine. Really, I am. I just had the wind knocked out of me. I had that happen multiple times when I was a kid."

Mrs. Brantley put a firm hand on his shoulder. "We need to get you checked out. I won't let someone drive away from Two Hearts injured."

He sighed and closed his eyes. "I can tell when I've been beat."

The emergency professionals examined him, applied the standard neck brace, and loaded him on the gurney. No one was family, so no one rode in the back with him, but they piled into their cars.

Paige had walked, though, so she was about to hurry up to her house to get her own vehicle when Mrs. Brantley said, "Come with me, Paige!"

Paige jogged over to the passenger door with Daisy beside her and had barely gotten it closed when the older woman peeled out. "I'd like to drop the dogs off in your front yard."

"That's fine."

She ground to a stop. Paige jumped out with her dog, with Mrs. Brantley doing the same. Seconds later, her driver had done a U-turn and chased after the ambulance. Paige could still hear the siren, but it had already moved out of sight. Holding onto the side of the speeding vehicle, she fired off a quick text to CJ to let him know he was dog sitting. When they turned onto Main Street, she could see the flashing lights in the distance.

Paige wasn't sure how to make conversation with Mrs. Brantley.

It turned out she didn't have to speak. Mrs. Brantley said, "I feel so guilty that this happened in my town. I should have anticipated it."

This put Paige in a different position when she became the comforter. "It certainly isn't your fault. It's the dogs'."

"We probably shouldn't have let them run without leashes." Under her breath, Mrs. Brantley murmured, "Maybe we need a leash law in parks in Two Hearts."

"I honestly don't think that leashes would have helped. They might have made it worse."

Mrs. Brantley turned onto the highway, heading north. "Why do you say that, dear?"

"Picture it this way: the dogs darting between people or the dogs with leashes trailing behind them darting between people. They jumped forward so suddenly that I doubt either of us would have kept our grip on the leash."

"Oh my! You are right. I can see the damage that could have caused."

"Everyone would have been down."

Mrs. Brantley shook her head. "Either way, the squirrel gets away."

Paige chuckled. When humor came back to the situation, she started to relax.

"He seemed to be okay, though, didn't he?" Mrs. Brantley asked.

"He certainly did to me. I didn't notice any cuts or abrasions."

"That handsome face of his did appear undamaged."

Ha! Paige thought she'd seen attraction when they had met. "He just had some bits of grass and dirt in that hair of his."

"Yes, that silver hair. He does have a silver-fox way about him. Dashing, debonair, and so handsome." Mrs. Brantley realized what she had revealed. "I mean, he looks like a model they'd use to advertise something targeted at middle-aged women, don't you think?"

"I do indeed."

It was unfortunate that the two of them lived so far apart. Mrs. Brantley was intrigued by him. He had also looked at her with interest. Maybe there would be some way . . . And then Paige realized that she was contemplating becoming a matchmaker.

Grinning, she watched the countryside roll by. They passed a farm with rows of pine trees. She'd always loved going to the Christmas tree farm when she was a kid. She and her dad had cut their own tree when their location allowed it. The scent alone made her happy.

When Paige and Mrs. Brantley arrived at the hospital, they asked about James and went to the floor he was on. The others came in soon after. They clustered together in the waiting room chairs. Mrs. Brantley had already gone over to the nurse's station and tried to get information, but they wouldn't tell her anything.

Nikki arrived and got straight to it, casually leaning on the counter as she spoke to the nurse, and signing something with a big smile on her face. When she stepped over to them, she said in a hushed voice, "That worked out well. The nurse recognized me, and she's a fan. She said she wasn't allowed to give much information, but she could say that he was okay. And there's nothing serious."

Paige felt relief pass through the group. Twenty or thirty minutes later, a doctor came out and said, "He's asked for someone named Nikki."

The singer followed the doctor out of the room and returned looking happy. "It's exactly as the man in Two Hearts said. A mild concussion and a sprain in his right wrist and left ankle. There doesn't seem to be anything else wrong, but he needs to rest for a few days." She paused for a moment. "He may have a concussion because of the fall. And that means that he can't drive, and he has to be watched for a day or so. Longer if any symptoms show up."

Mrs. Brantley asked, "Nikki, what do you know about James? Is there someone at home that can take care of him?"

Nikki paused for a moment. "He has photographed me for years. I know he was married, but his wife passed away probably four or five years ago. He dove into his work after that."

"Then we'll manage this another way." Mrs. Brantley turned on her heels and went to the nurses' station.

"What do you think that other way is?" Nikki asked.

"With Mrs. Brantley, it can mean anything," Paige said. "That woman could organize any situation."

Hospital staff wheeled their patient out not long after that.

Mrs. Brantley, who had been quietly seated and making notes on a small pad since her talk with the nurse, stood. "We're going to get James into my car, and I'll take him back to Two Hearts, where I can watch him and be his caregiver for the 24-hour period."

He looked up at her, startled. "That isn't necessary."

Paige wasn't sure if he thought it wasn't necessary or if he didn't want to go there.

Either way, Mrs. Brantley said, "James, it's my understanding that you currently live alone. You have to be observed. This happened in Two Hearts, and that's where your car is. Give me a better option." She stepped back and crossed her arms over her chest.

It wasn't more than ten seconds later when James said, "You're right. I don't have one. I accept your help. Um, will those dogs be there?"

They all laughed.

"Only one of them. The black-and-white dog. But I'll make sure she's in the backyard when you're up and about, if that makes you more comfortable."

He gave a single nod. The man didn't know it, but he was going to eat better than he ever had in his life. She couldn't imagine a finer cook or baker than that woman.

Soon after, he was sitting in the back seat of Mrs. Brantley's vehicle, and the three of them were headed toward Two Hearts.

"If you give me your car keys, I'll move the car over to where you're staying."

He tried to slip his right hand into his pants pocket, but pulled it back. "Ouch. This will take getting used to." Then he reached across his body with his left, retrieved a brass key ring that had a tiny camera dangling from it, and dropped it in her outstretched hand.

Paige helped get him settled on the living room couch. She and Mrs. Brantley went from there to the kitchen, where the older woman shooed her toward the back door. "I know you have plenty of things to do. If I need any help, I'll reach out to you or Greg or Cassie. Somebody. Don't worry."

"If you're sure?"

"I am."

Even though Mrs. Brantley could organize an army, she might need something. "I'm going to come by to visit later today. Let me know if there's anything you want me to pick up at the store."

She assured her she was fine, pulled a pan out of the kitchen cupboard, and started getting ingredients out of the cupboard. Yes, James would eat well.

The morning had been interesting. If the afternoon had any similarity, this would be quite the day.

CHAPTER TWENTY-SEVEN

*N*ikki had gone directly from the hospital to Nashville for a meeting, but they had assured her that James was in good hands and that everything was under control.

And everything did seem fine until Paige was getting out of his car at Mrs. Brantley's house, and James' camera equipment in a bag on the floor caught her attention. "Oh, no!" She hurried into the house and followed the voices to a downstairs bedroom. It was obviously the one Mrs. Brantley normally used, judging by the level of decoration and the floral patterns on the curtains and bedspread.

James was already lying down with his shoes on the floor beside the bed. Paige tapped on the door. "I brought your car over, James. Mrs. Brantley, could I have a quick word with you before I head out?" Paige dropped James' keys on the nightstand.

In the living room, Paige said, "He can't do the wedding photography. Can he?"

She gasped. "Oh my goodness, Paige. You're right. The wedding is just a few days away."

"A mild concussion could be okay."

"I watched him move just now. That sprain in his right wrist will make it so he can't hold a camera. And the left ankle would leave him unstable for photography." Mrs. Brantley glanced at the bedroom door. "What are we going to do?"

Those words from someone who planned everything to within an inch of its life startled Paige. If Mrs. Brantley didn't know, they really did have a problem. Before Paige could get another word in, Mrs. Brantley produced a plan. "Get together CJ, Bella, Micah, Greg, and Cassie, if you could, and have everyone meet over here for dinner. We'll figure it out."

"Should we just ask Nikki? It's her wedding."

"You heard her. James is her photographer for everything. But I'm sure Cassie knows dozens of photographers. We'll offer Nikki options."

Over a dinner of roast chicken with potatoes and fresh green beans that Mrs. Brantley conjured up with little notice, the group discussed it. Paige wanted to speak up time and time again, but stopped herself. She did know how to take pictures, and she had taken photos of weddings. Everyone had loved them. She'd won awards for her work, including one for a wedding photo. But someone like Nikki needed a professional.

When they got Nikki on the phone, Cassie spoke first. "I'm not going to lie to you. It is going to be really hard—close to impossible—to find an experienced photographer at this late date."

Nikki said, "I must have a photographer."

CJ said, "Paige is an excellent photographer. She just doesn't believe she is."

Cassie said, "I'm digging for someone right now."

Paige felt the conversation swirling around her like she wasn't really part of it.

CJ stood up. "We can solve this. Why don't you get your

laptop, Mrs. Brantley, and let's look up the images that Paige has online?"

Mrs. Brantley frowned. "That she has online?"

CJ stared at Paige, almost daring her to speak. "The photos she won awards for. And the photos that are still up from a wedding she did earlier in the year."

Cassie turned to her with a different expression. "You've never mentioned that you had done weddings before."

Paige had to either move forward or stay in her corner. She swallowed hard. "Most were for friends and family. But that wedding earlier this year was a friend of a friend. I was paid for that one."

CJ pulled out his phone. "And look at what she did here with Daisy." He held up the photo he'd asked her to send to him.

Cassie looked at it, and a smile came over her face. "Please bring your laptop, Mrs. Brantley. I do want to see what Paige has done."

Mrs. Brantley went down the hall and returned quickly with the computer open. She handed it to Paige. "This is your time," she whispered as she leaned down and gave it to her. She added, "Shine."

Paige brought up a handful of photos, each in different windows, and then passed the laptop to Cassie.

"These are wonderful! Why haven't you done this for your career?"

Paige looked around the group sitting here. If she confessed about not being good enough, it would be so much worse with all these people.

Cassie continued clicking through the photos. "You've captured the bride and groom in different ways. Here they're smiling, then they're more serious, and here they're playful. Nice job, Paige."

Nikki spoke from the phone, "Do you want to photograph my wedding, Paige?"

Before she could allow herself to talk herself out of it, Paige jumped to her feet. "Yes! I would love to photograph your wedding!"

Everyone looked up at her, wide-eyed.

Cassie said, "You're always so quiet."

Paige nodded. "I didn't have something that I felt this passionate about." She stepped closer to the phone. "Nikki, I don't have the expertise that James has. Are you sure you want to do this?"

Without hesitation, Nikki replied, "If you want the job, it's yours. I trust you, Paige." Conversation echoed behind her. "My sweetie's here, and we're going to talk over some of the places we want to see in the next six months. I haven't gotten to spend time in snow in so many years that I think we might start there."

She hung up, and Paige's new direction was sealed. She was going to have to spend the next day online researching wedding photography for any tips she could pick up. This was a huge leap forward compared to what she'd done in the past.

Cassie focused on Paige. "You and I can sit down and talk about the shots that I'd like for you to get."

Did Cassie not trust her? That made her more nervous.

"It's a standard thing I do. I look at the locations, and I envision where the best photos will be taken and with whom. I am a hundred percent open to what you want to do, though. If your idea is better, I am on board."

"I already have ideas. When I saw that church, I saw the possibilities. And the park will be fabulous. I can already see it."

Mrs. Brantley spoke up. "I do have one suggestion: The man down the hall can probably give you some great tips once he's had a chance to rest."

Paige sat down in the chair. "I would love that." How her life had changed. It felt like it had done so in the blink of an eye. One minute, she was a photographer on the side, dreaming of doing bigger things someday, but ready to open a bed and breakfast. Now, she was the photographer for one of the biggest country music stars, and the possibility of a bed and breakfast was fading away.

The next day, Paige drove to Mrs. Brantley's. There was no way she wanted to arrive for what felt like a business meeting sweaty from a bike ride. She found Mrs. Brantley inside her kitchen, bustling around industriously, as she seemed to do all the time. Paige tapped on the wooden frame of the screen door, and Mrs. Brantley said, "Come in." When Paige had, Mrs. Brantley added, "I'm making some chocolate chip cookies." She looked up from her work. "They're Jim's favorite."

Interesting. The famous photographer James had become Jim.

Paige eyed the cookie batter that was getting chocolate chips dropped into it right now. "Will the cookies be ready while I'm here?" She certainly hoped.

Mrs. Brantley laughed. "Of course. I'm sure you'll be talking to Jim for longer than it takes a cookie to bake. Now, you just go on down the hall."

Paige opened the door to the bedroom and did indeed find Mrs. Brantley's guest propped up on pillows in bed. He looked healthier than Paige had thought he would.

"I'm glad you're here. Have a seat." He pointed to a chair that was a few feet from the bed. Paige did as instructed and then looked at the man again. He was wearing pajamas made from a rust-colored print featuring fishing rods and reels. The colors fought mightily with the lavender sheets on the bed.

"I see you staring at me." He raised a hand when she started to protest so as not to embarrass him. "I need to get this out in the open that these are not my pajamas. I came to town for a simple meeting. I was going to stop at what I'd heard was a fabulous place to have pie, and then I was supposed to go back to the city. I wasn't considering staying overnight. Emmaline borrowed these from one of the neighbors, whom she apparently knows well."

Paige was about to comment on how many people Mrs. Brantley knew in town when James interrupted her thought. "I am sure that woman knows everybody. She can recite the names of their children and their grandchildren. She probably knows two generations back on top of that."

Paige laughed. James had figured out his caregiver's personality pretty quickly.

"I actually think that's one of the most wonderful things about Emmaline—her way with people," he continued. "She's quite amazing, don't you think?"

Paige could answer that honestly. "She is. In the short time I've been here, I've seen her go from being a new mayor to taking charge of so many wonderful things for the town."

"She's the mayor?"

"That's why she was at the meeting."

"I had no idea. Not knowing makes me sound like a fool, doesn't it? Here I thought she was just someone who was kind and enjoyed helping."

"She is that and so much more."

"Enough chit-chat. Let's talk about wedding photography before she comes in with something else wonderful for me to eat."

Paige grinned. "I understand you enjoy chocolate chip cookies."

"She didn't bake some, did she?"

Paige chuckled and nodded. "She did. They should be here soon."

The man started to rub his hands together with glee and then winced. "I'm going to have to watch that maneuver for a while." He sniffed the air. "It's probably because you just mentioned the cookies, but I smell them baking."

"No. You're right. It's wonderful." Paige thought of the very different scent when she baked.

"I may gain weight while I'm here, but I don't care. Now, let's get down to work."

Ten minutes later, Mrs. Brantley came in with a tray that held a plate of cookies, a cup of coffee, and one of tea.

She reached over and patted his good hand. "I'll leave you two to talk. And if you don't mind, Paige, I'm going to step out to get a job done for the city and return in plenty of time to prepare dinner. Would you stay and watch Jim for a while?"

"I would be happy to do that."

"He's only supposed to talk for so long, though. You've got to make sure you let him rest."

"Yes, ma'am."

After she left, they sat eating cookies and drinking their hot beverages. Paige paused and said, "I need to apologize one more time for what happened with Daisy."

"The corgi?" When she nodded, he continued. "Don't give it another second's thought." He glanced toward the door. "Do you think she's gone?"

"I'm sure she is. Mrs. Brantley seems to do exactly what she says she's going to do."

He dropped his voice anyway. "Then I'll tell you this. I have never eaten so well in my life. She's made me laugh, and she's made me smile in ways I didn't think were possible after I lost my beloved Betty five years ago."

There seemed to be a bit of romance in the air, along with the scent of the cookies.

Paige grinned. "She's a special woman. If you're saying what I think you are, you'll have the same problem that Cassie and Bella did. The city is an hour and a half from here."

"I have been considering cutting back on the number of weddings I do for several years. I still enjoy my work, but I want to see what else life has to offer. And I'd be happy to drive to the city every once in a while for an event. It would give me an excuse to get out."

"You've given this some serious thought in a short amount of time. After a brain injury," she added hesitantly.

He laughed again. "A *suspected* brain injury. They weren't sure I had a concussion—just that I had fallen and been briefly knocked out. I actually feel fine. I'm looking forward to getting out and exploring this town. What I saw looked good. That park was gorgeous."

Somebody had to tell him. The words rushed out of her. "Two Hearts has been a dying town for decades. It's only starting to come back now because of weddings."

"I noticed a shift taking place. I like what I see." He set his coffee cup on the nightstand. "But about Nikki's big day. I want to work with you, share everything I can about wedding photography, to help you succeed with this event."

Paige tried to keep her face in a neutral, professional expression, but a grin fought through. "I appreciate it."

"I see talent in your work. We could start collaborating on it now." He winced.

"Are you okay?"

"Slight headache. And I'm getting a little tired. I will take that nap as instructed. We'll talk later today. By the way, do you think I'm getting the cart before the horse with Emmaline?" She remembered hearing her grandmother use that expression.

"I think the heart does what the heart wants to do."

Just like with me and CJ. Paige sat there in shock. What had her heart done? She kept saying that she and CJ could never be more than friends. But that wasn't true. She'd fallen hard for him. It was time for her to decide what she wanted and see if maybe—just maybe—he'd be interested in a future with her. If she could keep him here in Two Hearts.

First, there would be a wedding for Nikki, and she had to focus on that because she couldn't let everyone down.

CHAPTER TWENTY-EIGHT

*T*he day of Nikki's wedding came quickly. Paige had only had a few days to go from enthusiastic amateur to professional photographer. Nikki had insisted on paying her the same rate she would have paid James. James had refused to take a penny of it, so Paige's fortunes had just changed. She could now not only update the electricity in the house, but she could also finish off a couple of the bedrooms. And Cassie had promised her more work if today went well. Maybe, just maybe, she was about to become an actual wedding photographer.

Paige checked her appearance one last time in the mirror before she left her house. What did a wedding photographer look like? Professional but also unobtrusive. She had to take photos of the entire ceremony and not be in the way. James had been quite clear about that. She thought her black top and pants would help her fade into the woodwork, and she'd pulled her hair back so that it was completely out of her face.

Last night's trial run at the rehearsal dinner in Nashville had been a strange warm-up to this event. The hotel where they had held it had a taped-down outline of the church that sat just a few blocks from her, along with some decorations that would be brought over.

Still uncertain, she collected all of her gear—both what was hers and what James was loaning her. It had felt like such an intrusion to go into his Nashville home the night before with his key, but he had been insistent. He seemed quite happy to be nursed back to health at Mrs. Brantley's house.

Paige drove over to the church and parked a short distance away near Wedding Bella. The bus filled with guests arrived from Nashville just as she did, so she hurriedly began snapping pictures as the well-dressed men and women came down the steps and onto the sidewalk. Laughter and a happy buzz of conversation filled the group. She hoped to capture that feeling with her camera.

Inside the church, she found organized chaos. Cassie was firmly in charge.

"There was a bit of a problem in the bridal room this morning. But we got it under control." Cassie looked like she could get anything under control. "Head in to take photos of the groom first."

Paige did as told. This was Cassie's show.

The handsome contractor wore a black tuxedo with a white shirt and an aqua patterned tie. Nikki had, without a doubt, chosen it to go with her color scheme.

Paige tried to be official-sounding. "Okay, everyone. It's time for some photos."

Groans went up from the men.

Paige's confidence slipped. After taking a deep breath, she pointed to Griff. "Thank you for helping me. I need you here, you next to him." She pondered the arrangement. "And you in the back because you look to be a little taller."

The men joked with each other about "Shorty in the front." She put the groom in different positions amongst his best man and groomsmen. When she was done, they all thanked her for the good job, and she walked out of the room with her head held high.

Cassie grabbed her as soon as she came out. "There isn't much time. Get over to the bride's room and take as many photos as you can."

Paige hurried over there and found the room calm—with the exception of a woman who must be the mother of the bride. She hadn't been at the rehearsal last night, but Paige remembered hearing that her plane had been delayed.

"I can't believe you chose to get married here over that elegant church in Nashville. What were you thinking, Nikki?"

Paige wanted to jump in and defend Two Hearts, even though that was the last thing she should do. Nikki took care of it for her.

"Mom, I love this little town. The people have been so good to me. They don't treat me like I'm some star up on a pedestal. I'm just a person. I love that. And by having my ceremony here, I get the wedding of my dreams. This little church that we're standing in is a lot closer to my vision than that big, fancy place in Nashville. I also get to help breathe some life into this town. That makes me feel better than you can even begin to imagine." By the time she was done, she had her hands on her hips and fire shooting out of her eyes.

Her mother—apparently used to her daughter's passionate remarks—simply said, "Okay. Let's do this."

Nikki dropped her arms to her sides and smiled widely. "It's going to be fabulous." To Paige, she said, "I'm glad you're here. Let's take photos of the girls and Mom together. After that, I can pretend to get ready and maybe put the flowers on my head. Something so we have action shots. What do you think?"

Paige processed the quick directions. Again, she felt like shrinking, but this time, she felt stronger inside. She could do this. Standing straighter, she said, "I think there are some great photos to be had here. I love the light over by that window. Why don't you move to there, Nikki, and we'll see what that does for the camera? Everyone else, if you could sit around in a casual way, we can get some photos snapped of you. I think you'd like them more casual than formal. Correct, Nikki?" They had already discussed this, but she was repeating it for everyone else in the room.

Nikki smiled. "That's exactly right. It's as though you can read my mind." With a wink, she sashayed over to the window and posed. This woman had been photographed so many times that she was easy to take pictures of.

When Paige had all she needed, she turned around to face the rest of the room and realized arranging the others might not be quite as easy. But when she had all the photos she wanted to take, she was satisfied. Cassie tapped on the door and opened it. In a firm voice, she said, "The groom is about to move to the front of the church. We are three minutes away from you walking down the aisle, Nikki. Everything looks good." She glanced at Paige, and Paige nodded.

"We're done here."

Cassie smiled encouragingly. "Then why don't you go to your location for the ceremony, and let's get this wedding going?" She grinned. Paige could tell this must be one of Cassie's favorite parts of a wedding.

Nikki made a stunning bride as she came down the aisle toward her groom, wearing her satin wedding dress that Bella had somehow managed to pull off in that short amount of time. Beading trimmed a few of the edges and caught the light.

Paige took a few pictures of the bride and then turned to snap some of the groom. He was mesmerized by the beauty of his wife-to-be. The ceremony passed quickly, with Nikki and Griff making vows they had written themselves—words that promised forever. And, from the looks on their faces, she thought maybe they just might make it.

Before long, Nikki went back down the aisle—this time, on

the arm of her husband after a kiss that had made the audience swoon. When he'd bent her backward over his arm, there had been "ahs" among the guests. Nikki had let out a "whoop" when he stood her upright.

Paige hurried outside and positioned herself beside the brick church steps, waiting for the bride and groom to leave. When they did, well-wishers showered them with flower petals. The shots she got would be absolutely gorgeous.

Once they'd finished the after-the-ceremony photos with the wedding party, the bride and groom climbed into their limousine, and Paige hurried back to her car to drive home. After freshening up, she walked from her house to the park. When she got there, her heart swelled with pride. The ratty, overgrown, barely there park she'd driven past when she'd first arrived had disappeared.

The rose bushes were still blooming and flowers had been added by Nikki's florist. It was an outdoor wonderland. When Paige looked up, she saw lights strung from trees and wondered how on earth they would power those, but then she spotted a small generator off to the side. This would be an evening this couple would never forget.

At the reception, Paige looked up to see CJ watching her. Seeing him there brought a smile to her face. Wait until he heard about the money that James had agreed to pay her for this. Nikki, really, but James had said to give it to her. He'd helped her learn, and then on top of it, he'd made sure she would get the money she needed.

She and CJ had never danced together. Maybe they'd be able to do that later. She was there because she was the photographer, but the bride had insisted that CJ accompany her as her plus-one. No matter how many times she told Nikki that she and CJ were just employer-employee or friends, Nikki had smiled, patted her on the arm, and said, "You believe what you want" or something similar. The thing was, in the end, Nikki was right. Paige couldn't imagine her life without that man. Didn't even want to try.

Nikki laughing with friends pulled Paige out of her daydreams. She hurried over to snap some photos. This was the most fun she had had in her life. It was also one of the longest days on her feet. But she didn't care. She got to share in this couple's big day. To capture it forever. What she was doing now mattered.

This was her dream, had always been the dream she'd kept safely tucked away.

As she stood there contemplating that startling thought, Nikki stepped up next to her. "Thank you for doing this."

"Thank you! This is so much fun." She held up the camera so that Nikki could see the last photos she'd captured.

"Those are good. I knew you'd be great at this."

Paige was glad Nikki had confidence in her, even if Paige had first thought it was misplaced. "I have a question for you, and you may need to think about it. Or you may not even have an answer." Paige felt like she was going in circles.

Nikki seemed to agree, because she said, "Just say it. What do you want? That's the way I got what I wanted in my life. You've got to stand up and go for what you want."

Nikki was right. Everything good that had happened in Paige's life since she'd decided to come here—including that original decision—had been because she had been bold, and she had taken the steps she needed to in order to make things happen. "I'm wondering if I can survive as a wedding photographer—if I don't need to run a bed and breakfast."

"I thought that's what you wanted more than anything. Did you change your mind?"

Embarrassment surged through her. She knew she sounded

flaky and uncertain. "There are some problems with my being a bed and breakfast owner."

Nikki stared at her and waited for her to continue.

"I don't mind having people in my house. That part is fine. The bed part of bed and breakfast works. The breakfast causes me a few issues."

"Like what? You just make some scrambled eggs, bacon, and toast, and you call it done. Maybe give them a little bowl of some fresh fruit you've cut up."

This was hard to say. CJ knew her secret, but very few other people did. "I'm a horrible cook, Nikki."

Nikki laughed. "It can't be that bad. Tell me one thing you can cook."

"It is that bad. I can't cook anything. I almost always burn scrambled eggs. The bacon, oh, the bacon. That was a disaster. And baked goods? They are bad. They're charred. They're flat. They're ugly. Even when I use a mix, it's like I just can't get past it. I've even burned toast. And CJ won't drink my regular coffee! I had to get one of those individual-cup brewers so that he would take a break and have a cup of coffee with me." She realized that she'd rambled. "That's probably more information than you needed."

"Oh my. I didn't know. But maybe you could get frozen foods or something like that for the breakfasts."

"I have tried that, but you still have to heat them up. The real block is that I'm starting to feel like my heart isn't in it. I chose that dream to survive here, but photography was always my real dream."

Nikki said, "Then chase your dream. Chase it all you need to."

Paige looked up and saw Cassie not too far away with Bella at her side, and Nikki's gaze followed hers.

"Those two ladies found their dream in this small town,"

Nikki said. "Maybe you can too. I spotted that handsome CJ not long ago."

Paige's face heated.

"I know you keep telling me there's nothing there—"

Paige fidgeted for just a few seconds. "You were right. I was wrong."

"Are you now saying that there's something going on between the two of you?"

"I think so."

"Then you'd better go find your man."

Nikki's new husband smiled at his wife from across the park. Paige watched her light up and hurry over toward him without so much as a goodbye. Paige didn't mind for a second. They were so cute together.

Now she needed to find CJ and tell him that maybe she could survive here. And maybe she'd find a way to tell him that she'd like to survive here with him at her side.

CHAPTER TWENTY-NINE

*P*aige put a box on the bed. She grabbed an armful of clothes from her closet and unceremoniously dumped them inside it. Then she returned for a second. She couldn't stay here.

When she'd woken up this morning, still happy about the wedding and the money she'd earned, she realized that it would pay for repairs to her house. But she had only done one wedding with the possibility of more to come but no guarantees.

Then CJ had texted her to say that he would be a little late because he had to finish a project at his rental before he went to Alaska.

It was time to move on. She would need a lot more experience before she could call herself a professional wedding photographer anywhere but here. And if James did fall for Mrs. Brantley, then he'd be in Two Hearts. This town couldn't support two wedding photographers. Anyone with half a brain would choose him with his long history of taking bridal photos.

When that box was filled, she set a second box beside it and continued. Halfway through, she sat down on the bed and put her head in her hands. "What have I done? I saved for so many years to get a house, and then I leaped at the first one. 'Leap and a net will appear' is garbage."

The thought that maybe she had done the right thing popped into her mind. She had been the photographer for Nikki Lane's wedding. The pictures were going to be in every magazine and on TV. Maybe that would be enough to help give her a start, even in a big city like New York. There must be hundreds of weddings there every day. Maybe someone would take a chance on a new photographer.

But that wasn't Two Hearts. And that wasn't anywhere near CJ.

Then again, unless she wanted to go to Alaska, she wouldn't be anywhere near CJ, anyway.

Her phone rang, and she pulled it out, almost dismissing the unknown caller, but accepted the call.

"Is this Paige?" The male voice sounded familiar, but she couldn't quite place it. Then she realized it was James.

"Yes. How are you doing today?"

"So much better. I'm not sure if it's the passage of time, medicine, or just the homemade chicken noodle soup and chocolate chip cookies I've been eating." He chuckled.

"She is a wonderful cook."

He muttered something that sounded like, "She's simply amazing." Then, louder, he said, "I have an idea. I don't want you to dismiss it without hearing me out."

"Okay," she said slowly. Usually when someone said that, they were about to make a bad suggestion. Like matchmaking.

"I've been thinking about retiring for several years. I've done well. I'll tell you that, Paige. I don't need the money. It's more creative expression at this point."

"If I were to be in Two Hearts, would you be interested in

letting me mentor you as you learn the wedding photography business? We could work together. I've wanted to have a protégé for the longest time, but the circumstances never seem to turn out right."

Had he just said what she thought he had? "Excuse me?" When he didn't immediately reply, she wondered if she'd offended him. "Did you offer to teach me what you know about wedding photography?"

"I did. Are you interested in that?"

Without hesitation, she answered, "Yes! I would love to learn from you."

Thoughts of the boxes piled on her bed and the stack of things to go inside them brought her back to reality. "James, I can't afford to live here. I went through my money faster than expected when rehabbing the house. New electric wiring was the final straw."

"You were paid by Nikki, right? I was fairly sure she was going to give you that money."

"Oh yes, she paid me, and that's how I paid the electrician." Then Paige realized that everything had changed. If this building didn't need to be a bed and breakfast, she could live here. There was nothing wrong with the house now. It had bathrooms and a kitchen; it was warm and had a solid roof. The electrical system was certainly in good condition. "Wait! I can stay if I'm going to earn money from photographing weddings. That is what you're saying, right?"

He chuckled. "That is what I'm saying. We do the weddings together, and you get the money."

"Oh, I can't take all the money." He would be vital to the entire experience. "Besides, the brides trust you because of your amazing portfolio and resume."

"Paige, remember what I just said? I don't need more money. What I need is someone to take over my business and to run it in a way that honors what I've done. That respects my career and my past, while moving forward. I have been looking for someone like that for years. I found her in you."

Tears welled in her eyes, but the smile on her face felt glued in place. This was the most amazing thing that had ever happened to her. "Then I accept. I can't imagine anything I would enjoy more."

"You do need to know that I'm going to be hard on you. I'm not letting you get away with anything. You and I are only going to do the best, to be the best."

Her smile widened. "That suits me perfectly. I don't seem to have a halfway button."

"I thought as much. Then we can get started when I'm back on my feet."

"There is the slight glitch of my living in Two Hearts and you being in Nashville."

"I would need you to come to town for occasional training and weddings. Mostly for the weddings that are already set up, because I book out a year in advance. But I may be getting a house here in Two Hearts. The place does tug at one's heartstrings, doesn't it?"

Paige heard a female voice in the background. Mrs. Brantley must have entered the room.

"I'm told that it is time for tea and brownies."

Paige said in a low voice, hoping it wouldn't carry over the phone to his caregiver, "That's going to be hard to leave."

"I have already figured that out."

They ended the call with a promise from him to discuss their future working relationship more the next day.

Paige grabbed clothes out of a box, threw them in the air, and watched them fall to the floor. Then she reached for another batch. Racing around the room and the mess she'd made, she shouted with glee.

CJ hurried in.

"What's going on?" His gaze fixed on the boxes on the bed. "Are you packing?"

"Not now. I'm celebrating. This is the best news ever." She ran over to CJ, pulled him into a hug, and kissed him. Stepping back, she said, "I get to stay here."

CJ's hand went up to his mouth.

Then she realized what she'd done. "Sorry about that."

He shook his head. "I'm not. I have to leave, though. I made a promise."

She wished he'd change his mind, but maybe he was as stuck in his plans as she had been in hers before her new mentor's call.

He gestured to the mess on the floor. "What was going on here?"

Paige looked around in a daze. Had she imagined the call? She took out her phone and quickly looked at it, finding the call from James. "CJ, I have been offered the deal of a lifetime. James is going to mentor me in wedding photography."

"That's great!" He sounded enthusiastic, but she could tell it was forced. "When do you start?"

"We'll begin as soon as he's better. If I'm remembering correctly, he was originally told that was going to be a week. He may not be able to use his hand and ankle well, but he would be able to start teaching me. How long does your Alaska job last?"

"A minimum of a month. Maybe more."

Silence stretched between them. CJ didn't mention anything about returning to Two Hearts after that. He finally said, "I'd better get back to work."

"Yes. I guess you had better do that."

Why couldn't she ever get all the good things to come together at one time? He was leaving, and once he was gone, he'd forget about her. For all she knew, he'd stay in Alaska and never set foot in Tennessee again.

Just before lunchtime—if she'd been in the mood to eat—Nikki showed up at her door. "I got the good news!" The singer pulled Paige into a tight squeeze of a hug, lifting her to her toes.

When her friend let her stand on her own again, Paige asked, "What good news?"

Nikki frowned. "Didn't James make you an offer? I hope I'm not coming in early on that."

Paige sighed. "Yes, that is amazingly wonderful news. But aren't you supposed to be on a honeymoon right now?"

"I'm not working. Griff's out on a golf course. I know it isn't conventional, but we want to relax and have fun. We'll be together tonight." She wiggled her eyebrows. Then her friend narrowed her gaze. "That's enough about me. Why are you sad?" Leaning closer, she said, "Is CJ here right now?"

"He is." Paige pointed with her thumb behind her. "He's finishing up some last details in the kitchen. He said he'd be upstairs working on one of the bedrooms after that."

Nikki tugged on her arm. "Let's move out front to chat."

What on earth was going on? She loved Nikki like a sister. It was amazing how quickly you could make some friends. But she could be a little intense—like right now.

On the porch, Nikki spun around to face her. Shaking her finger in her face, she said, "James' offer should have lit up your world. What's wrong?"

Paige swallowed hard and fought against the tears that started to pool in her eyes. Blinking, she looked down. "I am thrilled to be learning the wedding photography business with James' help."

"Honey, that is the furthest thing from thrilled that I have ever heard in my life. Give!" Nikki motioned forward with her hand.

The story rushed out of her. "CJ's leaving. He took a job in

Alaska. He's going to be gone for a long time, and I don't think he's coming back. He says he wants to finish up everything in the house so he won't feel guilty for leaving things undone."

Nikki's eyes widened as Paige spoke. "So, the two of you are still dancing around each other. I understood that correctly, didn't I?"

Were they? "Define dancing around."

"Each of you crazy about the other one, but neither one willing to step forward and say anything about it. Then when one of you gets closer, the other one backs away." She rolled her eyes. "What is wrong with you?"

Her friend's passion stopped Paige's crying. "I don't know what to do, Nikki."

"Let's sit in these rocking chairs and see if we can figure out a plan. I need to know exactly what's going on. I do my best planning with all information in hand."

In spite of the situation, Nikki made her smile. Paige heard CJ's footsteps in the house, so she closed the door to keep their conversation private. Then she heard a window opening, and then another, followed by a saw. Fortunately, that was brief.

Nikki set her rocking chair in motion. "I'm waiting."

"CJ fixed up the backyard for me, and we had a terrific night out there. Right after that, I found out I had to replace all the wiring in the house. That was going to take all of my money, so I couldn't have my bed and breakfast anymore." As she said that, her heart sank. "James working with me is a game-changer, though. I can stay. But CJ has already moved on. Or he will be moving on."

"Besides, he's just a friend."

Nikki doubled over with laughter. When she got control of herself, she said, "Honey, you passed 'friends' a long time ago. You are so in love with that man, and he is totally in love with you." In typical Nikki style, she said that loudly enough for the neighbors to hear—if there had been neighbors. Fortunately, CJ was upstairs and busy at work.

"I don't think that's true. I mean, I might quite possibly have realized that I am in love with him, but he hasn't said anything to me about his feelings."

Nikki's gaze bored into her. "You haven't told him either. You two are worse than fifteen-year-olds trying to sort out relationships, and you're in your thirties. Just tell the man!"

Paige shook her head. "No. He's leaving. He likes to travel. He doesn't have roots anywhere other than where he grew up. I just need to accept that. Besides, he accepted a job. He's going to fly in to the middle of Alaska in the winter and will be stuck there for a month or more."

"Snow?"

"From what I understand, quite a bit of it." Paige shuddered. "I spent so much time in the north that I'm looking forward to a more pleasant winter here. They tell me it can snow, but it's not going to stick around for long."

Nikki said wistfully, "I grew up in Minnesota. I miss cold northern winters. Cross-country skiing and snowshoeing. Ice fishing. Snuggling close to someone you love next to a roaring fire on a cold night." She sighed. Standing, she said, "Let's go have lunch at Dinah's. My treat. I'll even throw in a piece or two of pie. Let's see if that can help heal your wounds."

Even Dinah's pie wouldn't make this better. Paige didn't really feel like going, but being around Nikki did seem to make the world a brighter place.

CJ stepped back from the window as the women went down the porch steps and toward the street. He didn't want them to know he had overheard their conversation. Paige's softly spoken words had been a little hard to hear, but Nikki had more than made up for it with her booming voice. The woman probably didn't need a microphone when she was onstage.

Paige *loved* him. He let that idea sink in. Paige. Loved. Him. He made a whooping sound and pumped his fist in the air. "She loves me! Now we can . . ."

They couldn't do anything. He had told Mark—given his word to a man with a pregnant wife—that he would be in Alaska soon. He only had a few days before that promise had to be fulfilled.

Either he had to go, or someone at his skill level or higher had to take his place. The problem was that he didn't know anyone who had free time to do that. And most people wouldn't want to bring a family out there. He wasn't even sure if the homeowners would want the carpenter's kids and pets on the jobsite.

No. He would just have to go to Alaska and send Paige a letter every day a plane came in with supplies. It wouldn't be very often, but maybe she would believe in them, in their future, for that amount of time. Of course, she was building a new life here as a wedding photographer. Would he even fit into that life by the time he returned?

After a quick trip to the hardware store for supplies, CJ arrived back at Paige's house. He grabbed the bag of screws and went to the gate, where Daisy enthusiastically greeted him. After her usual belly rub, she ran off to play.

This would be one of the last times he was here. The pink Victorian was both a beauty and a money pit. He did hope the big money things were all taken care of now, though, for Paige's sake. When his phone rang, he took it out of his pocket and leaned against the side of his truck. "CJ."

"CJ? This is Griff, Nikki's husband. I still feel funny saying that." He gave a self-conscious laugh.

CJ waited for what the man wanted.

"Anyway, she said that you've accepted a job in Alaska."

This was an odd conversation to have with someone barely more than a stranger. "Yes, it's for a man I worked with in Colorado. He's a contractor up there now. Do you want me to ask if he has something interesting for you?" CJ heard rustling on the other end.

"Nikki just poked her head in here to see if I'd called you yet. I told her I was working on it. You know, we're guys and we don't like to talk about these things, but Nikki has told me that you and Paige would be able to get together if you weren't heading out of town."

That did sound like something Nikki would say. "I don't usually stay in one location for a long period. It's probably time for me to move on." Even as he said the words, CJ wasn't sure his heart was in them. Actually, he was positive it wasn't.

"Well, if you think that your friend would accept me in your place, you are completely off the hook. I make my wife happy— one of my main goals in life—and you get to stay in Two Hearts and figure out whatever this is that you and Paige have going on."

Hope surged through CJ. "Seriously? Don't mess with me about something like this if it's not true!"

Griff chuckled. "A snowy and remote cabin seems to appeal to Nikki right now after being on the road so much. And it sounds really rewarding to be my own boss for a while. I know I still have a client, but I doubt those clients are going to be looking over my shoulder."

CJ said, "From what Mark told me, they aren't even planning to go anywhere near their new home until it's done and the snow is gone." He'd promised Mark, but he also knew Griff's reputation. It didn't get any better. CJ was still building up his client list, but this man was well established, not only in Nashville, but throughout Tennessee and the surrounding states.

"Should I have you tell me about the situation? Or do you want me to just talk to your friend?"

"I'll give him a call and pass on your contact information."

"Sounds good. I'll wait to hear back."

CJ stared at his phone. He never walked away from things he'd agreed to do. Never. He brought up Mark's number and, after a second's hesitation, called him. "Mark!"

"Please tell me you aren't going to call to cancel. My wife will not be happy."

Should he tell him? He turned and faced Paige's pink house. "I actually should stay here. But don't worry"—he heard sputtering from the other end as Mark started to speak—"the man who has offered to take my place is far more experienced." CJ gave him the name and then sent him a text with Griff's contact information. "Check him out online. I'm sure you'll like what you see."

"I just brought him up. You were right. And here's a picture that says he just married Nikki Lane?"

"Yep! They got married right here in Two Hearts. She'd actually like to come along. She's been wanting some solitude and snow."

Mark chuckled. "I can certainly provide both. I'm scrolling through this man's credentials. He looks good. I'll give him a call and get back to you to tell you how it went."

CJ stared at his phone after they ended the call. He didn't want to walk inside until he knew what was going on. It wasn't five minutes before his phone rang.

"It's a deal! I'm sorry that you won't be coming up to Alaska right now, but thank you for finding the replacement. My clients might be excited to know they had Nikki Lane in their home for construction. I'll cancel your ticket and get tickets for them. I hope to see you up here some time."

"Or you down here in Two Hearts."

"You're staying there? I thought you weren't going to stay anywhere."

CJ caught a flicker of movement through one of the windows. "I think I found the right place."

CHAPTER THIRTY

eading into the house, CJ's smile grew wider and wider. He marched up the front steps and opened the door. "Paige!" he shouted.

Footsteps pounded toward him. Then he saw her looking over the railing from upstairs. "Is something wrong?"

"I have exciting news. Could you come downstairs?"

Paige descended the stairs at a slower pace. Probably because his last great news would have sent him thousands of miles away. When she reached the bottom, she stood there and didn't approach him. He couldn't blame her.

"Paige . . ." CJ took a step in her direction.

Paige held up her hand to stop him. "You're going to Alaska. There's nothing more to say."

"Nikki and Griff are going there instead." He slowly walked toward her.

"Nikki? Why?"

"Apparently, it has the perfect mix of snow and solitude that she's been looking for."

"She did mention to me that she wanted that." More softly,

she said, "Nikki? Then, if they're going, you're not going, right? I'm hearing all of this correctly, aren't I?"

She stayed where she was, but he took several long strides and ended up right in front of her. Reaching out and taking both of her hands in his, he said, "It's all taken care of. I am staying here. In Two Hearts. Not just in the Lower 48."

"But you gave up the little house you were living in, didn't you?"

CJ grinned. "You may have left the big city, but you still brought some of that mindset with you. How many empty places are there in Two Hearts?"

"I imagine there must be dozens. Just based on the for-sale signs that I see and the lack of care of so many houses." And then, it seemed to dawn on her. "So, you can find a new place to live quickly."

"I can rent the place I was in or find something better."

She wrapped her arms snugly around him. "Are you really going to stay in Two Hearts?"

Her words were slightly muffled, but he could understand them just fine. "I'm staying."

"The town won you over?"

This was the moment he'd been both dreading and looking forward to. "*You* won me over, Paige."

CJ felt Paige's rapid heartbeat against his chest. "I'm so glad you're staying."

He let out his breath in a whoosh. "We'll get to spend more time together."

"The house has been a bit of a challenge, though, hasn't it?"

CJ nodded, and his chin brushed against her soft hair. "It has. You know, you don't have to keep this house. It has been a money pit. There are a lot of cute little houses in town."

She thought about it for a moment. "It has been a lot of work. But we should be past the big expenses, shouldn't we?"

"We should."

"If I'm staying in Two Hearts, this is the house I want. The work we have left is mostly physical labor, right? I mean, other than the price of paint or wallpaper. Not that I ever want to wallpaper anything again after taking off all that was in here. But just the pretty part will cost. The other part is only labor, right?"

"Yes." Where was she going with this?

Paige snuggled closer to him. "Then I do have a question for you." She paused for a moment. "If you and I were the ones doing the labor, eventually, wouldn't it be easier if we were both sharing the same home—the same roof?"

He stepped back and held her at arm's length, looking into her eyes. "I don't see you as someone who would want to live together before marriage."

"You are seeing me correctly."

He cocked his head to the side as he looked at her for a moment before answering. "Are you asking me to marry you?"

Paige nodded. "I believe I am."

He grinned. "Then I may have to accept."

"My house just became *our* house."

"Will you marry me soon?"

She smiled up at him. "I think I can do that. Yes," she nodded thoughtfully, "I believe I'll marry you next week."

Instead of panicking about settling down in one place, he felt more love toward Paige. He knew that this time he was in the right place. "Proposals usually involve an engagement ring. Would you like to go to Nashville tomorrow to buy one?"

She threw her arms around his neck. "Yes," she whispered.

"And they're usually sealed with a kiss. I love you, Paige Conroy." He scooped her into his arms.

EPILOGUE

*C*assie watched the wedding from the edge of the lawn. The pink Victorian house had come to life for the best party it had seen in half a century. A wooden dance floor covered part of the backyard, with tables and chairs scattered about the rest of the open area from the house to the lake.

Paige's father and stepmother had surprised her by flying in from Japan yesterday. CJ's entire family had descended on Two Hearts the day before that. The families were spread among several tables and chatting amongst each other.

The bride and groom danced beautifully together as a band Nikki had recommended played a sweet love song.

Cassie scanned the room, watching to see if anything needed her attention. Nick, the caterer and a good friend of Micah's, carried a pan filled with what looked like mashed potatoes from the kitchen at what was now CJ and Paige's home to a buffet table on the lawn beside the porch. A wedding cake covered in pink roses rested on a separate table next to that one.

Simone, her friend and wedding cake master, sat on the edge of the porch. "I'm going to rest here for a few minutes."

Cassie sat beside her. "Congratulations! You managed another gorgeous miracle cake."

The baker put her hand over her mouth as a loud yawn escaped. "Sorry. I already had a full schedule for the week, so I squeezed this one in." The usually spunky baker leaned against a porch column and shut her eyes. "I finished about 4:00 a.m."

"Oh, no! How did you drive here?"

"Didn't. I knew Nick was catering, so I called him. He has a better van for transporting, and I needed another person to help me load, anyway."

Cassie turned toward the caterer.

"Don't think it. My eyes may be closed, but I know you're considering matching us up."

"No? He's handsome and nice."

Simone ignored her comment. "This was purely a business decision. Running off the road with a cake would make an interesting news story. I don't want to be the baker who does that." She straightened. "If you wouldn't mind, I'd love to run away from here to go to sleep in your comfortable guest room."

Cassie hugged her friend. "Thank you for making this cake."

"For a while, you have to find clients who plan months in advance." Simone shook her finger at her. "But speaking of weddings, when are you and the handsome sheriff tying the knot?"

Cassie searched the room, found Greg, and motioned him over. "Soon."

"You seem to be hesitating about saying 'I do.' Is anything wrong?"

Cassie sighed. "No. I'm just wedding shy after my last experience. But the good news is that I know how I want you to decorate the cake."

Simone laughed.

Greg heard the last word. "Do you want me to get you a piece of cake?"

Cassie chuckled. "Thank you, but no. Would you take Simone to my house?"

"Sure."

Simone patted her arm as she jumped from the porch to the ground. "Thank you!"

Bella stepped over as the two of them went into the house. "Simone's leaving?"

"Cake decorating until just before dawn."

"I'm glad my profession allows me to finish work in advance."

"Paige's dress is amazing!" The bride whirled around the dance floor in her groom's arms.

Bella grinned. "It's a pleasure designing for a tall woman. I could add embellishments that would overwhelm a bride my size."

"The oversized, organza bow on the back adds a whimsical touch. When they moved their wedding date from one week to three, you must have breathed a sigh of relief."

"Yes! She would have had a simple dress otherwise. And CJ's yard work and painting the house made this a wonderful place for the wedding."

"Am I the only one who's surprised he painted it pink —again?"

Bella laughed. "A man in love does surprising things."

"Walk with me while I do another pass through the crowd."

Bella kept pace with her as they wove between tables and around the yard.

"Everything looks wonderfully issue free." Cassie picked a paper napkin up from the ground and deposited it in a trash can.

"They're such a cute couple." CJ and Paige left the dance floor hand-in-hand.

"We did a good job with them."

Bella snorted. "Are you kidding? They matched themselves up."

"True. But Paige told me that we pushed them into it with our terrible matchmaking attempts."

Bella grinned. "The new deputy was engaged? You didn't think to ask?"

Cassie winced. "That was a slight oversight."

They both laughed.

The newly married couple separated and moved about the room, speaking to guests. Paige stopped beside James, where she appeared to receive another lesson in wedding photography. Their new friend drank in every word the older photographer said, then snapped a few photos with him at her side.

"Paige took surprisingly good pictures at Nikki's wedding. Quite a few were featured in magazines and online sites, all to glowing praise. It will be wonderful having a wedding photographer right here in town."

"We would have anyway with James moving here."

Bella chuckled. "I think he's serious about retiring. He usually appears more interested in Mrs. Brantley than anything else."

"That's the truth. When they arrived here together, she giggled as they talked. It's adorable!"

"By the way, where is she?" Bella glanced around. "I haven't noticed her for a while."

"She insisted on managing the inside of the house, so she's giving tours, because everyone's curious. I told her I could hire someone to do that, but—" Cassie shrugged. "She is a great organizer. The matchmaking is the only thing I've seen her fail at."

"I have a feeling we'll be doing a wedding for her and James, eventually."

"You may be right. We didn't need to be matchmakers for

them. With her as my future mother-in-law, I wouldn't have dared, anyway."

"You know . . . Simone and Nick would make a cute couple."

Cassie stopped and faced her. "Don't think it! We were disasters."

Bella sighed. "You're right. Those two are on their own."

1.You have options. (I love options!) If you enjoyed Paige and CJ's story, you'll love BRIDESMAID OR BRIDE? It's about Michelle from Dinah's Place and book 3.5 in the series. Readers kept asking for her story, so I was happy to write it. She's always the bridesmaid and never the bride. Until now.

AND

2. You can also go to book 4 in the series, WAITING FOR A WEDDING. Nick and Simone both work with food, he a restaurant owner and caterer, she a wedding cake designer. Falling in love should be easy for these two . . . but it isn't.

3. Nikki's friend Carly has her own story: *HOW TO MARRY A COUNTRY MUSIC STAR*. She's a down-on-her-luck country music star, and Jake is the wealthy man who hires her to be his housekeeper. Get it FREE at cathrynbrown.com/marry.

ABOUT CATHRYN

Writing books that are fun and touch your heart

Even though Cathryn Brown always loved to read, she didn't plan to be a writer. Cathryn felt pulled into a writing life, testing her wings with a novel and moving on to articles. She's now an award-winning journalist who has sold hundreds of articles to local, national, and regional publications.

The Feather Chase, written as Shannon L. Brown, was her first published book and begins the Crime-Solving Cousins Mystery series. The eight-to-twelve-year-olds in your life will enjoy this contemporary twist on a Nancy Drew–type mystery.

Cathryn's from Alaska and has two series of clean Alaska romances. You can start reading those books with *Falling for Alaska*, or with *Accidentally Matched* in the spin-off series which includes *Merrily Matched*.

Cathryn enjoys hiking, sometimes while dictating a book. She also unwinds by baking and reading. Cathryn lives in Tennessee with her professor husband and adorable calico cat.

For more books and updates, visit cathrynbrown.com

Printed in Great Britain
by Amazon

38087576R00158